Oper Fishwrapper

A Jock Miles WW2 Adventure
By
William Peter Grasso

Novels by William Peter Grasso:

Operation Fishwrapper
Book 5 in the Jock Miles WW2 adventure series

Operation Blind Spot
Book 4 in the Jock Miles WW2 adventure series

Operation Easy Street
Book 3 in the Jock Miles WW2 adventure series

Operation Long Jump:
Book 2 in the Jock Miles WW2 adventure series

Long Walk To The Sun:
Book 1 in the Jock Miles WW2 adventure series

Unpunished

East Wind Returns

Copyright 2015 William Peter Grasso
All rights reserved
ISBN: 978-1517128173

Cover design by Alyson Aversa

Operation Fishwrapper is a work of historical fiction. Events that are common historical knowledge may not occur at their actual point in time or may not occur at all. Apart from the well-known actual people, events, and locales that figure in the narrative, all names, characters, places, and incidents are products of the author's imagination and are used fictitiously. Any resemblance to current events or locales or to living persons is purely coincidental.

Author's Note

This is a work of alternative historical fiction. In actual events, MacArthur's forces invaded the island of Biak at the end of May 1944 as part of their continuing quest to neutralize the Japanese in Dutch New Guinea and secure airfields to support the invasion of the Philippines. The fighting on Biak raged until early September of that year, when the last Japanese retreating westward across the island in a brutal war of attrition were finally subdued. While the story in this novel adheres loosely to the timeline of actual events, the events depicted, the units and weaponry involved, and the intelligence ploys used to achieve an American victory are fictitious.

In no way are these fictional accounts meant to denigrate the hardships, suffering, and courage of those who served.

Contact the Author Online:
Email: *wpgrasso@cox.net*

Connect with the Author on Facebook:
https://www.facebook.com/AuthorWilliamPeterGrasso

Dedication

To Peg, still the only reason all this is possible

DUTCH NEW GUINEA

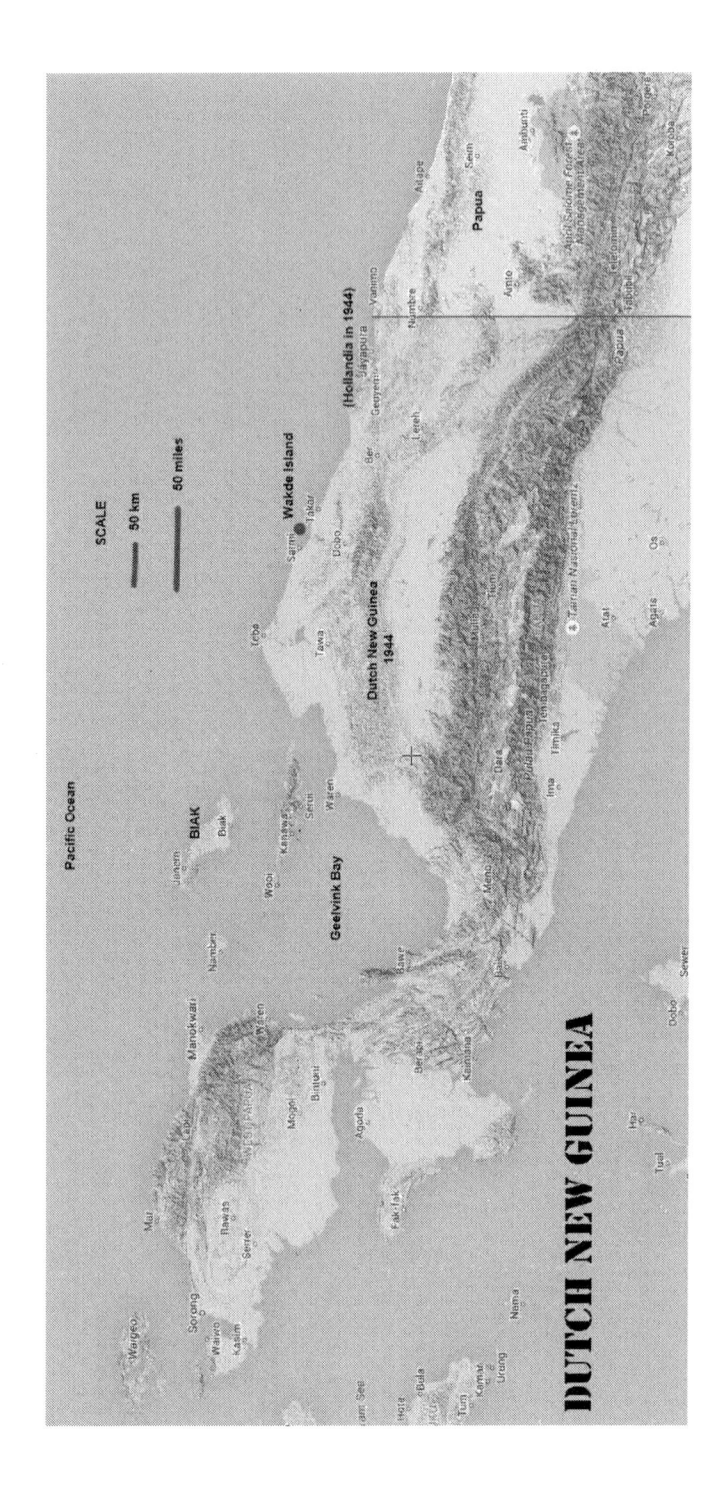

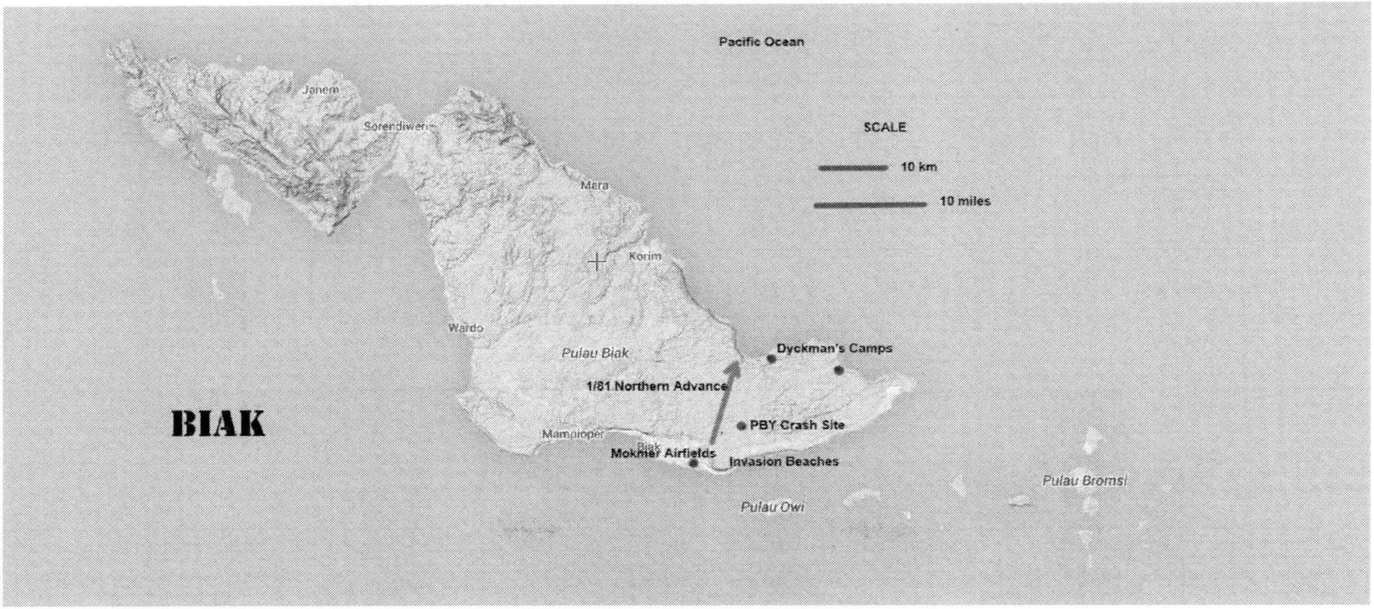
Pacific Ocean
SCALE
10 km
10 miles
Janem
Sorendiweri
Mara
Korim
Wardo
Pulau Biak
Dyckman's Camps
1/81 Northern Advance
BIAK
PBY Crash Site
Mamboper
Biak
Mokmer Airfields
Invasion Beaches
Pulau Bromsi
Pulau Owi

PART I

BROKEN WINGS

Chapter One

June 10, 1944

2300 hours

The US Navy crew of the PBY Catalina was used to night missions. They'd been flying them for months, using their radar to find and attack enemy ships seeking refuge with the only friend the Imperial Japanese Navy had left: darkness. Two symbols stenciled below the pilot's window—each an outline of a sinking ship—meant this aircraft had been credited with sending two enemy vessels to the bottom. But this US Navy *Cat* had rarely worked as a solo ship before—and never with an Army officer onboard, calling the shots.

That officer—Jock Miles, Major, US Army—peered over the shoulder of the PBY's navigator, a lieutenant j.g. named Becker. Together, they watched as the dial on the radio direction finder crept slowly toward the aircraft's port beam. "About fifteen seconds," Becker called to the pilot. "Then turn left to heading one-three-zero…on my count."

Becker turned to Jock and said, "Well, Major Miles, let's hope and pray the signal from Darwin isn't bending a whole lot tonight." Then, stopwatch in hand, he began the countdown:

"Five…four…three…two…one…MARK."

The lumbering flying boat dipped her left wing and began a southerly turn. When she leveled off at her new heading, the radar operator stared intently at his scope and said, "Well, that looks pretty good, Major Miles. We've got a coastline about five miles off our port wing and nothing but sea return ahead. Wanna look?"

Jock leaned closer to the radar scope. "Like you said, Baum, it's *a* coastline. With a little luck, it's Biak's coastline."

"Don't sweat it, sir," Petty Officer Sid Baum replied. "Mister Becker hasn't gotten us lost too badly yet."

The PBY droned on for twenty minutes more, slowly losing altitude until they were 3,000 feet above the sea's surface. In the pale glow of the cockpit lighting, Jock could read the tension on the face of the pilot, Lieutenant Arthur Simpson.

"You sure it's safe to be down this low, Major?" he asked Jock. "Mountains jutting out of the sea in the dark are a great way to get us all dead."

"Yeah, I'm sure, Mister Simpson. Been over this place three times in the past week."

"But that was in broad daylight, Major...and you were probably a hell of a lot higher, too."

Simpson was right about that: those missions on *Photo Finish*—an Army Air Force B-24 bomber converted for the photo mapping role—had been flown at 8,000 feet, with the comfort of escort fighters to ward off Japanese interceptors. None had risen to the challenge, though—and the photos hadn't shown anything to suggest a significant Japanese build-up on the island of Biak. The pilots had called those missions *milk runs*.

"And I'm still a little fuzzy what the Army expects to see at night it couldn't see in broad daylight, sir," Simpson said, and then laughed as he added, "oh, wait...the Army doesn't do much night flying. They get lost real easy once the sun goes down. Maybe you should've gotten the Aussies to fly this mission, Major. MacArthur usually gives them all the shit jobs, doesn't he?"

Without taking his eyes off the navigator's plot, Jock replied, "Mister Simpson, I'm *married* to an Aussie, so I don't need to be hearing that crap from you, too. Now come left five degrees. Let's get a little closer to the coast."

As he put the big flying boat into a shallow bank, Simpson mumbled a skeptical, "Aye aye, sir."

They were barely out of the turn when Simpson said, "Major Miles, you'd better have a look at this."

There was a bright glow in the distance, just visible over the Cat's nose, like the lights of a small city. They were flying straight for it. Simpson asked, "What the hell do you make of that, sir? Fires or something?"

"Nope," Jock replied, "those are floodlights. Just what I was afraid of."

"Afraid? Why?"

"Because, Mister Simpson, the natives don't generate electricity. Those are Jap floodlights."

"But sir, why would the Japs be stupid enough to light up the place like it was Christmas?"

"They're in too much of a hurry to care right now, Mister Simpson. We figured they'd be building airfields around the clock down there on Biak. But I still can't figure out why we never saw any of that on the daytime recon flights."

"Well, now we know they're building *something*," Simpson said. "And now that we've seen it, we can get the hell out of here." He was already pushing the throttles forward and beginning a turn that would take them away from the coastline.

" Negative, Mister Simpson," Jock said. "Hold your course and altitude."

"But that's going to take us right over the Japs!"

"That's exactly what I want. Now throttle back, for cryin' out loud—let's not make this big black airplane easy to spot by blowing flames out her exhausts. I'm going back to the blisters for a better look...and to get some pictures."

Jock had barely stepped from the cockpit when Sid Baum, the radar operator, yelled, "Holy shit! I'm getting returns like crazy, five miles dead ahead, maybe a little less."

"Dammit," Simpson said. "A mountain! I knew it! We don't know where the hell we are!"

Lieutenant Becker replied, "Begging your pardon, Skipper, but I've got a pretty damn good idea where the hell we are...and there aren't any mountains ahead of us."

"Mister Becker's right, sir," Baum added. "This sure as hell isn't any mountain I'm looking at. It's got to be ships. Lots of them."

We figured that, too, dammit, Jock told himself. *Ships bringing troops under cover of darkness. Lots of ships bringing lots of troops.*

"Hold this damn course, Lieutenant," Jock yelled to Simpson. Then he continued aft to the gun blisters, passing below the flight engineer at his panel in the stubby cabane strut that joined the fuselage to the wing. The engineer, a crusty CPO named Atticus "Buzz" Parmly, called down, "What the hell's going on, Major? The lieutenant can't seem to decide whether he wants to climb or stay put. He's playing hell with my fuel calculations."

"We're staying put, Chief. We may have hit the jackpot."

"Jackpot, eh? We gonna win the war tonight, Major?"

"Right now, I'd settle for not losing it, Chief."

When Jock reached the aft compartment, he found Minsky and Benedetto, the two gunners, staring intently out the left blister. Benedetto asked, "What the hell's going on down there, sir? It's lit up like a fucking carnival."

"Looks like the Japs are building airfields," Jock replied. "That lit-up area's got to be between Mokmer and Sorido. It's the only place on Biak where there's a plain flat enough for airfields but close to the sea for easy resupply."

Minsky asked, "All the rest is mountains and jungle, right?"

"Pretty much."

"And the Army's hot to invade it, ain't you, sir?"

"Afraid so," Jock replied. "Pretty soon, too…maybe too damn soon. But that's not for publication, understand?"

"Aye aye, sir."

As the Cat flew closer to the shoreline, the floodlights, though trained on the ground, reflected an unwelcome glow across the plane's lower surface and into her cabin. The scene below looked as if it was being played out in the bright sunlight of high noon. Trucks, steam rollers, and gangs of men—hundreds, maybe a thousand—were toiling to clear and level long, narrow strips of land in three distinct areas.

"Three separate airfields, spread out over about five miles," Jock said as he snapped photos and jotted notes on a map. "They'll be able to launch hundreds of planes, enough to do some serious damage to our amphibious assault before it even gets near the beach. No wonder we couldn't see any of this during the day—they're working under camouflage netting. Looks like miles of it."

Flying directly over the shoreline now, they could see ocean-going troop barges nestled against makeshift floating jetties and the sparse patches of beachfront the mangroves had failed to claim. Each barge was huge, meant to carry fifty to one hundred troops or tons of equipment. Jock counted at least three dozen offloading men and materiel. The rectangular shapes of countless other barges lurked in the offshore darkness, barely visible yet betrayed by the glow of their wakes as they circled, waiting their turn to be guided through the reefs.

Jock didn't need to see any more. He hurried back to the cockpit. Grabbing the message pad on the radio operator's desk, he began to draft the message to 6th Army HQ: a warning that Biak was not the easy pickings MacArthur had pronounced it to be.

Then the first jolt rocked the Cat.

Even though they'd expected it, to a man they wanted to pretend it hadn't happened. But they couldn't pretend for long, not as the harsh, industrial racket of flak punching through their ship continued. They dared to look and saw the orange glints in the dark sky — looking deceptively like the harmless blink of a photographer's flash—as anti-aircraft shells exploded all around them. They could hear the explosions, too, their dull *poomfs* too close for the drone of her engines to mask—quickly followed by a sound like angry waves of hail against a tin roof as still more iron fragments ripped through her thin aluminum skin.

With a sickening lurch, the Cat yawed left. The steady, comforting drone of her engines turned into the cyclic moan of mismatched rpms as the port engine began to falter. Chief Parmly struggled with the dying engine, gently playing her controls, trying to restore at least some of her power, while he offered a silent prayer for the continued health of the good starboard engine.

"I CAN'T CLIMB ON ONE ENGINE, DAMMIT," Lieutenant Simpson yelled. "WE'VE GOT TO GET THE HELL OUT OF HERE."

He jerked the control wheel hard to the right, hoping to turn his lumbering ship back over the sea, out of harm's way.

Nothing happened. The Cat didn't turn right. She just kept drifting left, over the Japanese on Biak.

What the hell? he thought, and gave the wheel an experimental spin fully to the left. The Cat didn't respond in that direction, either.

Staring in bewilderment at the useless controls, he said, "Son of a bitch...we've got no ailerons. Flak must have cut the cables. Right rudder's already to the floor fighting this crapped-out engine...and we're still slipping to port."

His co-pilot, a cocksure rookie named Steve Richards, tapped his finger against the altimeter and muttered, "Shit...shit...shit." The instrument was slowly winding down, dragging Richards' confidence down with it.

Lieutenant Simpson gave a tentative backward tug on the control column. The ship's nose began to rise. "At least the elevators still work," he said, watching as the airspeed—already dangerously low—began to bleed off. "But if we don't keep the nose down, she's going to stall."

He turned to his radio operator and said, "Morales, send out the *mayday*. Tell them we're going to end up in the drink somewhere south of Biak."

"No," Jock said, still writing on the message pad. "If we're going down, we've got to get this intel report out first. Too many lives are at—"

"Bullshit on that," Simpson interrupted. "I'm not taking a dunk in the Pacific without them knowing where the hell I am."

Becker, the navigator, asked, "And where exactly are you going to be, Skipper? We don't have a clue where we're going to splash. Not yet, anyway."

"*Ballpark*, Mister Becker. Just get us in the damn ballpark."

"One hell of a ballpark," Becker mumbled as he drew a big goose egg on his chart south of Biak Island.

"We're wasting time," Jock said, thrusting the message pad toward the radio operator. "How about it, Morales?"

Hector Morales looked at Jock, and then his pilot. Grabbing the message pad, he said, "Begging your pardon, Mister Simpson, but the major here is right. And if you gentlemen would stop measuring your peckers for a minute and leave me alone, I could get off *both* these messages no sweat." He hunched over his telegraph key and began to send the intel report.

"Dammit, I gave you a *direct* order, Morales," Simpson said.

"Yeah, I know you did, sir, but he outranks you."

He kept right on sending Jock's report.

"Dammit, I'm in command of this aircraft," the pilot said. "You'll do as I—"

Jock cut him off. "No he won't, Mister Simpson, because I'm in command of this *mission*. Every man in your crew seems to realize that except you. Just fly the fucking airplane."

The moaning of the out-of-sync engines stopped, giving way to a shrill squeal like metal against a grinding wheel. The cockpit lit up with an orange glow as the damaged port engine trailed a comet's tail of sparks. In seconds, it burst into vivid flames, which swept aft across the wing.

Before Simpson could scream *Feather it...shut her down*, the engine seized, her propeller blades coming to an abrupt halt in a startling display of centrifugal force that tore the engine halfway off its mount. It dangled crazily, a useless, drag-inducing appendage on a barely controllable ship that needed every bit of that lost streamlining just to stay airborne a few minutes more.

At least the fire had gone out.

Ensign Richards was still watching the altimeter wind down. "We're going to be on the deck in a little over a minute," he said. "We've got to hit level, or we're going to bury a wingtip and cartwheel...and I can't keep her straight with the rudder anymore."

"No shit," Simpson replied. "Looks like there's only one way to pull that off now..."

He yanked the throttle of the undamaged starboard engine to idle. The Cat became nothing more than a reluctant, muttering glider, wings level at least, but sinking steadily back down to earth.

The floodlights of the Japanese airfield builders were now behind them. Below was nothing but an indefinable darkness.

"We can't possibly be over water again," Simpson said.

"Believe me, we're not," the navigator replied. "There's miles of Biak still ahead of us."

"We're putting the tip floats down, anyway," the pilot said.

Wishful thinking...

The first new sound was an intermittent scraping, as if a stiff brush was scouring metal.

The second was a sickening *CRUNCH*, like a boat being smashed against rocks by an unforgiving sea...

Followed by the violent deceleration that swirled everyone and everything around the cockpit like rag dolls...

And then nothing but a damning stillness.

Chapter Two

As Jock regained his senses, one thing became obvious: they hadn't crashed in the water. His hands found a flashlight; its beam revealed they weren't quite on the ground, either—at least not the forward fuselage. It had sheared from the rest of the airframe and was wedged high amid a stand of trees, its nose angled sharply upward. The first challenge would be to not fall to earth through the gaping hole where the cabin bulkhead used to be once he freed himself from his seatbelt.

As he struggled with the buckle, one thought filled his mind: *This was supposed to have been a desk job...a game-legged infantryman helping the Air Force make better maps for us dogfaces.*

Nobody, though, had forced him to fly recon missions like this one, which had just come to its unceremonious end. Going on flying status had been his decision and his alone.

But aside from aching like he'd just taken a thorough beating in the boxing ring, he knew he wasn't badly hurt. Even the leg seriously wounded months ago—the wound that was supposed to keep him out of combat—still felt serviceable.

Hell, I hardly limp at all anymore.

Reaching beneath his seat, he was relieved to find his Thompson submachine gun still there, its strap still wrapped around the seat frame.

And these Navy guys gave me funny looks when I brought this tommy gun on board, like it never occurred to them we might land in the wrong place and need some serious firepower. All they carry are those sidearms...and I bet they can't hit anything more than five feet away with them.

Making the uphill climb through the cockpit on hands and knees, he found Hector Morales helping Sid Baum from beneath the wreckage of his radar set.

"You guys okay?"

"Yeah, I'm fine, Major," Morales replied, and then asked Baum, "You sure you're not hurt, Sid? There's a hundred pounds of crap laying on you."

"Nah, Hec, I'm good, I think. Nothing's broken. Ain't heard much out of the officers, though."

Jock climbed farther into the cockpit and found out why: Becker, the navigator, was dead. His head lay against his chest as if attached by nothing more than rubber bands.

Broken neck, the poor bastard, Jock told himself.

Simpson, the pilot, and Richards, the copilot, were just coming around, moaning softly, still strapped to their seats. They were covered with plexiglass splinters from the shattered cockpit windows. Miraculously, neither appeared to have suffered more than superficial cuts. Jock went to work freeing Simpson from his seat harness.

The pilot's return to lucidity was as abrupt as if a switch had been thrown. He fixed Jock in an accusing glare and announced, "This isn't my fault, you know. It was all your idea."

"Save that crap for the pilots' lounge," Jock replied, helping him from the seat. "Nobody gives a shit whose fault it is at the moment. Now hang on to something real tight or you'll slide right out of here. We haven't figured out how far it is to the ground yet."

"Yeah, we have, Major," Morales' voice replied out of the darkness. "We played out some rope, and we're about twenty-five feet up. But we've got other problems…the chief's hurt. Looks like he busted his arm. Must've hit his head, too, because he thinks he's back in Cleveland. And I just got a pretty good whiff of hundred octane."

"EVERYBODY OUT," Lieutenant Simpson said, pushing past Jock in a great rush to slide down that rope.

"Not so damn fast," Jock said, holding him by the arm. "You and Mister Richards take the thirty cal from the nose turret. Grab as many ammo belts as you can carry, too."

"NO TIME! WE'RE GONNA BURN, DAMMIT," Simpson replied. "WE GOTTA GO."

"There isn't anything in this part of the airplane to burn, Mister Simpson," Jock said. "In case you haven't noticed, the wings aren't with us anymore. They got ripped off—and if memory serves me right, all the fuel is in those wings." He tightened his grip on the Navy man's arm. "Now get ahold of yourself, Lieutenant. Welcome to the ground war. The fun's just getting started."

They left Becker's body in the cockpit. "We'll get him out and bury him once we get our bearings," Jock told the others.

It wasn't hard to find the rest of the airplane, even in the dark. Jock took Baum and backtracked down the line of broken trees that extended some fifty yards from the severed forward fuselage. It was all there: two torn-off wings, forming a ragged *V* with the tail section inside. The battered bodies of Minsky and Benedetto, the two aft gunners, were there, too, lying amid the wreckage. The odor of aviation gasoline Hector Morales had detected while they were still hanging in the trees was overpowering; leaking fuel was forming widening pools on the ground.

As they dragged the dead gunners clear of the twisted metal and puddled fuel, Baum asked, "You're going to get us out of here, aren't you, Major Miles? I mean, Mister Simpson may be a decent pilot and all, but down here, well…"

His voice trailed off. Further explanation seemed unnecessary.

Before Jock could answer, they heard the growl of a motor vehicle engine, barely above idle, far off but growing louder.

"Shit," Jock said, "I think someone heard our arrival."

Baum asked, "Shouldn't we be seeing some glare off his headlights or something?"

Jock replied, "Ain't that funny? They've got their airfields lit up like Times Square, but a solitary vehicle driving around in the bush is practicing blackout discipline. That's why they're going real slow…they can't see a damn thing in front of them."

"How far away do you think that truck is, sir?"

"Can't tell for sure. Maybe half a mile. Leave these poor guys here for now. Let's get back with the others."

They didn't have any trouble finding *the others*—Simpson, Richards, Morales—in the darkness of the rainforest. All they had to do was home in on the racket those three men were making.

Three men. There should have been four.

"Knock off the noise, dammit," Jock said. "We've got company coming. And where the hell is Chief Parmly?"

"Don't know," Simpson replied. "We were trying to make a splint for his arm, and he just kept babbling about going to some bowling alley to meet some dame. Next thing we knew, he was gone."

The pilot was all jittery motion, ready to vanish like his flight engineer. "We heard that truck," he said. "It's coming this way. We've got to get the hell away from the ship."

"Hold on a minute, Lieutenant," Jock said. "The truck's not that close. Not yet, anyway. Maybe you'd like to hear about the rest of your crew first, so you won't be worried you lost track of them, too?"

"What? Are they dead?"

"Yep."

"Their fifty cals...can we use them?"

"No, they're all twisted up in the wreckage. Besides, they're too heavy for the handful of us to carry around. The thirty cal from the nose is a lot more practical."

Richards, the co-pilot, wasn't even a shadow of the cocky young pilot he'd been in the air. He whined, "But don't we need a tripod to fire that thing?"

"Believe me, Mister Richards, we won't need a tripod. Who's the best shot with it?"

All the Navy men pointed to Hector Morales.

Jock said, "Good. You handle it, Morales. Everybody else, strap a belt of ammo around yourself, just like this..." He draped one around his own torso to demonstrate. "Now, did you get everything else we need out of the plane?"

"Yeah," Simpson replied, "we've got the survival kit, the canteens, the code book, the Very pistol...but we've got two more little problems."

"Only two? Now there's a miracle. So what's the deal?"

"Well, first off, Ensign Richards has lost his forty-five."

"Yeah," Richards said, "the stupid thing must've fallen out of its holster when I was sliding down the rope." Like a confused schoolboy, he added, "I can't find it in the dark."

Jock took the .45 from his own holster and handed it to Richards. "Here, use mine," he said. Unslinging the submachine gun from his shoulder, he added, "I'll get by with Mister Thompson here. What's the second problem?"

Simpson replied, "Morales never sent that mayday I ordered him to. I'm going to make sure he rots in the brig as soon as we—"

"*Balls*, Lieutenant," Jock interrupted. "Do us all a favor and put a lid on that bullshit right now. You sound like some *shithouse lawyer*—and the law doesn't mean a whole lot out here in the bush. Neither do those pilot's wings."

"Oh yeah? Then *enlighten* me, Major...what *does* mean *a whole lot* in the bush?"

"Watching out for each other's asses and not doing anything stupid, Mister Simpson."

The vehicle was close enough now to hear the driver grinding its gears.

"C'mon, let's go south," Simpson said, checking the compass in his shaking hand. He looked ready to break into a sprint.

"No," Jock replied. "That would be one of those *stupid* things I was just talking about. We're not running anywhere...not in the dark. It's bad enough the chief's already stumbling around out there."

Simpson's whispered reply sounded like a muffled shriek: "So that's your plan, Major? Stay here and die?"

"No, Lieutenant, that's not it. Now listen up—first, we're going to get about fifty paces from this nose section and set up a perimeter."

"But there's only five of us."

"That's plenty, Mister Simpson. Everyone, follow me."

***

They could hear the Japanese shouting in the darkness. "Sounds like they've found the wreckage," Jock whispered. "Just remember...if they come at us, let the thirty cal do the talking. Those pistols will be useless unless you can reach out and touch the bastard."

He crawled closer to Morales on the machine gun and added, "If you've got to shoot, keep it low. Good troops will go to ground at the first shot. Make sure they stay there."

"Got it, sir. But the tracers...won't they give our position away? I tried to swap them out but there's not enough time...and I can't see what the hell I'm doing."

"Don't sweat it, Morales. Close as we're going to be, they'll see the muzzle flash, anyway. That's good thinking, though. Keep it up."

A *crack*, like a footstep crunching through the underbrush, very close.

A man's scream from the other side of the perimeter.

Multiple shots from a .45 pistol, GI issue.

And then the insane racket of so many different weapons, shooting wildly.

More men screaming, near and far.

Bullets flying, ricocheting off the ground, the trees, the mangled metal that used to be the Cat.

The strobe-like flash of Morales' machine gun, its tracers etching lines of brilliant light as they deflected like speeding pinballs off invisible bumpers.

Jock's mind sorted the chaos with a swiftness born of hard experience: *The Japs aren't on top of us...they're by the wings and tail.*

In the middle of all that gasoline...

He grabbed the Very pistol, slipped a flare into its chamber...

Skip it like a stone, Jock.

The flare was startlingly bright as it streaked from the pistol, a low line drive piercing the darkness that concealed the wreckage, dipping, bouncing...

But the broad circle of fire that erupted as it careened through puddles of fuel seemed brighter still.

They watched in open-mouthed awe as the dark silhouettes of men danced crazily in the flames...

Until they seemed to evaporate, drifting with the embers into the night sky.

The only shots being fired now were the random cook-offs of rounds caught in the blaze, aimless but no less deadly.

"Keep your asses down," Jock said, "and follow me."

They'd only low-crawled a few yards when Sid Baum moaned, "Oh, geez..."

He'd bumped into the lifeless body of Chief Parmly.

Baum hesitated for a moment, wondering what to do, until he realized there was only one choice. He left the body where it was and scurried away after the others.

Once they'd escaped the fire's light, they got up off their bellies and walked as swiftly as the darkness and the rainforest allowed. Jock led; the Navy men followed, each with a firm grasp on the shadowy form in front of him. To lose that grip—and become lost, separated from the rest—could be as good as a death sentence.

Thick undergrowth snagged their feet constantly. Each man had tripped and fallen countless times, pulling down the man in front and behind like a sagging chain. Every tumble sapped a little more of their ebbing strength. Jock called them to a halt. They needed a break.

"Give me a perimeter just like we had back at the wreck," Jock said.

They complied without a word, too terrified to do anything else.

Baum began to say, "The chief...he's—" before Lieutenant Simpson cut him off.

"We know, Baum. We know...he's dead."

Even in the dark, Simpson could feel Jock's eyes boring into him.

"You have a problem with me, Major?" he asked.

Jock replied, "Just wondering who popped off with the .45 back there and started that little shitstorm."

"What are you saying? You think I shot Chief Parmly?"

"I'm not saying anything, Lieutenant. But ears don't lie. It came from your side of the perimeter. What were you shooting at?"

"Dammit, I don't know...I saw something—*someone*," Simpson replied. "He was right there"—he held out his arm to indicate the closeness—"and you were the one who said *don't shoot unless you can reach out and touch the bastard*."

Morales mumbled, "Even if the bastard was one of our own guys?"

Mumbled or not, everyone heard it.

"Now just a damn minute," Simpson said, "I've had about enough of you, Morales, and—"

"Shut up, Mister Simpson," Jock interrupted. "Here's the deal—you fucked up when you lost track of Chief Parmly. If he'd been where he should have, he might not be dead right now. You understand what I'm telling you?"

Simpson gave a barely perceptible nod.

"I take it that's a *yes*, Mister Simpson?"

"Yes...sir."

He may have hesitated to say it, but his use of the word *sir* managed—finally—to convey every ounce of respect the term deserved.

"Good," Jock said, "because there's nothing we can do about the chief now, just like there's nothing we can do about Mister Becker, Minsky, or Benedetto. Let's see if we can get the rest of us off this rock while we're still drawing breath. Any questions?"

There were none.

"Okay," Jock continued, "let's get reorganized. Anyone have any pistol ammo left?"

Aside from Hector Morales, who'd been firing the machine gun, none of the Navy men did. They'd shot every last bullet they had.

"Morales, divide up what's in your magazine to the others," Jock said. "That'll give you a couple of shots each. But don't waste them. I've still got one full magazine for the Thompson…and it looks like we've got a belt and a half for the thirty cal."

"That's not a whole lot, sir," Simpson said.

"You've got that right," Jock replied, "so let's try and stay out of trouble."

They were ready to move again in minutes. Lieutenant Simpson asked Jock, "What's the plan, sir?"

"We're going to head east."

"Why east, sir? The south coast is a lot closer."

"Because the south coast's got the best beaches for an amphibious landing, even better than where we saw the Japs landing a couple of hours ago."

A couple of hours ago—already it felt like *a couple of years*, Jock thought.

"The Japs know a good beach when they see one," Jock added, "so they'll be in force down south, waiting for MacArthur to come. We'll take our chances going east. Intel says some Dutch planters may still be hiding out there. If they are, maybe we can hook up with them."

"Are you going to be able to walk very far on that leg of yours, sir?"

"Just watch me, Mister Simpson."

Chapter Three

With the sunrise came the ability to pinpoint their position. All one of them had to do was get his head above the dense rainforest so he could see Biak's prominent mountain peaks. "I'm not the tree climber I used to be," Jock said, "not with this leg. So who's it going to be?"

Arthur Simpson didn't look like much of a candidate. He was burly, looking every bit the tackle he'd played on the Annapolis varsity. Sid Baum was a big bruiser, too—an urban brawler if there ever was one.

Either one of them would probably snap the top of a tree right off, Jock thought.

Wiry guys made the best tree climbers—that got the list of candidates down to Steve Richards and Hector Morales.

"I'll do it, sir," Morales said, sounding positively eager.

"No," Lieutenant Simpson replied. "This is an officer's job. Mister Richards, you do it."

Steve Richards looked terrified at the prospect.

"Don't worry," Jock told him. "You're a better target down here in the open than you'll be up there."

That didn't seem to comfort Richards at all. But he took the compass Jock offered and, with great reluctance, swung himself onto a lower branch. Jock said, "Just get us good azimuths to the two highest peaks. They should be hard to miss once you're up there."

Using branches like ladder rungs, Richards got about halfway up the tree trunk—thirty feet or so above the ground. From that point on, the branches would be too thin to support a man's weight. He'd have to shimmy up the trunk to reach the top.

He made the mistake of looking down...and froze.

Jock asked, "Something wrong, Mister Richards?"

"I...I can't, sir. I can't do it."

"Why the hell not?"

"I...I just can't."

Sid Baum offered, "I think I know what's wrong with him, sir. He's afraid of heights."

"Are you shitting me? A *pilot* who's afraid of heights?"

"Seen it before, sir. A good pal of mine couldn't even climb a ladder or ride a Ferris wheel when we were kids, but that didn't stop him from becoming a bomber pilot with the Army. Got a letter from my wife last week that said he did his twenty-five missions over Europe and now he's back home."

Jock puzzled over that one for a moment before saying, "That doesn't make a whole lot of sense."

"Maybe not, sir, but it's the God's honest truth. As long as the thing he was riding wasn't attached to the ground, it was no problem. Looks to be the same story for Mister Richards."

"Well, I'll be a son of a bitch," Jock said. "Morales, go and get him down."

Arthur Simpson seemed just as startled as everyone else. He responded to Jock's accusing glare with an earnest shrug that said, *Hey, I didn't know! Really!*

Good thing, Jock thought, *because setting a man up like that—one of* your *men, to boot—would make you an even bigger asshole than I already think you are.*

Once Richards' feet were firmly back on the ground, Hector Morales shot to the top of the tree with astonishing ease. The compass shots took less than a minute and then he, too, was back on Mother Earth.

"The highest peak on the north island is shrouded in mist," Morales said, "but I still got a pretty good estimate where it is, sir. Couldn't be off more than a degree or two. The other peak I shot dead on. I can still see smoke from where we burned the plane, though. We're not as far from it as I thought...a mile or so, probably. I'd hate to get caught in a forest fire we set ourselves."

"Don't worry about that," Jock replied. "The wind's blowing away from us...and it'll rain buckets before you know it. That'll put the fire out, for sure."

Plotting Morales' azimuths on the map, Jock said, "That puts us here, halfway across the southern plateau, about three miles north of the southern coast...in the middle of this big, empty green glob. This old map sure isn't real big on surface features, is it? No rivers, no streams, no contour lines...*nothing*. I guess we should count ourselves lucky it showed those two peaks, at least."

Arthur Simpson took a good look at the map and replied, "I thought you said the Japs would be in force near the south coast, sir. It seems deserted around here."

"Are you complaining, Mister Simpson?"

"Hell, no, sir."

"Don't sell the Japs short, either," Jock added. "Just because we don't see any at the moment doesn't mean there's not a regiment or two nearby." He made a small circle on the map along Biak's east coast. "Let's shoot for this area here. It's only about a seven-mile walk...if we can believe this map, that is."

Simpson asked, "Why there, sir?"

"Because if I was looking for somewhere to hide out, I'd pick a place like that. Nothing but rainforest, supposedly. Maybe the Dutch think the same way."

"You mean if they're still even on this island, sir...and alive, right?"

"Well, Mister Simpson, I'd say you have an excellent grasp of the situation. Pull your gear together—we move out in two minutes."

Steve Richards didn't need to say a word. All it took was one look at him to know he was mortified by his tree-climbing failure. Jock walked over to him; Richards' eyes wouldn't meet his.

"Don't sweat it, Steve," Jock said quietly, hoping only Richards would hear. "I can't climb a tree, either. And I sure as hell can't fly a plane...so I guess that puts you one up on me."

Lieutenant Simpson was too close not to hear it, though. He hovered, with what Jock thought to be a smirk on his face, looking ready to mock his copilot...

But Simpson read the forbidding look on Jock's face correctly: *Don't you fucking dare.* He turned away and said nothing.

They hadn't walked far before the downpour came, just as Jock promised it would. The jungle rain promptly drenched them, and its loud *hiss* made it impossible to speak softly. "Use that rain catcher from the survival kit," Jock shouted. "Catch every drop you can."

"But we've still got lots of water, sir," Baum replied.

Jock laughed and said, "You flight crew guys don't get out in the hot sun very much, do you?"

"No, sir, not really. We're either flying...or cooling our heels."

"Well, just wait until this squall passes and the sun starts to bake us. You never have enough water in these parts. Fill us up...every container we've got. When you're done with that, everyone use some rainwater to wash yourselves up."

Jock decided this was a good time for the rest of the jungle hygiene lecture. He gathered the Navy men close: "I don't see any Halazone in that kit, so don't drink any—and I mean *any*—water from streams we might stumble across. We don't need anyone laid low with *the shits*. And while we're on the subject, if you do have to shit, don't wipe yourself with leaves. You've already bought enough trouble without your ass itching and burning, too. There any toilet paper in that kit?"

"A little," Baum replied.

"Well, when that runs out, use whatever paper you don't need...ration wrappers, notebook pages, whatever you've got. Just don't use one of these damn maps, in case they actually turn out to be at least a little accurate. And one more thing..."

They all looked at him like they'd heard quite enough already.

"Whatever paper you use, bury it. We don't need to leave any calling cards."

The rain shower lasted only a few minutes, ending as if heaven's faucet had been abruptly shut off. Jock asked, "Any of those forty-fives get wet in their holsters?"

The Navy men all shook their heads.

"Good. Now let's hold up and dry out the thirty cal." He pulled the small oil bottle from the stock of his

Thompson. "When you're done, get a little of this on those moving parts in the casing. As soon as that gun's up and running again, I'll dry out my Thompson. That way, we don't lose all our firepower at once."

It wasn't even 0900 but the heat and humidity were already taking their toll. "I think I see what you meant about the water, sir," Sid Baum said, slurping from his canteen once again. "How long you figure until we hit the coast?"

Before Jock could answer, there was a shriek from farther back in the column—one high-pitched *yelp*—the sound of a startled and terrified man. Jock turned around to see Arthur Simpson some ten yards away from a native man, who was clad only in khaki trousers but carrying a Nambu pistol. That weapon was pointed straight at the Navy pilot.

The native shouted something—Jock couldn't understand what he said.

Arthur Simpson was jerking around as if receiving electric shocks. He was trying—and failing—to pull his own pistol from its holster. His panicky hands couldn't seem to get the motion right.

Before anyone could take a breath, the native fired…

Simpson flinched but didn't go down. And he still hadn't drawn his weapon.

"DOWN!" Jock yelled. Everyone but Simpson hit the ground.

The native fired again.

Again Simpson flinched but didn't fall. He began backpedaling as fast as he could...

Until he tripped over Sid Baum.

The native took a step back, putting a tree between him and Jock, and fired a third time.

Racing to clear his field of fire, Jock told himself, *If I don't take this guy down, nobody will.*

The *BUPBUPBUP* of a three-shot burst from Jock's Thompson...

The red spray of blood and body tissue as the three bullets hit the native squarely in the chest...

And he fell backward in a heap.

His Nambu clattered to the ground.

"ANYBODY HIT?" Jock asked.

No one answered. But Jock could see Morales and Richards clearly. They seemed shaken, but physically all right.

"Stay sharp, you two," Jock told them. "There may be more of them around."

He had to take a few steps to see Simpson and Baum. They weren't hurt, either...but Simpson looked like he'd just witnessed his own death. Baum just looked confused. He asked, "What the hell's going on, sir? I never saw nothing."

"Take a look over there," Jock replied, pointing to the man he'd just shot.

Baum took a few tentative steps toward the motionless body. The native wasn't dead yet—he was still gurgling softly—but he would be very soon. The blood flowing from his wounds was nearly invisible as it pooled on the wet ground.

"Where the fuck did he come from, sir? That's a Jap pistol, ain't it?"

"Yep. Looks like Jap Army pants he's wearing, too."

Tucking the Nambu into his belt, Baum said, "So it looks like the natives ain't necessarily friendly, are they?"

"Maybe not. Let's get the hell out of here...before some of his friends show up."

Helping the ashen-faced Simpson to his feet, Jock added, "It's a hell of a lot harder to kill people when you're face to face, isn't it? Not nice and easy like dropping bombs on them, eh?"

Simpson couldn't find the words to reply.

"Well, at least you didn't piss or shit yourself. Probably didn't have enough time. C'mon...let's get moving."

As he took the lead once again, Jock found himself mumbling: *Fucking flyboys.*

Chapter Four

Colonel Dick Molloy walked briskly into the old plantation villa at Hollandia, New Guinea, trusting no one but himself with the delicate task at hand. He passed the GIs nailing a sign above the entryway and thought, *They're sure not wasting any time getting set up here. They only flew in from Port Moresby yesterday.*

The sign read:
SUPREME ALLIED HEADQUARTERS,
SOUTHWEST PACIFIC
OFFICE OF CIVIL AFFAIRS

This is where he'd find Jillian Forbes—actually, Jillian Forbes *Miles*, Jock Miles' Australian wife. She'd been given the job *Assistant Australian Advisor for Civilian and Refugee Affairs.* Dick Molloy had been the prime force behind that appointment, lobbying for her until General Sutherland, MacArthur's Chief of Staff, finally relented and decreed the job was hers. After all, who could provide better guidance on the needs of resettled civilians and refugees than a woman who was both of these things—and an ex-POW of the Japanese, too?

Or, as Sutherland dismissively put it, *Oh, what the hell, Molloy. She knows all about sea transport and the darkies, right?*

Molloy had chafed at the mandate she'd be *Assistant* Australian Advisor, since there didn't seem to be any *Senior* Advisor at Supreme Allied Headquarters. But he'd take what he could get; he fully understood that a woman would never be the boss of anything in MacArthur's kingdom.

He made his way across the worn hardwood floors of what was once an opulent parlor before the Japanese occupied it. They'd first used the villa as a division headquarters. Later, as American and Australian forces bore down on them, it had become a hospital and, finally, a charnel house as Hollandia fell to the Americans.

Now it served as a bustling office that seemed much too clean and fresh to be part of a forward Allied headquarters. *Those Army engineers did a hell of a job fixing this place up after what it went through*, Molloy told himself, trying to lighten just for a moment the weight of what he was about to do.

She was sitting at a desk in the middle of the room, sifting through stacks of paperwork. As soon as she saw the look on Colonel Molloy's face, she had no doubt: *Something's wrong...terribly wrong.*

Her stomach knotted as if it had been punched, knocking the wind from her, forcing her to whisper:

"What happened? Is he...?"

"We don't know anything, Jillian. He was along on a night recon mission."

Molloy hesitated, feeling as if he was betraying a secret Jock had very much wanted to keep from her. A betrayal for sure—but a necessary one now. As far as he knew, Jillian had no idea her husband was doing anything other than an Air Force staff job on Wakde Island, just over a hundred miles to the west. *Intelligence liaison* between Army and Air Force, as Jock had described it. A safe job, out of combat and firmly on the ground.

"A *flying* recon mission, of course." Her voice had returned but sounded disembodied, as if she was having a discussion with herself.

"You knew, Jillian? You knew he was flying?"

"How bloody stupid do you think I am, Colonel? Of course I knew."

Molloy looked surprised...or perhaps confused, so she added, "I work for your bloody Army, remember? I know how to find things out. So where do they think he is?"

"We don't know. They radioed in over an island called Biak. That was the last thing heard from them."

A male voice—officious, impatient—boomed from an adjacent office, saying, "Missus Miles, I need those figures on Dutch POW repatriation on the double."

Through the office's open door, Dick Molloy could see the speaker, an aging, pudgy, and sweating captain—the type of rear-echelon pencil-pusher who considered himself the complete soldier because he was dumb enough to wear a necktie in the tropics—seated like a petty tyrant behind a desk too grand to be GI issue. It must have been the property of the original Dutch plantation owners.

"I'll take care of that jackass for you," Molloy told Jillian as he turned toward the office.

"No," she replied, "it's all right. I'll be fine, sir."

She scooped up some of the papers from her desk and started her own trek to the captain. Over her shoulder, she mouthed the words, "Leave the wanker to me."

At the doorway, she stopped and looked back at Molloy. Her brave face cracked for just a moment as she asked, "You'll tell me the minute you know, won't you?"

And then she strode to the captain's desk, unafraid, as always, of self-important little men.

Chapter Five

Arthur Simpson finally got his .45 out of its holster. Once they'd started walking east again, it never left his right hand. He intended to be ready for the next encounter.

"Remember," Jock told him, "you've only got two rounds in that pistol. Make 'em count...hold it straight out in both hands when you fire. None of that movie cowboy *shooting from the hip* bullshit."

"Yeah, fine, sir," Simpson grumbled in reply.

It was just past sweltering noon when Hector Morales said, "Sir, how much longer do you figure we've got to walk?" He was sagging beneath the weight of the .30-caliber machine gun.

"Maybe another hour."

"I don't see how you doggies manage all this walking, sir."

"You mean *infantrymen*, don't you, Morales?"

"Yes, sir, that's what I meant. No disrespect or anything..."

"None taken. Tell you what, though...let Baum carry that weapon for a while."

Morales started to protest but thought better of it. His heart may have been willing, but his body was crying for some relief.

Sid Baum shouldered the machine gun and said, "It's okay, Hec. Take a break. You earned it."

They walked on. Fatigue made the now-thin rainforest an enemy: an endless and monotonous maze that hindered their progress, providing only random patches of shade that offered no shelter from the broiling heat. Vines tore their flesh and snared their feet. They were nearly out of water again.

When he first caught sight of them, Jock thought he was hallucinating. There were dark men—*natives?*—directly in front of them, just yards away yet nearly invisible...

And then the dark men stepped forward—very real now, a dozen or more, obviously natives—with empty hands held high over their heads in a gesture of surrender. Their garb was typically native—most clad only in shorts, a few in loin cloths. Not a hint of a Japanese garment this time.

Arthur Simpson had taken Jock's earlier instruction to heart. He held his .45 straight out, in both hands, its muzzle just a few feet from the face of a cringing native. Definitely not *cowboy bullshit*.

"NO!" Jock yelled. "DON'T SHOOT THEM!"

Simpson hadn't pulled the trigger yet, but his aim didn't waver.

"This could be a damn Jap trick," he said, his voice high-pitched and breathless, like a man scared half out of his mind. "Fuck it, let's kill them all."

"No, Mister Simpson. Put down that weapon. If this was an ambush, we'd be dead already."

"So what the fuck do we do?"

"We accept their surrender."

A tall native turned to Jock and said, "*Leider?*"

"I think I know what that means, sir," Sid Baum said. "It's Dutch. He's asking if you're the leader."

Jock nodded *yes*.

"Good," the tall native replied. "Come...come see *Meneer* Dyckman."

Jock turned to the Navy men and said, "I think we might've just hit that jackpot, lads."

Andreas Dyckman seemed less than pleased to have the Americans in his camp. Jock's first impression of the man: *His head looks like it's on fire!* The hair and beard were a vibrant red, slowly turning a brilliant orange in random places as it whitened with age. This tall and burly Dutchman—senior to all present by many years but fit as a much younger man—held court over his collection of fugitives from the Japanese. They numbered twenty-four European men of various ages—plus the sixteen native men and women loyal to the Dutchman. The village of huts they had created on this high ground overlooked the plateau that covered most of southern Biak. In outward appearance, it looked no different than a native village. Only the collection of white faces within its confines betrayed it.

In crisp English, Dyckman told Jock, "We fled here when the Japanese first arrived two and a half years ago. They have little interest in this part of the island. All the harbors and good land for airfields are on the opposite coast. Keeping hidden from them is not terribly difficult." He pointed to the tall native who led Jock and the Navy men to his enclave. "Josiah tells me that despite the islander you killed, you were not followed. That is the only reason you are allowed to be here." His tone was less than welcoming. Almost hostile.

"And we're most grateful to be here, Mister Dyckman...but I'm a little confused. Aren't we all on the same side?"

"I once thought that, Major Miles...until the deaths of our wives and children at the hands of your pilots changed my mind." The Dutchman glared at the two naval officers as he said it. The golden pilot wings on their chests had indelibly marked them as enemies.

"But perhaps you can be of some use to us," Dyckman said. "We saw the flames of your crash—"

"That fire wasn't from the crash," Jock interrupted. "We started it to get away from the Japs who showed up."

"No matter," Dyckman continued. "Did any of your radios survive the crash, Major?"

"Maybe...if they didn't burn."

"Well, we'll know shortly. My men will be back from your wreck before nightfall."

Glancing toward the boar being roasted on a spit, Dyckman added, "Come and have some supper. You and your men must be starving."

The reason for Dyckman's interest in the Cat's radios became apparent in short order. Jock was led to a hut containing a radio station, complete with multi-band receiver, transmitter, a bank of storage batteries, and a hand-cranked generator. Everything was in perfect working order...except the transmitter.

"It hasn't broadcast a single dot or dash in two years," Dyckman said. "We're not sure what's wrong with it...we're copra farmers, not radio experts. And we don't have spare parts, anyway."

"Two of the men with me *are* radio experts," Jock replied. "Maybe they can get this set back on the air."

Jock imagined Dyckman would be as enthused as he was at that prospect, but the Dutchman's words didn't reflect it: "For all the good it did last time."

"What do you mean?"

Dyckman settled slowly onto a stool. He voice took on a softer, doleful tone as he said, "February 1942, when the Japanese began sweeping down from the Philippines, we planned to escape. But we had only a few small boats, so we sent the women and children first. They set out just before nightfall. It's just a short sail to Japen Island—not even fifty kilometers—and an even shorter one from there to New Guinea. We were in radio contact with the Dutch military at Sarmi and told them refugees would be coming over the water. It did no good."

"Why? What happened?"

"They weren't even out of sight when the planes attacked them."

"And you think they were Allied planes? Hell, back then American planes weren't even here yet...just a few Aussie and Dutch. How can you be sure they weren't Japanese?"

"American, Australian, Dutch, it's all the same to the dead. At any rate, Major Miles, when the slaughter was over the planes flew south, back toward New Guinea. Japanese planes would have flown north or west."

"Well...I can see your point there, Mister Dyckman."

"Yet, we clung to the faint hope they'd somehow survived. Days went by before we learned they never arrived. Our escape plan was a total failure: they're dead, we're trapped here."

Radio static and snippets of voices in a jumble of languages filled the hut as the Dutchman spun the dial through the shortwave bands. "Let's see if your General Eisenhower has been thrown back into the English Channel yet," he said, settling on an Australian station.

"I don't think that's going to happen, Mister Dyckman," Jock replied.

"I wish I shared your optimism, Major."

Chapter Six

It was nearly dawn when Andreas Dyckman's scavenger team returned from the Cat's crash site. The team's leader—a young Dutchman named Hans—was the closest thing Dyckman had to a radio *expert*. The five natives under his direction had stripped anything that looked remotely like communications gear from the wreck and lugged it back to the camp.

Dyckman had begun to despair they'd never return. "What took you so long, Hans?"

"We had to wait until some *gekken* went away," Hans replied.

Jock asked, "What the hell are *gekken*?"

"Crazy people, Major," Dyckman replied. "It's what we call islanders who are enamored with the Japanese and try to emulate them."

"Like that one I killed yesterday on our walk here?"

"Yes. You were fortunate you ran into only one. They usually come in groups...islanders who banded together over some grievance against the Dutch. The Japanese invasion was the spark that ignited their rebellion."

"And the Japs give them weapons?"

"No, Major...even the Japanese are not that stupid. But like any other sprawling organization, their military *loses* things from time to time..."

"*Loses*...as in *gets stolen*?"

"Perhaps, or they simply leave stuff behind by accident when they relocate. The Japanese are ruthless but far from perfect."

"I see," Jock replied, "but the Japs I've fought—if they caught you with their stuff, you'd be executed on the spot."

"Of course. The Japanese on Biak are no different."

"So why the hell would a native walk around with a Jap weapon?"

"That's one of the reasons we call them *gekken*, Major Miles."

Morales and Baum walked into the radio hut. Both let out shrill whistles of surprise when they saw the Cat's radio gear—some of it still trailed several feet of wiring crudely hacked from the plane by machetes.

"Gee, this stuff didn't get burned hardly at all," Morales said, "but damn...it looks like you guys took an ax to it."

"Our tooling for this sort of work is quite limited, sir," Hans replied. "We had no choice. My apologies."

"Ahh, no apology necessary. And you don't have to call me sir." Morales pointed to the two chevrons stenciled on his sleeve and added, "I work for a living." Then he grew serious and asked, "Was Mister Becker still there?"

"There was a dead American flyer still in his seat, if that's who you mean."

"Yeah...him."

"Shit," Sid Baum muttered, "sure wish we could have buried him...and the other three guys, too." But then, like a man possessed with renewed purpose, he said, "So speaking of tools, you at least got a couple of screwdrivers so we can dig into this transmitter of yours and see what's what?"

As the two Navy men went to work, Jock had another question for Andreas Dyckman. "Those sympathizers…the *gekken*, as you call them…do they know you're here? And if they did, wouldn't they report you to the Japanese?"

"I suspect they have," Dyckman replied, "but the Japanese have far bigger problems than a tiny group of Europeans hidden away in the forest, wouldn't you say?"

Hector Morales wiped his sweaty brow and announced, "It's no use. We can't get this transmitter of theirs working, sir. We need some final amp tubes, but our sets don't have the right ones, so we can't cannibalize them. But we've got another idea…"

Jock replied, "What's that?"

"Simple…we can jury-rig their generator and power supply to *our* transmitter from the Cat. It'll take a little doing…we'll need to come up with some kind of soldering iron. Sid may already have that one figured out."

Sid Baum was holding a foot-long iron rod filed to a point. "If I make a wooden handle for the blunt end so I can hang onto the darned thing once it gets hot, we can stick the pointy end into a fire for a while and *voila*…we've got a soldering iron. It'll be a slow process, going wire for wire, but it should work. We don't have a roll of solder, so there won't be much of it on the connections…only what we can salvage from what's already there. They'll be a little brittle, but if we're gentle with it…"

"Sounds like a hell of a plan," Jock said, "but how *slow* do you figure this *slow process* will be?"

Baum replied, "We can probably have it up and running sometime tomorrow...Right, Hec?"

Morales nodded in agreement.

That sounded like good news to everyone except Andreas Dyckman. Deep in troubled thought, he stuffed his hands into the pockets of his tattered shorts and shuffled out of the radio hut. Jock was right behind him.

"That transmitter may save you, Major Miles," Dyckman said, "but it does me and my people little good now."

"What are you talking about? It'll get you and your people off this island."

Dyckman's initial reply was a few beats of skeptical laughter, soft and mournful notes trapped behind a tight-lipped smile. Then he said, "You put me in an awkward position, Major. If the Americans come now and drive off the Japanese, there is no point in my leaving. I must stay and reclaim my property. But you say the Japanese are far stronger here than your generals suspect, and you wish them to delay their invasion."

"Not for long, Mister Dyckman...just until we've prepared better."

"How long would that be, Major?"

"That's really not for me to say...a month, maybe two."

This time, Dyckman's laughter turned derisive. "And you believe that your fears—and yours alone—will persuade your generals to delay their precious plans? And here I thought you military officers were serious students of history. Didn't the last war teach you anything at all?"

"I'm just trying to do my job, Mister Dyckman."

"I have no doubt of that, Major, and I won't stand in your way. That gives me another problem, though..."

"What's that?"

"If we keep transmitting from the camp, the Japanese will come after us for certain. We can't push our luck too long. We'll have to relocate...and frequently. Will you be capable of that, Major?"

"Capable? Why wouldn't I be capable?"

"Your leg...is that an old wound? It seems to be bothering you."

"Don't worry yourself about my leg, Mister Dyckman. It'll get me wherever I need to go."

Sid Baum and Hector Morales had put up with the annoying presence of their two pilots all day. Lieutenant Simpson and Ensign Richards, hovering over them like fidgety shadows, had proved just as irritating—and just as useless—as the swarms of flying insects pestering the radiomen struggling to get the Cat's transmitter back on the air. The sun was going down now, forcing the tedious work to continue in the dim firelight. Sid Baum had finally had enough of the officers' needless *supervision*.

The soldering iron grew cold and useless again. Reheating it in the fire for what seemed like the hundredth time, Baum said, "You know, gentlemen, you're not really bringing a whole lot to this party. Watching us like hawks isn't helping you or us a damn bit."

Simpson replied, "We just want to make sure we get the hell out of here, Baum, as quickly as possible."

"That's what we want, too, sir...but dogging us won't make this job go any faster. We've got to be *real* careful what we're doing here. We hook up a wire wrong and this whole thing can go up in smoke...and then we're all really fucked."

He hesitated, weighing his next words carefully before finally saying them: "So, unless you gentlemen know something about wiring up a radio, how about you cut us some slack and get lost? With all due respect, of course."

"*Due respect,* my ass, Baum. I tell you what...we'll *get lost*. But you'd better not fuck this job up, or..."

"Or *what*, sir? How could we be in more trouble than we are right now?"

Simpson grumbled something unintelligible; Baum and Morales were sure they heard the word *brig* in there somewhere. He motioned for Richards to follow him, and they both beat a hasty retreat.

As they did, the pilots felt sure they heard Baum mumble something unintelligible, too. They were sure they heard the word *shithead* in there somewhere.

He couldn't sleep. Jock lay on a mat outside the hut, trying to count stars. The burning, haggard feeling in every exhausted sinew of his body was nothing new. Every combat soldier had learned to deal with it:

You'll sleep when you're dead.

Exhausted or not, his mind was in overdrive, planning what the first radio message would say—if and when the transmitter worked.

Even more difficult: planning what to do if the transmitter wouldn't work.

He wasn't the only one who couldn't sleep. Andreas Dyckman appeared out of the shadows and sat down beside him.

"If we move," the Dutchman said, "we should head north, into the mountains. They can only come at us from one direction then."

Jock nodded. He'd been thinking the same thing.

"Of course," Dyckman continued, "if you're lucky, you'll be long gone. It won't be your problem."

Jock had been thinking that, too. And more: "You know, even if we get picked up, you can still be a big help to our invasion force with that radio, funneling intel our way."

"Forgive my lack of enthusiasm, Major Miles, but a radio has never brought me anything but sorrow."

"You confuse me, Mister Dyckman. If you're so down on having a working transmitter, why did you bend over backwards to salvage one from the crash?"

"That's very simple, Major. I did it on the slim hope that if we can tell them where we are, then maybe we, too, won't be attacked by your planes."

Dyckman rose to his feet. "I'll let you sleep now, Major."

"Ahh, who's sleeping? But hold on a minute. I need to tell you something. I've been in a situation just like the one you're in."

"You have?"

"Yeah. I thought my wife was dead, too, lost at sea off Buna. I finally gave up and resigned myself to it…and I let a little bit of me die, too."

"But she wasn't dead?"

"Nope. Turned up a year later on Manus Island in a Jap POW camp. She's back in New Guinea now, working at Allied Headquarters."

"And your point in telling me this?"

"My point is this, Mister Dyckman: *never* give up hope."

"I appreciate your trying to cheer me, Major Miles…but I know what I saw."

Chapter Seven

In war, good news always seems to come with bad news attached. For Colonel Dick Molloy, the good news was that Jock Miles was alive and well on Biak. Even better, he was transmitting fresh intel the general staff needed to know immediately.

The bad news: that intel showed just how badly they were underestimating the strength of the Japanese force they'd soon face.

The Japs are turning that rock into a damn fortress, with enough air power to sink a big chunk of our invasion fleet before they even get near the place.

Biak will be like Buna all over again. Maybe worse.

He barged into the office of General Willoughby, MacArthur's intelligence chief, the message from Jock in hand. Willoughby's aide jumped out from behind his desk and blocked the open doorway to the general's inner sanctum.

"You can't go in there, Colonel," the aide said.

Molloy was about to shove this obstruction wearing captain's bars out of the way when Willoughby's irritated voice boomed from within the office.

"*At ease*, Colonel," the voice said. "You'd better have one hell of a good reason for this rude behavior, dammit."

"I believe I do, sir," Molloy replied, striding up to the general's desk. "I've got bad news—*real* bad news—from Biak."

Willoughby let out a frustrated sigh. "What is it this time, Richard?"

Molloy began to fill the general in on the details of Jock's report. He wasn't halfway through when the general held up his hand: *stop*.

"That Miles of yours...he keeps popping up like a bad penny, Richard. What I don't understand is why you're getting sucked into all his hysteria. Of course the Japanese will have airfields on Biak...and this is old news, anyway. His first report—the one when they were still airborne—was duly noted."

"*Duly noted*, sir...and promptly ignored."

The general's eyes flashed with anger. "*At ease*, Colonel. I won't tell you again."

"Begging your pardon, sir, but I know what we'd like to believe is the Jap situation on Biak, but it just doesn't add up to what Miles saw. We're facing an air and ground defense far more formidable than—"

Again, the general's hand went up.

"What he saw *at night*, Richard...*at night*, from a couple of thousand feet up. You know as well as I do the tricks the eye can play on an overactive imagination under those conditions."

"Begging your pardon, General, but Jock Miles is no rookie at this game. I think General MacArthur needs to be informed of the changing situation immediately."

"Oh, *do you*, Colonel? The last time I checked, you were a *regimental commander*. You wouldn't be trying to do the G2's job—*my* job—too, would you?" He pointed to the brass plate atop his desk, adorned with name, title, and two silver stars.

"No, sir. Of course not, sir. But we need to delay the Biak landings until—"

The hand went up once more.

"This is what you're going to do, Richard. Get with our Air Force people. Have them set up a bombing run on those *alleged targets* Miles identified for tomorrow." He'd sneered as he said the words *alleged targets*.

"But sir, it would take a raid by a hundred heavy bombers, at least, to take out all those airfields at once. That's way beyond Fifth Air Force's capabilities."

"Nonsense, Richard. They'll do the job with what they've got, just like they always have. And then, the Biak landings—*Operation Alamo*—will take place as planned, eight days from today."

"It's no good, sir," Molloy replied. "We've got to delay."

The general shook his head. "We're driving an enormous ship, Richard, at very great speed. You just don't stop it—no, you *can't* stop it—every time someone thinks he sees the boogey man."

He went back to shuffling the papers on his desk. Molloy stood in place, ramrod straight, struggling to find the words that might turn that *enormous ship* around.

"Why are you still here, Richard? You've been dismissed."

In reluctant retreat, Molloy was halfway to the door when General Willoughby said, "Oh, and one more thing, Richard. As long as Miles is already there, have him give us a bomb damage assessment after the raid. Nothing like having eyes on the ground."

"Isn't that what the photo recon boys at Fifth Air Force are supposed to do, sir?"

With a sarcastic smirk, Willoughby replied, "You mean the photo recon group that hasn't yet managed to take *one measly picture* of what Miles claims is there?"

Molloy ignored the jab. "But he and the Navy crew have been through a crash, sir...and they've been evading the Japanese ever since. We should really have the Navy pick them up ASAP."

"Negative, Richard. We've all been through worse, and you tell me this Miles of yours is a very resourceful boy. He's apparently healthy and in a position to be quite useful. You have your orders. Carry on."

Jillian hung up the phone and stared blankly into space. The young GI—a PFC mail clerk—who'd been standing beside her desk waiting for the call to end, asked, "You okay, Missus Miles? You look like you're a million miles away." Then he laughed and added, "Actually, a million miles from Hollandia sounds like a great place to be."

"I'm not so sure," she replied. "I'm trying to figure out if I've just gotten good news...or bad."

"About your husband, ma'am?"

She nodded.

Gently, he placed a stack of envelopes on her desk. Ordinarily, he would have just dropped them with a loud *plop*. He decided not to this time, though; it would have seemed a cruel intrusion into her privacy. "Well, I sure hope it turns out to be good news, ma'am," he said, and pushed off on his rounds.

So do I, laddie, she told herself. *So do I.*

She tried to turn her focus back to work but found it impossible. Now that the shock of knowing he was in hostile territory had worn off, a rage began to seethe within her.

They're going to just leave him there and put him back to work? I thought they were supposed to rescue downed airmen. They do it every day...one bloody submarine in the dark is all it takes. I've got a good mind to—

Jillian stopped herself—ranting would do no good.

At least both of us know the other is still alive. That's more than we've known for most of the past two years. Go outside...take a walk for a bit...clear your head...

And then get back to your job.

The walk around the headquarters compound did Jillian a world of good. Returning to her desk, she dove back into the discrepancy she'd found before that phone call derailed her:

Something's wonky with the figures from the Aitape resettlement camp. Looks like there are about sixty fewer Dutch refugees reported to be living at the camp than were transported there.

She double-checked her figures. Same result.

Walking into the office of the sweating, pencil-pushing captain, she laid her evidence on his desk. He didn't seem in the least bit concerned.

If this bloody wanker spouts "no big deal"—that tired excuse for Yank sloppiness—I just may have to bash his brains in.

But he surprised her by saying, "We simply cannot have a discrepancy of this nature. It makes it look like this department doesn't know what in the Sam Hill it's doing, and I will not have that. We must account for *those people* to the last head. You do realize, Missus Miles, that the Supreme Commander has made it a top priority to account for every last Dutchman—military and civilian—in these parts?"

She told herself, *How touching that tosser MacArthur cares so much about the Dutch when he doesn't give a shit about his own troops.*

But she replied, "Of course I realize it, Captain. Sorting out the refugees is my bloody job, after all."

"I'm certainly glad you realize that, Missus Miles. So tell me…what do you propose we do about this little problem?"

"How about I go to Aitape and solve it, for starters? Teach you Yanks how to count, if necessary."

And get me away from you for a while, you fucking pompous imbecile.

Andreas Dyckman was growing more nervous by the minute. "We've already waited too long," he told Jock. "You've broadcast three times. They'll find this location for sure…and soon."

The Dutchman's camp was a frenzy of activity as his people packed their scant belongings, hoping to begin their trek north to the safety of the mountains before darkness fell. He hurried to the radio hut and began to hover anxiously over Baum and Morales as they struggled to dismantle the gear.

"Dammit, we're going as fast as we can, Mister Dyckman," Baum said. "These *Rube Goldberg* connections we made are fragile enough. We break something now and we may never get this set back on the air."

"Getting *back on the air* will be the least of our worries if the Japanese come walking in on us," Dyckman replied. "Please, gentlemen…finish with all possible haste."

Jock huddled over a map with the Dutchman's scout, Hans. They were preparing for a walk in a different direction: back to Mokmer on Biak's west coast for the bomb damage assessment ordered by Headquarters at Hollandia. The raid by the planes of Fifth Air Force was scheduled for 0900 tomorrow. They'd have to walk all night—coast to coast, clear across the Biak plateau—to be in position on the bluffs above Mokmer's airfields. When the raid was finished, they'd have to walk all the way back across Biak, hopefully to find Dyckman and his people once again.

Hans asked, "Will we be taking the radio with us, Major?"

"No," Jock replied. "Much too heavy…and much too fragile. We need to travel light."

"But that means we cannot report to your generals in Hollandia what we saw until we return to *Meneer* Dyckman's new camp."

"Yeah, that's exactly what it means, Hans. I've already told HQ to expect about a twelve-hour delay in reporting. If we need another raid…and I'm betting we will…they wouldn't be able to fly it before the next day, anyway."

Something about the plan still bothered Jock, though. "Are you sure we can set up on the bluffs without the Japs seeing us?"

"Quite sure, Major."

"All right, then...let's take two more guys besides you and me. How about one islander and one Yank?"

"Fine. Do you remember Josiah, the man who found you?"

"Yeah...he'll be good."

"Yes, he will, Major. But what Yank will you choose?"

"I'll let you know in a couple of minutes."

Arthur Simpson answered a question still unspoken. "No fucking way, Major Miles. I'm not going."

"To be honest, Mister Simpson, I wasn't planning on asking you."

Steve Richards didn't wait for Jock's question, either. "Sure, I'll go, sir," he said. "Be glad to do it."

"Great, Steve. Pull your gear together. We leave in thirty minutes."

Simpson leaned against a tree, sulking. "I don't see why you don't take the Jew or the Mexican instead. Foot patrols sound like an enlisted man's job, anyway."

"That's funny...I could have sworn you were the guy who said *climbing a tree* was an officer's job. The Navy seems to have pretty interesting ideas about division of labor. Anyway, I wouldn't take *Petty Officers* Baum or Morales, Mister Simpson, because they've got a very critical job of their own, tending to that radio. Something only they can do."

As he turned to walk away, Jock added, "Mister Simpson, didn't the Navy teach you a little respect for your men and their abilities goes a long way?"

Simpson's shake of the head was not a *no* but a rejection of Jock's premise. "I don't answer to the US Army, Major Miles."

"Maybe not, Lieutenant. But since you're staying with the others, you *will* be answering to Mister Dyckman. Try and be of some use to him."

Chapter Eight

Jock did a last check of the three men going with him on the all-night walk to Mokmer. They were armed lightly, their weapons more a token offering to the danger they might face than a serious defense against it. Jock carried his Thompson, deadly at close range but uselessly inaccurate beyond. Hans and Josiah toted ancient, bolt-action Mannlicher rifles, slow-firing and cumbersome. Steve Richards had only his .45 pistol.

"Remember," Jock told them, "we're a recon mission. We're not looking to get into any fights. Nobody get itchy on the trigger."

Richards asked, "Shouldn't we be taking the thirty cal, sir?"

"No...Dyckman's people will probably need it worse than we will."

They hadn't even cleared the camp's perimeter when *CRUMP*—the first mortar round landed in its midst.

"Get back with the others...*NOW*," Jock yelled.

A few rapid heartbeats later, the second *CRUMP*.

Dyckman and his people were frozen in fear, half-crouched, their wild eyes searching for a safe haven nature couldn't provide. Hector Morales crouched behind the .30-caliber machine gun, ready to fire...but he could see nothing to fire at.

"EVERYBODY DOWN, DAMMIT," Jock called out. "KISS THE GROUND."

Another *CRUMP*, and Jock said, "Rate of fire's real slow. Can't be more than one mortar out there...and it's a light one. Probably not too far away, either."

He crawled to Dyckman. "Any of your people hit?"

"I don't believe so, not yet," the Dutchman replied. "Where is it coming from?"

Jock pointed west. "That way. I'm going to go find it."

Dyckman recoiled in horror. "Shouldn't we run?"

"No, keep your people down. If we run, they'll just follow us. Don't think there's very many of them...not if they're using a mortar right off the bat. Better we get them off our backs right now."

Telling Hans to follow, Jock low-crawled out of the camp. Once out from under the mortar rounds, they regained their feet and moved swiftly through the forest. As the *CRUMPS* of impact grew fainter, they began to hear the *poomf* of the mortar being fired.

It was coming from somewhere on their right...

A few dozen yards away...no more than that.

They were on their bellies again, crawling closer.

Ahead, a sight unseen in nature: bushes twirling, moving back and forth...a repetitive, energetic activity...

Not bushes at all, but poorly camouflaged men feeding rounds into a mortar tube.

"Bingo," Jock whispered. "I count four...what about you?"

"Yes, four."

"I'll take them," Jock said. "Cover my back in case there are more around."

The Japs looked comical as Jock crawled closer—men adorned with branches and leaves like children at play...

Confident they were blending with their surroundings...

But standing out all the more.

Jock was ten feet away when the first Jap saw him. By then, it was too late.

Two quick bursts from the Thompson.

Four dead Japanese soldiers. One corporal, three privates.

One silenced mortar, still smoking.

"Should we bury them?" Hans asked.

"No time," Jock replied, his words hurried. "There's got to be more of them around somewhere."

Hans nudged a lifeless body with his foot. He was relieved when it remained dead. "Why did they stay so far away, sir? Why didn't they come close and snipe at us?"

"Probably got a gander at the thirty cal over Morales' shoulder and preferred to keep their distance."

Jock took in the full panorama of the forest. There was nothing to see but trees. "I guess Mister Dyckman must be right. The Japs really are spread pretty thin in these parts."

He picked up a rucksack fashioned as an ammunition carrier. There were still four mortar rounds inside. He picked up the corporal's binoculars, too.

"Take the tube, Hans. A knee mortar might come in handy later."

"A *knee mortar*, sir?"

"Yeah, that's what we call these little fifty-millimeter jobs. Seen them plenty of times before. Even used one a couple of times."

"What are we going to do with it?"

"Take it with us," Jock replied. "We could use a little more firepower for our little trip to Mokmer. Now c'mon…let's make sure the others are okay."

Dyckman breathed a sigh of relief as Jock and Hans returned, but his troubles were far from over. "By some miracle, none of my people are injured," he told Jock, "but your troublesome Mister Simpson is missing."

"I saw him," Sid Baum added, pointing into the rainforest. "He was running like a scared rabbit. You went one way, Major, looking for that mortar, and he went the other..."

He mumbled a few more inaudible words. Jock was fairly sure *chickenshit* was among them.

Dyckman was already shepherding his people onto a trail. "I don't have time or daylight to go looking for him," the Dutchman said.

"Neither do I," Jock replied. "But he couldn't have gotten far. I'm pretty sure he'll turn up again before long...if he doesn't get himself killed first."

"Now *there's* a thought," Baum replied, hoisting a piece of radio gear to his shoulder. Then, with a big smile for Jock and Richards, he added, "With all due respect, of course, gentlemen. See you tomorrow night...I hope."

Then he joined Andreas Dyckman's column as it began to head north while Jock and his three-man team set out for Mokmer.

It had been dark for several hours when the heavens opened up. Jock and his men paused for a few minutes to fill their canteens with the cool, fresh rainwater, ate a few bites of the emergency rations they'd salvaged from the Cat, and then pressed on. They had no time to waste.

Steve Richards asked, "How's your leg, sir?"

"It's fine. I wish everyone would stop asking me that. Just because I limp a little doesn't mean I can't cut the mustard."

Cutting the mustard also meant ignoring the burning eyes and drained muscles that felt like elastic bands stretched beyond their limits—all the products of living on little or no sleep.

When did I sleep last? Dammit, I don't even remember. I've got to get my mind off how tired I am. Think about something else...

Something else turned out to be the disappearance of Arthur Simpson.

Jock asked, "Hey, Steve...have you flown with Simpson for a while?"

"On and off for a couple of months, sir."

"So why do you think he cut and ran? I mean, hell...he's been under fire before. We hit worse shit when the Cat got knocked down. Strange that a little popgun mortar would push him over the edge."

Composing his thoughts, Richards paused before replying, "It's different in the airplane, I guess. There's nowhere to run."

"But you didn't run. Baum and Morales didn't run, either."

"I can't speak for the other guys, sir, but I was too scared shitless to run anywhere. Did you ever feel like that, sir?"

"You mean *scared shitless*, Steve?"

"Yes, sir."

Jock laughed as he said, "All the time, Steve. All the damn time."

The path Hans and Josiah had chosen took them not through the rainforest but scrubland, with only occasional patches of scrawny trees topped by sparse crowns that looked ghostly in the gray moonlight. Jock fumed as he thought, *Of course, according to this damn map, all the terrain on this part of the island is supposed to be dense rainforest. Haven't seen much of that yet...and I doubt the terrain has changed any since they drew this map at the turn of the century.*

The open country had been a blessing for walking in the dark. It allowed for good speed without the constant stumbling and falling a nighttime trek through the forest usually guaranteed. In daylight, though, open terrain like this—without cover or concealment—could be a death sentence. Once they reached the area where the Cat had crashed, Jock knew the terrain would turn back to rainforest and offer them protection. But they weren't there yet...and the eastern horizon had begun to show the pale pink band of the coming dawn.

"How much longer until we hit some real trees, Hans?" Jock asked.

"We're very close, Major. A few more minutes."

"And that tree cover will last all the way to the bluffs overlooking the airfields?"

"Yes. Absolutely."

Hans knew his business well. In short order, they were within the shelter of the forest, just as rays of the early morning sun began to cast their shafts of orange light through the tall columns of trees.

One of those shafts of light fell on a strange object some distance ahead...something no one had expected to encounter: a Japanese tank, motionless, silent, and seemingly unmanned.

By definition, it was just a light tank. Even a small-caliber anti-tank shell would turn it inside out.

But to a foot soldier, it looked like a dreadnought.

Jock, Hans, and Josiah scurried for cover behind a broad tree trunk.

Steve Richards sprawled face-down in an open patch far from any tree, a flatter yet clearly visible target. The captured knee mortar he carried made a resounding *thump* as it bounced off the ground.

"Crawl over to that tree, Steve," Jock said, his voice an urgent whisper. "And for fuck's sake, stay behind it."

Hans watched Richards do as he was told, then turned to Jock with a curious look as if to say, *What's wrong with that man?*

Even unspoken questions needed answers. "He's a sailor and an airman," Jock said, "and neither profession knows how to fight on dry land."

Using the binoculars he took from the dead mortar crew, Jock surveyed the steel obstacle in their path. "Ahh, shit. A soldier just popped out. He's barely dressed...just in one of those loincloth-things they wear for underwear. Looks like he just woke up. Doesn't seem like he heard us, at least. Wait, there's two more..."

The three soldiers started a small fire beneath a kettle hung from a makeshift tripod. Each threw a handful of what looked like pellets—probably kernels of rice—into the kettle. Then they sat on the ground, their backs against the road wheels of a tank track, in no hurry to go anywhere or do anything. They didn't even bother putting on their uniforms.

The Japs aren't any different than any other army, Jock told himself. *When there's no one in charge, they'll just sit around and goof off.*

Hans asked, "Why do you suppose that tank is sitting out here in the middle of nowhere, Major?"

"I think it's broken down. If their tanks are anything like ours, that'd be pretty typical."

Hans took a look through the binoculars. "Yes, I see what you mean. There's some kind of hatch open at the back end...and there are tools scattered all around."

"Yeah, the back end's where the engine is. And if it's not running, it can't chase us. All we've got to do is sneak around back and be on our way."

Retracing their path, they retreated to the edge of the forest and then turned north. Once out of sight of the broken-down tank, they turned west again, toward the bluffs overlooking Mokmer...

But a new and terrifying sound sent them scurrying for cover: the rumble of vehicle engines bearing down on them from the north...

Still unseen through the trees but their sound growing closer.

Maybe only a hundred yards away.

And then, there they were—tanks.

Just like the broken-down one they'd skirted.

Three of them in column, close together.

Shit, Jock thought, *just what the landing force doesn't need. A whole bunch of Japanese armor. If we've seen four of them already, I'll bet there's a battalion, at least.*

On the lead tank, its commander was perched atop the turret, his feet dangling into the hatch. Casually smoking a cigarette as if out for a Sunday drive, he was clearly on an administrative movement. The freedom to forget he was caught up in a war was his, if only for this brief moment.

The tanks' decks were laden with personal gear, ammo boxes, tools, and spare track parts.

"This isn't some patrol or training exercise they're on," Jock whispered to Hans. "They've got all their crap with them. They're just repositioning, probably to the southern beaches. I guess MacArthur's intentions aren't so hard to figure out, after all."

The tanks were rumbling closer now—close enough to spy through binoculars the sergeant's insignia on the collar of the lead tanker's shirt. In a few seconds, they would split Jock's party in half.

Jock and Hans would be a few yards to the tanks' right, Josiah and Richards a few yards to the left.

Trapped in a lethal game of hide-and-seek, they slithered in small arcs around broad tree trunks.

The tanks were almost close enough to touch when the leader stopped.

Jock dared to peek around the tree...

And saw the knee mortar Richards had been carrying lying on the ground, squarely in the lead tank's path.

Jock wanted to scream, *Dammit, Steve! Can't you hold on to that damn thing?*

The tank commander was sliding off the turret to his vehicle's forward deck.

One quick jump and he'd be on the ground, just a few feet away...

With an eye-level perspective on the area.

There'd be no way to hide from both him and the men still on the tanks.

Fingers tightened around triggers, preparing to fire a shot that could be a death warrant for the shooter as well as the target.

Before the tanker could jump to the ground, Josiah was standing in the middle of the trail. Wisely, he'd left his rifle stashed out of sight.

He reached down, picked up the mortar, and approached the lead tank.

When he got there, he bowed, and then—as if making an offering to the gods—held up the mortar with both arms outstretched.

The tank commander took the mortar, looked at it for a second, as if wondering what the hell to do with it, and then tucked it under a rope holding down some gear.

With great impatience, he motioned for the black man to step out of his way.

Josiah bowed low once again and cleared the path.

One by one, the tanks passed, engines growling and tracks clanking. Josiah waved farewell to each in turn.

No Japanese tanker bothered to wave back.

The sound of their engines faded to a distant growl. Jock and Hans emerged from their hiding places to join Josiah, still standing in the open.

"That was some real quick thinking, Josiah," Jock said. "Great job."

The islander seemed surprised the American major thought praise and thanks were necessary.

"It had to be done," he said, as if his action had been the most ordinary thing in the world. "None of you could do that. Only me."

"Yeah, that's for sure," Jock replied. "But where the hell's Richards?"

Josiah pointed to the base of a tree. "Behind there, Major."

Jock found Steve Richards right where Josiah said he was, slumped against the trunk. He was shaking, his eyes full of tears. Whether they were tears of fear or shame Jock couldn't tell.

"I fucked up again, didn't I?" Richards said, his voice barely above a whisper.

"Yeah, you did, Steve. But it's all spilled milk now. Forget about it."

He pulled Richards to his feet.

"Funny, though," Jock added, "I figured that mortar would come in handy. I just never imagined it would be *that* way."

He tapped the rucksack still slung over Richards' shoulder—with the four mortar rounds still in it—and said, "Ditch the sack, Steve."

"But maybe we could still use them like grenades, sir."

"Theoretically, I suppose we could, Steve....but I've never done it with a Jap round and this isn't the time to be experimenting. Anyway, with your luck, you'll probably just blow yourself up. Like I said, ditch the sack."

Jock checked his watch. It read 0730.

"C'mon," he said, "we've got about ninety minutes to get into position."

"Plenty of time, sir," Hans replied.

"Let's hope so."

Chapter Nine

The OP Hans and Josiah had selected was nothing short of excellent. It sat on the edge of a bluff some 500 feet high, among trees offering good cover and concealment, and looked down on the airfields around Mokmer—the closest about a mile away—and the narrow dirt road winding its way along the coast. That road was clogged with Japanese trucks and troops on foot, making their way south to the broad beaches where MacArthur's invasion forces would undoubtedly come.

"No wonder their tanks are going cross-country," Jock told his men. "That road down there is one big traffic jam. The tanks'll make better time, and use a lot less gas, driving right down the plateau. I just hope there aren't a whole lot more of them than the ones we've seen already."

There was another revelation, too. The faces of the bluffs to the north were studded with caves, each now the home of a large-caliber weapon able to throw shells out to several miles offshore. "That stuff looks to be forty millimeter or better," Jock said. "They've got all the ground down there covered with fire. Our troops will be fish in a barrel."

At a few of the gun positions, rope hoists were pulling crates of ammunition up from the base of the bluffs.

"How the hell did they get those big guns up there?" Steve Richards asked.

"Same way they're pulling that ammo up," Jock replied. "A lot of pulleys, a lot of guys, and a lot of hard work. Did you ever hear the stories of how the Aussies got their artillery over the Kokoda Track?"

Richards nodded. Jock added, "Pretty amazing what you can do when you have a mind to, isn't it?"

"Yeah, and some banzai bastard's got his sword up your ass."

As they spoke, Jock was trying to correlate the terrain they were seeing with the map he held. He'd come to a conclusion: "This map isn't worth a shit. If you believed it, you'd think men could just mosey up these bluffs like it was a walk in the park...instead of the mountain-climbing expedition they really are."

"The map doesn't look so bad to me, sir," Richards said. "The coastline's pretty accurate, at least."

"Gee, you must be in the Navy, Steve...and a flyboy, too. Coastlines, water depth, and the elevation of the highest peak are all you care about. For the guys who have to walk and drive on land, though, it's all about the fine details. Good maps mean your artillery lands on target, planes bomb and strafe where you tell them to...and maybe your commander doesn't order you into some fucking death trap."

"You mean like *Into the Valley of Death Rode the Six Hundred*, sir?"

"Yeah, something like that."

"But I thought that's what your job is, sir—working with photo recon to make better maps for your guys."

"That's exactly my job, Steve...but we've been focused on redrawing the ones for the southern end of the island, where our landings will be. We haven't quite gotten to updating the rest of these relics yet."

Jock turned his binoculars back to the airfields. The biggest one was closest to the seaside village of Mokmer.

He could count two dozen aircraft parked under camouflage netting, mostly fighters, the rest a mix of single and twin-engined bombers. The nets that had concealed the runway from daytime aerial observation were down, concealing nothing.

"Maybe they're getting ready to receive more airplanes," Richards said. "That strip can hold plenty more. Look at all those empty parking ramps."

"I think you're right," Jock replied. He focused now on the other two airfields, trying to count the aircraft parked there. But those fields were farther to the north, their details less clear.

"I'm going to guess fifteen planes at Borokoe," Jock said, "and maybe ten at Sorido, with plenty of room for more at both of them, too." Richards nodded when asked, "You agree?"

Jock checked his watch. It was 0855. "Almost showtime…if all goes according to plan, that is."

Hans and Josiah had been anxiously watching and listening for the American planes ever since arriving at the OP. Josiah had even climbed a tall tree to get a better view to the east, the one direction in which the forest blotted the sky. The only bombing raids they'd ever seen were by Japanese planes when Biak fell in 1942. Then, the Dutch opposition to the invaders had been almost nonexistent. It had taken only a handful of Japanese airplanes to claim the skies over their island. They had high hopes the American bombing raid would be far more impressive.

Jock did, too.

The American planes didn't come at 0900. The only things flying in the brilliant blue sky were seabirds gliding on the thermals rising from the warming earth below.

"Which direction will they come from, Major?" Hans asked. "*If* they come."

"Don't give up hope quite yet," Jock replied. "Military time can be a little *variable* sometimes. With the linearity of the targets and the prevailing winds, though, I think they'll come out of the south. Better get Josiah out of that tree now."

"Why, Major?"

"Because they're not always on target. He's got no cover up there."

But the bombing raid was already twenty minutes late. He didn't want to let on that maybe he, too, was beginning to lose hope. Something his mother always said crossed his mind: *Good things come to those who wait, Jock.*

Well, okay then, Mom...I'm waiting. Now let's see something good.

At first, they were just specks in the southern sky. Then they could hear them, their sound still faint but unmistakable: the guttural growl of aircraft engines, steadily growing stronger as the specks evolved, sprouting tiny silvery wings and twin tails.

"B-25s," Richards said. "I count...oh, I don't know...eighteen? Twenty?"

"Twenty sounds about right," Jock replied. "About two squadrons' worth. Dammit, I was hoping for more. A lot more."

"They're awful high, sir, about eight grand, I'd say. I hope to hell those bombardiers have damn good wind data or they won't hit a fucking thing."

"No shit, Steve."

Jock trained his binoculars skyward. "They've got fighter cover, too...way, way up...about half a dozen P-38s. Can't hardly see them."

He ran the numbers in his head: *twenty bombers, four to eight bombs per ship. Eighty to one hundred sixty bombs...to cover about four square miles of target. That isn't nearly enough...*

And a lot of those bombs will miss.

The sound of air raid sirens drifted up the bluffs from the plain below.

"Those Japs aren't getting much of an early warning," Richards said. "They won't even get those fighters down there cranked up, let alone into the air."

"Yeah, but the gunners are getting a full minute, maybe a little more," Jock replied. "That should be more than enough for them."

It certainly seemed to be enough. The guns in the caves were being traversed and elevated, trying to target the approaching American planes. Richards wondered aloud, "Do you think those are the guys who knocked us down?"

Jock didn't answer. He was focused on the B-25s, waiting for the leader to start his drop. Once he saw that first bomb start its plummet earthward, he'd be able to make a guess where it, and all the rest, would land.

He only had to wait a few seconds. *Bombs away.*

In the instant its freefall began, that first bomb was little more than a tiny black dot.

But it quickly grew in size as gravity imposed its relentless acceleration...

And then threatened to vanish into its own blur if Jock so much as blinked.

He counted down the seconds: *one one thousand...two one thousand...three—*

The flash of impact lasted only a millisecond but spawned a crushing shock wave, a ring of hot gases racing outward from its epicenter...

A beguiling vision, seemingly benign from this distance, like the circular ripple of a stone dropped into a pond...

Not adding a sound of its own to the *THUD THUD THUD* of anti-aircraft fire and the drone of engines...

Until the soft *poom* of the first bomb's impact made its five-second odyssey to the OP—and then all the other *pooms* in rapid sequence, like the sustained roll of a distant drum, its beats too numerous to count.

Then it was over.

Their bomb bays closed now, the American planes continued on their way, seemingly untroubled by the scores of black puffs floating in the sky around them like soiled cotton. Lingering reminders of flak bursts that had failed to take down even one aircraft.

"Ain't that something," Steve Richards said. "They can't hit one plane out of twenty in broad daylight, but we got knocked down flying all by our lonesome in the dark of night."

"Fate's a cruel mistress, Steve."

"How cruel was she to those Japs down there, sir? What are you seeing?"

Jock didn't reply right away. He hadn't finished scanning the broad target area below with the binoculars.

When he did finally speak, he sounded anything but pleased.

"Well, those flyboys moved a bunch of dirt around and kicked up plenty of dust, but...ahh, shit." He handed the binoculars to Richards. "Here...have a look for yourself."

What Richards saw almost made him jump for joy. "But sir, look at those craters they put in that runway. That airstrip's out of commission. We blew the shit out of them!"

"Bullshit, Steve. They'll have that fixed tonight. And I only see a couple of aircraft knocked out."

"But there's probably damage to a lot of the other planes we can't see from here, sir."

"That's faith, Steve, not hard intel. Let Hans and Josiah have a look."

After his turn with the binoculars, Hans said, "They missed the road, too. Completely."

He was right. Not one vehicle seemed so much as disabled, let alone destroyed. Drivers and foot soldiers who had sought refuge off the road were returning to it now and resuming the march south.

It was time for Jock and his men to leave. The radio was a day's walk away on the far side of the island. Jock knew all too well what the bomber pilots would tell G2 as soon as they landed: *The drop was dead on target. Three airstrips badly damaged. No opposition from Jap fighter aircraft. Flak ineffective.*

And like the Navy pilot Richards had said only a minute ago, so would the Air Force pilots conclude their debrief: *We blew the shit out of them.*

In other words, a perfect misrepresentation of the enemy situation on Biak.

One I must correct, Jock told himself.

They were packed up and ready to leave the OP. Josiah lingered, taking one last look with the binoculars. What he said didn't surprise Jock at all:

"The Japanese, Major...they're already working to repair the runways."

They'd only been walking for an hour. Jock was already lagging far behind.

Steve Richards asked, "Your leg...it's acting up, isn't it, sir?"

There was no point in lying. There wasn't even a way to put an optimistic face on it.

He was in pain and everyone knew it.

"You guys better push on without me," Jock said. "Here...I've already written out the message we need to send. Take it, Steve. I'll try and catch up when I can."

If I can.

"Bullshit on that, sir. This is about where we ran into those tanks a while back, isn't it? What are you going to do when more come? Run away?"

The Navy pilot might've been just a beginner at ground combat but he made a good point.

"Then what do you suggest we do, Steve?"

Richards reached down and eased Jock to his feet. "I'm going to be your crutch, sir. And when I get tired out, Hans and Josiah will take turns, too."

"No good, Steve. I'll slow you down way too much. That message needs to get to Hollandia ASAP. Too many lives depend on it."

"A couple of hours one way or the other won't change a damn thing, sir. Your invasion isn't supposed to happen for another week, right? And didn't Hans say it's only about ten miles back to where Mister Dyckman's going to be, instead of the fifteen we had to cover going the other way?"

"Yes," Hans chimed in. "That is true. We'll be crossing a narrower part of the island. And the trail is better."

"It's settled, then," Richards said. "Now come on, sir...one foot in front of the other."

They'd only walked for a few minutes when they again heard the bellowing engines of tanks making their way south. There was no cause for alarm; the tanks were a good distance behind them, not even close enough to be seen. With each passing second, those steel monsters would drive farther away.

Jock caught Richards grinning and said, "All right, all right...so you made a good call about the tanks, Steve. Don't let it go to your head. We've still got a hell of a long way to go."

It wasn't meant as a reproach and Richards knew it. He kept right on grinning as he replied, "I'll take that as a *thank you*, sir."

Something had been bothering Steve Richards about this game-legged Army major ever since he boarded the Cat four days ago. He decided this was the time to clear it up. "Sir," he asked, "why are you still even here? Couldn't you have gone home with that leg wound?"

Jock was silent and pensive for a few moments, as if carefully composing his reply. Then he said, "This is my home now. Everything I care about in the world is right here. Like it or not, I can't get off this train until this damn war is finished once and for all."

Chapter Ten

The jeep was barely managing twenty-five miles per hour along the rutted dirt road. It had bounced and lurched for the past three hours but still had a long way to go in the choking dust and stifling morning heat. At the wheel, Lieutenant Jimmy Ketchum figured it would take another hour, at least, to reach Aitape, some one hundred miles down the New Guinea coast from Hollandia. He feared that hour would be spent in more awkward silence; this whole trip, the fierce-looking Australian woman sitting next to him hadn't said a word, despite his many attempts to break the ice. As if immune to the rough ride, she never looked up from the papers she was trying to study.

Geez...would it kill her to shoot the breeze a little?

Ketchum tried to crank up a conversation one more time. "You know, Missus Miles, I served under your husband at Buna. I was a green platoon leader and—"

Without looking up, Jillian interrupted, "I know, Lieutenant. You told me that before we even left."

"And I heard about all you did for us there, ma'am..."

She looked up—*finally!*—and fixed him in a questioning gaze.

"Go on, Lieutenant."

"And I just wanted to say I'm real, real sorry it worked out so badly for you, getting captured by the Japs and all."

"It came out a lot worse for the lads who didn't make it through, Lieutenant."

"I suppose you're right, ma'am. But I'll tell you what…if Major Miles asked me to, I'd go to hell and back for him all over again."

He could only steal glances at her; the bad road demanded so much of his attention. But the look he saw on her face in those brief glimpses was one he'd only seen on strong men in the throes of combat: a calm, steely-eyed resolve in the face of death, forged in fear but not bending to it.

That look quickly softened. A knowing smile took its place as she said, "I know what you mean, Lieutenant, but I reckon I already have gone to hell and back for him."

He expected her to return to the papers in her lap, but she didn't. Suddenly, it seemed like all she wanted to do was talk.

"How'd you end up being my chauffeur? Doesn't your Army have better things for its officers to do than drive an Aussie civilian around?"

"I'm *convalescing*, ma'am. Got wounded a few months back, at Aitape, of all places. Somebody's idea of a joke, I guess, that I'm being sent back there now. And I'm not just your driver…I'm supposed to assist you in any way I can."

She let out a roaring laugh. "Now *that* sounds exactly like your bloody American Army, Lieutenant. A job with no specific purpose."

It was Ketchum's turn to laugh. "Then maybe you can clear up for me what *your* purpose on this little trip is, ma'am."

"It's simple, Lieutenant. We're going to find the whereabouts of these sixty some-odd unaccounted-for

Dutch souls, so that bloody wanker I work for can balance *His Royal Majesty's* books for him."

"His Royal Majesty, ma'am?"

"MacArthur, Lieutenant. Your bloody General MacArthur."

"But sixty people, ma'am, give or take a few? Hell...they could all be in unmarked graves somewhere. We may never find them. They were probably all POWs, right?"

"That would make it easy for us if they were," she replied. "Japanese prison camps keep meticulous records."

"Why would they bother keeping records, ma'am? They didn't sign the Geneva Convention."

"True, but certain prisoners could be very useful for propaganda purposes. If they didn't know who they were, they couldn't take advantage, now, could they?"

He took her word as gospel, since she knew from hard experience.

"If they're on land, we'll find them somehow, Lieutenant. The sea's the only one who never gives up her dead."

They knew they were close to Aitape now; tall signposts had begun to sprout along the roadside, the top of each decorated with a thicket of arrows pointing this way and that, each arrow stenciled with an Allied unit's designation.

"Who are we looking for?" Ketchum asked. "The MPs?"

"Yes," Jillian replied, "the One-Oh-Sixth Military Police Company. They're responsible for keeping law and order around these parts…supposedly. Bloody thugs and head-bashers are all they are, if you ask me."

"I know exactly what you mean, ma'am. Have you ever heard that old Army saying?"

"You mean the one that says *I'd rather have a sister in the whorehouse than a brother in the MPs?*"

"Yes, ma'am. That's the one."

As if their joking had summoned him somehow, a GI wearing an MP armband stepped into the middle of the road, his outstretched hand commanding the jeep to halt.

"What's going on, Corporal?" Ketchum asked the MP.

"Nothing to concern yourself with, sir. You'll be on your way in a minute."

A bit farther down the road, the reason they'd been stopped was now in plain view. Three white people—two men, one woman—were being led under guard across the road. They were civilians by their tattered and filthy clothes, barefoot, and gaunt. Their hands were tied behind their backs.

Skin that seemed thin as paper stretched tight over their sinewy frames. Jillian doubted they'd had a decent meal in months. Maybe longer.

Each man had tattoos on his bare upper arm which Jillian recognized immediately: the marks of seamen. The woman's hair was a coppery red—dull and dirty, as if she'd been in the bush for a while, but unmistakably a *ginger*.

Jillian leapt from the jeep and brushed past the flustered corporal. A buck sergeant with the air of a bully was leading the parade of prisoners. She marched right up to him, and in a command voice that rattled the young man for just a moment, asked, "Just why exactly are these *civilians* being treated like prisoners, Sergeant?"

His surliness returned quickly. "Speaking of civilians, lady, just who the fuck do you think you are? You better get the hell out of here before I lock that big mouth of yours up, too."

She reached into her trouser pocket, produced a document, and thrust it in the sergeant's face. He got as far as *The Supreme Commander's* seal on the letterhead. There was no need to read further:

This skirt's got friends in real high places.

Jillian wished she had more time to enjoy watching this arrogant goon of a Yank turn to a sputtering idiot before her eyes. "What's your name, Sergeant?"

"Polito, ma'am...Louis T."

"Well, Polito, Louis T., let's try this again. Why are these *civilians* being treated like POWs? Shouldn't they be in the resettlement camp?"

"They're Jap sympathizers, ma'am. They escaped from the camp last night, trying to make it to them yellow bastards still holding out up in the mountains."

"*Really?*" she replied. "Jap sympathizers? Sounds a bit unlikely, Sergeant Polito."

"Don't matter, ma'am. I've got my orders."

"I'm sure you do. How do we find your company HQ, Sergeant?"

Pointing down the road, he replied, "It's the next turn-off...about a quarter mile down. You'd better check in with Sergeant Knox, ma'am."

"Actually, I'm looking for your company commander, a Captain Hutchins, I believe."

Polito let out a laugh. "Good luck finding him, ma'am. He usually makes himself real scarce. Like I said, ol' *Hard* Knox is the man to see. He runs the show around here." He pointed again down the road. "Now, if you'll excuse me, ma'am…" Almost an afterthought, he looked to Lieutenant Ketchum and threw a careless salute.

As the prisoners were led away, the woman looked back, wanting to say something. She was stopped by the blow of a rifle butt against her back. But the look on her face, the way her lips had moved—Jillian was sure she was begging *Help us…*

As they climbed back into the jeep, Ketchum asked, "You buy that bit about them being Jap sympathizers, ma'am?"

"Not for a bloody minute, Lieutenant."

To Jillian Miles, Technical Sergeant Franklin Knox was the walking, talking embodiment of everything she thought about military policemen: *bloody thugs and head-bashers, all of them.* Tall and stocky, with a barroom brawler's beer belly that strained the buttons of his khaki shirt, his eyes seemed as cold and merciless as a shark's.

No wonder that GI back on the road referred to him as "Hard Knox," she told herself. *Looks like a right mongrel to me.*

But she saw something else going on behind those dead eyes. *He's a schemer…he's at it right now. Either he's trying to figure out how to turn my visit to his advantage or how to stop me in my tracks. Why on earth would he want to do that?*

Unless he's got something to hide.

At the moment, Knox wasn't bothering to hide his distaste for rank or women. Looking right past Jillian, he told Jimmy Ketchum, "You can tell the lady this letter of hers don't cut a whole lotta ice around these parts..." Like an afterthought, he tacked "*Lieutenant*" to the end of that sentence. It carried the same lack of respect he would have lavished on titles like *dog catcher* or *shithead.*

"Negative, *Sergeant*. That letter has the full effect of an order. You and your organization are to cooperate with Missus Miles to the fullest."

The big sergeant sneered. He wasn't even going to bother saying *Yes, sir*.

"And I'm not sure why we're wasting our time with you, Sergeant Knox," Ketchum continued. "Take us to your commander, Captain Hutchins, on the double."

"Can't do that," Knox replied.

"Why the hell not, Sergeant?"

"Because it ain't my turn to watch him, *Lieutenant*, so I ain't got no idea where that man is at."

Ketchum was starting to lose patience. "You've got a pretty route-step outfit here, Sergeant. Not very impressive at all."

Knox just shrugged. "We take care of our business, *Lieutenant.*"

Jillian had had enough of the dick-measuring contest. "And I'm about to take care of *mine*, Sergeant," she said, "with or without your help or your bloody captain's. I'm sure your company clerk can provide me all the files I need to start the ball rolling."

She pushed past the looming sergeant and headed straight to a meek-looking corporal seated behind a typewriter in the corner of Knox's day room. At first, the corporal had trouble grasping the situation. Since he joined the Army, he'd never had to deal with a woman in an official capacity. Aside from the nurses, he didn't know there *were* women in any official capacity.

But it was obvious this Aussie lady wasn't just some clerk/typist for the brass: she was an undeniable force, a commanding presence sucking the air right out of the room. She hadn't asked him for a thing yet, but he just knew when she finally did, every word would be precise, proving the lady definitely had her shit together.

She ain't gonna ask no questions she don't already know the answer to, I'm betting.

It only took one more bit of rationalizing for the corporal to fall into step:

She works for the Supreme Commander, for cryin' out loud...hell, she's got herself a fancy title, too...and even Hard Knox knows damn well she's going to get what she wants, whether he likes it or not. That's why he didn't stop her from talking to me...

And hopefully, it's why he won't beat the shit out of me when I do what she says.

In short order, the corporal was handing over every document Jillian requested.

Hard Knox might've been silent but wasn't amused. He grew agitated when, after just ten minutes going over the files, she announced, "Sergeant Knox, there seem to be quite a few discrepancies here. If I'm to believe these figures, some sixty refugees who arrived at this resettlement camp can't be accounted for now. Can you explain that to me?"

"You're gonna have to talk to Captain Hutchins, ma'am."

"Then you're going to have to find him for me, Sergeant, and right bloody now."

The last person in the world Hard Knox wanted to find was Captain Hutchins: *That stick-up-his-ass rich boy would only fuck things up now. Better he chases skirt up at the hospital, keeps getting piss-drunk at the "O" club, and stays the hell out of my way, like always.*

He gunned the jeep onto a narrow side road which bore none of those arrows directing you to this or that unit. Soon, he came to a gate in a tall, barbed wire fence, manned by two American MPs who waved him through. Racing the short distance to a weather-beaten villa nearly hidden by trees, he slid the jeep to a halt at the back steps. A half-breed, light-skinned New Guinean—with the bushy hair of a native but the smooth features of a European—stepped from the house to greet Knox.

Sauntering like the cock of the walk, Fritz Van Flyss said, "Good afternoon, *General*. What brings you to our fine establishment at this time of day?"

"Shut the fuck up, *Fuzzy*," Knox replied. "We gotta talk. We got big trouble."

"So big the mighty US Army can't handle it?"

"No, you numbnuts…the fucking Army *is* the trouble."

They walked through the house—a *warehouse*, actually—where natives were busy breaking open boxes marked with bright red crosses and sorting their contents. Settling into a quiet back room, Knox refused the whiskey Van Flyss offered; that was enough to convince him the news his partner in crime carried was bad. Really bad.

"Never known you to turn down a drink, Sarge."

"No time right now, Fuzzy. Now listen and listen good..."

Knox told him all about Jillian being on the verge of blowing their whole operation sky high. He concluded with, "If she finds what happened to them people and why, we're fucked. So we gotta get rid of that skirt, and fast."

"You mean kill her?"

Knox bounced a meaty backhand off the side of Van Flyss' head. It nearly knocked him out of his chair.

"Oh, that'd be all we need, you imbecile—kill some Aussie split-tail working for MacArthur. This fucking place would be crawling with more brass than McNamara's band."

"So what are we going to do? And that hurt, by the way."

"Tough shit, Fuzzy. Now here's the deal—you're gonna get some of your *coons* to put a damn good scare into her. Fuck her up a little...so she won't never be coming back here again."

"But won't they just send someone else then?"

"They already did that once, remember? Those dumbass officers they sent couldn't find their asses with both hands. Gave my unit a glowing report. This skirt can add two and two, though."

"Let me get this straight, *Hard*...you want my boys to give her a beating?"

"Gee, you ain't so dumb, are you, Fuzzy? That's what I'm saying…beat her up real good…whatever it takes. Scare the shit out of her. Just make sure she can walk out of here."

Van Flyss thought it over for a moment, and then said, "I told you we should've killed those people."

Knox scowled at him. "I take it back, Fuzzy…maybe you *are* that dumb after all. I'll tell you one more time— if we killed them outright, it'd be a firing squad for us, for sure. But the way I got it set up, anything that happens to them is gonna be seen as God's will."

Van Flyss sighed and said, "All right. When do we do it?"

"Tonight."

Chapter Eleven

Thirst was driving Arthur Simpson slowly out of his mind. He'd yet to cross a stream or river from which to fill his canteen. In his solitary wandering toward Biak's southeastern shore, the only body of water he'd come upon was a stinking swamp—a glorified mud puddle. But even though he could no longer summon saliva to his mouth and he felt sure he'd be spitting out dried-up pieces of his esophagus any minute, he wasn't crazy enough to try and drink from it. Not yet.

He'd couldn't remember how long he'd been walking the edge of this bluff—at least two hundred feet high—looking for a safe and easy place to descend to the seashore. Simpson could see the Pacific now, and its forbidden water—infinite, undrinkable—seemed to be taunting him. The weather was taunting him, too. From his high vantage point, he'd watched two storms roll off the ocean, pouring their life-giving rain on the island far to the north and south. Not a drop had fallen anywhere near him.

Below the bluff, thick forest stretched to a rocky shoreline. He wasn't sure at first—*maybe my eyes are playing tricks on me*—but he thought he was looking down on a thin column of smoke rising above some treetops not far away.

A cookfire, I'll bet. Some darkies must be cooking up fish or a pig for supper…and where there's cooking, there's got to be a village…

And where there's a village, there's water.

Better hurry…it's going to be pitch dark in a couple of hours.

Abandoning caution and the laws of physics, he eased one foot over the edge and then the other...and began a clumsy and death-defying descent down the steep slope—slipping, falling, tumbling, bouncing off trees—only to somehow regain his feet, try a few more uncertain steps, topple over, and begin the head-over-heels journey all over again.

Bruising though it was, Simpson's unceremonious downhill run was a big timesaver—he reached the bottom in little over a minute. He took some small comfort in that fact:

I'm a little banged up but I don't think I broke anything...and now I've only got an easy little stroll to that village.

He staggered to his full, commanding height, threw back his shoulders—*Ow! Must've sprained something...*

And then, as the pain in his shoulders receded, he stepped off smartly, like a man on the way to reclaiming his rightful destiny.

When the huts of the village came into view, he stopped, crouched low, and began to recon the situation before him. As he did, he reached for his .45 pistol...

But the holster was empty.

Shit! Must've lost it falling down that fucking cliff. Ahh, the hell with it. Only had two damn bullets in it, anyway. Don't imagine I'd be able to shoot my way into getting a drink.

Simpson could see nothing but a group of busy women—*a dozen, give or take*—tending to children and the boiling pot.

Looks like they're cooking supper. Fish stew, I'm guessing. They're no threat...but where the hell are all the men?

He heard something behind him, a rustling sound, like an animal in the underbrush.

When Simpson turned, there was a man—an islander—standing before him.

In his hand was a large wooden blade—like a fraternity paddle...or a cricket bat.

There were more island men all around him. No bats for them, just long knives hanging from their waists.

Where the fuck did they all come from? They don't look too damn friendly, either. But at least there ain't no Nambu pointed at me this time. And those knives don't mean shit. Hell, every pickaninny in the jungle carries a knife.

Simpson held up his hand in greeting, like the actors pretending to be American Indians in the movies did when saying hello to white men.

The islanders made no gesture in return.

"US Navy," Simpson said, pointing to the gold wings on his chest. "Pilot...aviator...flyer."

Still no response.

He pointed skyward as he patted the wings. Pilot or not, he was making no impression on the grim-faced islanders.

"American," Simpson said. He smiled, confident he'd just played the trump card ensuring his salvation.

The batsman took a sudden step forward and, quick as lightning, delivered a knockout blow with that weapon to the side of Arthur Simpson's head.

The storms that bypassed Arthur Simpson were much kinder to Jock and his men. They'd been drenched twice, cooling themselves and refilling their canteens each time. Even if it hadn't rained they wouldn't have become parched: Josiah was adept at finding the thick vines that, when a cutting was hacked open, oozed enough thirst-quenching sap to keep a man hydrated.

The setting sun was casting its long, eastward shadows as they stopped to rest for a few minutes. Trying to make some sense of his map, Jock asked Hans, "How much longer do you figure? Best I can make from this piece of toilet paper is we're still on Biak, somewhere."

"We will reach our rendezvous within the hour," Hans replied.

Steve Richards added, "See? I told you, sir...you wouldn't slow us down hardly at all."

"Well, I sure appreciate the help, Steve." Then Jock stood and, for the first time since morning, took a few wobbly but unassisted steps on both legs.

"Whoa, sir," Richards said. "Give it a rest!"

"No, I'm okay. You guys have been carrying me all day long. I think I can finish up this trip on my own two feet. You could use the break...I know it isn't easy being somebody's crutch over all that distance."

"Hell, sir, it was only about ten miles. Sure, it was up and down a little, but..."

Jock laughed and said, "Steve, you're sounding more and more like an infantryman every minute."

"I'll take that as a compliment, sir," Richards replied. Then he pointed skyward and added, "But I belong up there, with the rest of the flyboys."

"Speaking of *flyboys*," Jock said, "your Lieutenant Simpson...there'll be a board of inquiry..." He had started to say *if we get back* but changed his mind and finished the sentence with "when we get back." Then he continued, "I've worked with pilots for a while now and I know how you like to cover each other's asses. What do you plan to say about him?"

Without a moment's hesitation, Richards replied, "I'll tell them he ditched us and ran away. Fuck him."

"Suppose he's back with Dyckman when we get there, Steve?"

"It doesn't change a damn thing, sir. Would it matter to you if he came back?"

"No, you're right, Steve. It wouldn't change a damn thing. Fuck him."

Arthur Simpson was fairly sure he was conscious now—still *woozy* but conscious. He could hear people talking in some strange language but couldn't see anything except vague shadows, more like sensing motion from behind a curtain than seeing animate objects.

That's it! I'm lying here with a sack over my head. Burlap or something.

He tried to lift his arms to remove it but he couldn't. Something was holding them to his sides. There was chafing pressure at his wrists, which worsened the more he tried to pull his arms free.

Shit. I'm tied up.

There were hands on him now, roughly pulling him to a kneeling position.

It felt like someone was untying something from around his neck, and then the bag over his head was whisked away.

He could see again, at least whatever the soft glow of twilight allowed.

The village. I'm still here.

Dark silhouettes paced around him as if performing a ritual dance.

But one silhouette remained stationary, directly before him...

And he's still holding that fucking bat.

There was something strange about the shape of the batsman's head...

He's wearing some kind of cap...but it almost looks like a hood.

The batsman drew close, crouched low, and stared right into Simpson's face.

His features were clear now...and so was that cap.

It's one of those a Jap soldier wears, with that drape on the back to keep the sun off.

On the cap's peak was the big star of the Imperial Japanese Army, normally red but grayish now in the fading light.

Ahh, fuck...Gekken.

The batsman slowly raised his weapon so it touched Simpson's cheek.

The edge was razor sharp, like a wooden sword.

He pulled that sharp edge along the pilot's cheek, causing a sharp pain and drawing blood.

Simpson could see the red trickle on the blade.

He tried to pull away but the hands of unseen gekken forced his head to be still.

The batsman seemed to be enjoying himself. He barked words that sounded like orders and sprayed Simpson with spittle.

The sack had been rolled into a slender length of rough cloth, like a kerchief...

Or a blindfold. It was quickly tied over Simpson's eyes.

In the quiet seconds that followed, the Navy pilot thought of the stories he'd heard of Allied flyers being executed—*beheaded*—by their Japanese captors.

But that can't be happening...not to me. These aren't Japanese. They're just some fuzzy-wuzzies playing dress-up games. And he doesn't even have a real sword.

Enough of this shit. I've got to get the fuck out of here...

He tried to stand...but couldn't.

His ankles were secured to the ground somehow. To stakes, a tree—he couldn't tell.

Puffing his chest out, he said, "Look, I'll give you my wings! They're nice and shiny, right? Shine like gold! You want them, don't you? Go ahead, take them."

It seemed such a short time ago he had not a doubt in the world he was all powerful, the master of his universe. A soaring god...

The master of *every* universe.

Now he was helpless, his fate in the hands of a stranger:

Some fucking darkie.

This is all the Army's fault. Let them ask me again to fly a mission for them.

They can all go fuck themselves, from that comic opera son of a bitch MacArthur right on down the line.

Arthur Simpson didn't even sense the disturbance of the air...

But he felt the bite of the wooden blade as it struck the back of his neck with terrific force.

It put him face down in the dirt. He couldn't move a muscle...

Couldn't feel his arms or legs.

But he could still hear the shrieking of the gekken standing over him.

A metallic taste in his mouth:

My own blood.

A second blow...

But his head remained attached to his body—there was less shattered spine and mangled tissue to hold it now, but it was still attached.

On the twelfth blow, the wooden sword splintered to pieces.

But the batsman was too caught up in his bloodlust to stop. He screamed for another *sword*.

Arthur Simpson was dead long before the seventeenth blow finally caused his head to roll free.

The winded but exultant batsman picked it up by a bloodied ear and displayed it like a trophy.

But all the other gekken were gone. For them, the Japanese ritual of execution they'd dreamed of performing on a white man for so long had proved too horrific to watch.

The batsman's solitary celebration didn't last long. He was soon confronted by a mob of angry village women. They demanded the white man's body—including his severed head—be removed. *Immediately*, the women insisted, before it began to rot and stink. Already it was attracting swarms of insects. The batsman had little choice but to comply; his mother was the mob's leader.

The rest of the gekken men joined him as he wrapped Simpson's body in a woven mat. Then they lifted it and headed off in the darkness, hoping to travel as short a distance as possible downwind from the village before ridding themselves of the corpse.

That distance turned out to be even shorter than expected; they had barely made it to the trail when they heard heavy footsteps coming the other way, sounds that could only be made by men with boots on their feet. Men wearing footwear could only be enemies.

The gekken had no intention of getting caught. They dropped Arthur Simpson and fled back to the village. They were long gone when the first soldier in the Japanese patrol tripped over their discarded cargo.

Chapter Twelve

They could tell they were getting near the edge of the rainforest. As the sun set at their backs, its light had grown dim among the trees through which they walked. But ahead, there was still a sense of pastel pink mixing with deep blue. That was where the labyrinth of the forest ended and the vista of sky and sea began.

"I'm guessing there's a pretty sharp drop to the water there," Jock said, "despite the *gentle slope* this useless map would have you believe."

"Yes," Hans replied, "about two hundred feet, almost straight down, I'm told."

Those last two words took Jock by surprise. He sputtered, "You're *told*? You mean you've never been here before?"

"No, not here, exactly, Major. But I've been close...and I do listen when others describe things."

"How *close* is *close*, Hans?"

"Within a few miles."

"What about Josiah? Has he ever been here?"

"Not that I'm aware of, Major. But I assure you, there's no cause for alarm. We know where we're going."

Josiah turned, as if to add his reassurances. But before he could say a word, he dropped to one knee, rifle at the ready, and raised his hand to the others: *Stop!*

Then he pointed toward the trees still ahead, wagging his finger back and forth...

Sketching a line of adversaries in their path.

Crouched low behind trees, the others couldn't see the Japanese.

But there were telltale sounds: the scurrying of feet...

The *clack-clack* of rifle bolts...

Then the first shot from an Arisaka splashed against the tree, just a foot above Jock's head. "STAY DOWN," he said. "DON'T WASTE A ROUND UNLESS YOU CAN SEE THEM PLAIN AS DAY."

Steve Richards shot him a panicked look. He wanted to fire, to do something—anything, no matter how useless—to try and buy his salvation...something—anything—to stop the angry lead splintering the tree which, for the moment, protected him.

Jock knew well the instinct flooding Richards' senses—and he knew well what a mistake it would be to follow it now.

"Just do what I say, Steve."

Suddenly, on the left flank, a Japanese soldier was running, trying to keep his bent body low to the ground.

But speed makes for poor cover. Hans picked him off with one shot.

"They're trying to get behind us," Jock said. "They'll be easy to see if they keep it up."

Another Japanese soldier tried, this time on the right flank.

It took two shots, but Josiah took him down.

"Outstanding," Jock said.

Richards was still nothing short of terrified. "What about your Thompson, sir? Let loose with it! Spray their asses!"

"When they're close enough for this thing to hit them, I will. Same thing for you with that .45. Now calm the fuck down, Steve, and stay alert. You remember what your quadrant is?"

"Hell, yeah!"

"Good. Stay glued to it."

It fell silent for a long, anxious moment—just long enough to allow for false hope the Japanese were retreating...

But then came the sense of something *hissing* through the air above their heads...

And a *thump* as the grenade struck the tree right behind Jock...

And dropped into his outstretched hand like an outfielder playing a long fly off the wall.

The grenade's *hiss* was a deafening whisper now as its fuze burned, spewing a plume of wispy gray smoke, marking the last instant to its destiny.

Could there really be any time left?

In one smooth motion, Jock's arm went from catching to throwing, hurling it back from where it had come.

The eyes of his three men watched it fly over their heads in stunned disbelief, anticipating the blast which seemed so long overdue.

Praying the grenade wouldn't bounce off yet another tree—and this time, land at their feet...

For they knew no hand would be quick enough to flick it on yet again.

It had dropped from sight when it finally blew up, its sound a muted *poof*...

Causing barely a ruffle of the surrounding trees.

More like a malfunction than a deadly explosion.

"A dud?" Richards asked.

"No," Jock replied. "That's what they sound like."

They waited for another grenade, more rifle fire—anything to indicate the Japs were still players in this lethal game.

"You killed them all," Hans said, a prayer more than a fact.

"I couldn't be that lucky."

He wasn't—and neither was Steve Richards.

The Japanese soldier seemed to pop right out of the ground before him.

Richards' .45 was only inches from the onrushing soldier's heart when he jerked its trigger.

They fell as one, in a swirling sense of misfortune and dread...

And stuck fast to the ground on which they fell.

Richards was on the bottom, flat on his back. The mortally wounded Japanese soldier's head lay prone on the flyer's chest, the stock of his Arisaka rifle standing above them like a grave marker.

The rifle's long bayonet had gone completely through the left side of Richards' abdomen. Its tip was planted firmly in the ground.

Their blood mixed, painting matching portraits of war's agony on their khaki shirts.

Jock raced to them, threw the Japanese soldier off and placed the muzzle of his Thompson against the man's forehead.

Never give these bastards the benefit of the doubt. Even the half-dead ones try to kill you somehow.

But he hesitated: *Don't waste the bullet. He's as good as dead already.*

Richards' hand clung to the forestock of the rifle nailing him to the earth, as if even its slightest movement might tilt the odds of living or dying even further against him. Jock slid next to him and said, "Just try to relax. I'm going to pull it out."

"NO! DON'T! IT'LL—"

There was no point protesting further. Jock had already done it.

"It'll *what*, Steve? Hurt?"

"Yeah."

"Does it?"

"No...not yet."

"Good. Now just stay put."

Pulling a pack of sulfa powder and a roll of gauze from Richards' musette bag, Jock stuffed a hastily fashioned dressing into the wounded man's shirt.

"I think you're lucky, Steve. You didn't get stuck anywhere serious."

Richards' breathless reply: "Oh, man...you're not going to tell me it's just a flesh wound, are you, sir?"

"Actually, I was. It's a big one, but—"

Two shots from a Dutch rifle cut his words off. A few seconds later, there was a third shot.

"Sit tight, Steve," Jock said, placing the .45 back in the flyer's hands. "Doesn't sound like this is over yet."

He stood and saw Hans not ten feet away. "No, Major," the Dutchman said, his words as unsteady as his stance. "I think it is over. Come and see."

Twenty yards away—where Jock had pitched the grenade—were the bodies of two Japanese soldiers. "They were wounded," Hans said, "and we finished them." He pointed to the bullet wound in each man's forehead in turn. Then he dropped to one knee and looked like he was going to vomit.

Ten yards farther, Josiah stood over the body of a third Japanese soldier. Unlike Hans, he didn't seem the least bit upset at having to take lives. "He was crawling away, Major," the islander said. "But he didn't get far enough. That makes six we killed." He took a look all around and added, "I don't think there are more."

"We can't bet on that," Jock replied. "Not after all the noise we just made. We'd better get the hell away from here…and we're going to have to carry Mister Richards. Which way do we go to find Dyckman?"

Hans wobbled to his feet. He looked terribly confused.

"What's the matter?" Jock asked. "Never had to kill anyone before?"

Hans shook his head.

"Don't feel bad. It hits everyone like that the first time…unless they're already crazy. But I've got to know, Hans…which way to find Dyckman?"

"We shouldn't have to go anywhere," Hans replied. "They were supposed to be right here."

"Well, of course they're not here, dammit. The place is crawling with Japs. Pull yourself together. I need your best guess where they might be, and I need it *now*, Hans. Don't make me flip a fucking coin."

Josiah walked over to Steve Richards. He bent down to help the pilot to his feet but then stopped, straightened up, and returned to Jock and Hans.

"What's the matter?" Jock asked the islander. "Why didn't you pick him up?"

"He cannot live like that," Josiah replied. "Better we leave him."

"Negative," Jock said. "You didn't leave me and we're not leaving him."

"You weren't bleeding like a speared animal, Major," the islander replied. "He is."

Jock wasn't sure what was infuriating him more: Josiah's intransigent refusals, the fact that he was spewing doom easily overheard by Richards, or that Hans was now useless, unable to come to grips with having to kill other men to save his own life.

"Look," Jock said, "it's bad enough we can't seem to find our way out of a paper bag right now…" He walked over to Richards and, with great difficulty, lifted him to his feet and became his crutch.

"You carried me all that way, Steve. Now it's time I returned the favor."

At first, it was all Jock could do to keep his weak leg from collapsing under the strain.

But anger—and adrenaline—were doing their work. He felt like a superman.

And he must've sounded like it, too, when he asked Hans and Josiah, "Now, are you two going to get your thumbs out of your asses and give me a hand here?"

Shame washed over Hans' face. "Forgive me, Major, but I do not know which way to go."

Jock looked to Josiah. "What about you? Any ideas where Dyckman is?"

The islander just shrugged.

It didn't matter now. Jock had made up his mind. "I'll tell you what…we'll head to the sea. That's what everyone seems to do when they're lost on one of these islands. Maybe it'll work for us, too."

They began to walk east, toward the sea. All except Josiah.

Jock looked back over his shoulder at the islander. He asked Hans, "What about our friend there? Is he with us, or what?"

"Don't fault him, Major. The island people are…how should I say?…very fatalistic in matters of life and death."

"That's all well and good, Hans, but fate be damned: Mister Richards isn't going to die. Not if I have anything to say about it."

In a pained whisper, Steve Richards added, "Sure glad you feel that way, sir."

Jock gave the islander one more glance, adding, "So unless you have some other urgent business to attend to out here, Josiah, we sure as hell could use your help."

It didn't seem like he was going to come. He stood in place, his face emotionless, as the three others kept walking east. Just when Jock was convinced Josiah really wouldn't be joining them, he called out: "I think you're all going the wrong way."

That was enough to stop them in their tracks. They turned to face Josiah.

"I think I know where *Meneer* Dyckman will be, Major." He was pointing north.

Jock asked, "Why north, Josiah? Why that way?"

"Because he, too, will go to the sea. The only way to get there without falling off a cliff is to go farther north."

"How much farther, then?"

"Not far, Major. Before nightfall."

That didn't give them much time. Josiah had already started his walk north. Jock and the others fell in behind him, all with the same hope and the same fear for Dyckman and his people:

They'll go north…if the Japs haven't already gotten them.

They hadn't walked far when Josiah abruptly dropped to one knee and signaled *Stop!*

For Jock and Hans, going to ground—and easing the wounded Richards down with them—was a much more delicate exercise. It seemed like an eternity before they got the flyer propped up behind a tree. Only then could they scatter to find their own cover.

Whoever—or whatever—was approaching didn't seem concerned with noise discipline in the least. They *clomped* through the underbrush like carefree animals—or careless men. Josiah's finger tightened around his trigger.

"No, don't," Jock told him, not bothering to keep his voice down. "We know who it is. Look..."

A tall, burly white man, in light blue shirt and denim trousers and carrying a .30-caliber machine gun, US issue, was at the head of a small group of men some forty yards away.

"That's Sid Baum," Jock said. "I guess they're out looking for us." He stood up and walked toward the Navy man.

"Thank God you're okay, sir," Baum said. "We heard all that shooting a while back. Thought you might need some help."

"Yeah, we do, Sid," Jock replied, pointing the big man toward Richards. "How far away is the rest of Dyckman's party?"

"A mile or two, sir...down the cliff toward the beach."

"Any sign of Mister Simpson?"

"No, sir. He's still gone."

"That's a damn shame."

"You thinking about looking for him, sir."

"He's the last thing on my mind right now, Sid."

"Yeah. Mine, too, sir. But you guys must be starving, right? Well, there's great eating down there. Everyone's chowing down—crabs and stuff."

"Outstanding! We polished off the last of those emergency rations a long time ago, so *hell yeah*, we're starving. Now take off your shirt, Sid."

"How come, sir?"

Jock was already taking his off. "With yours and mine, we've got enough GI shirts to make a stretcher for Mister Richards. First, we need some sturdy branches, about six feet long or so..."

In just a few minutes, branches were found and slipped through the buttoned-up shirts; a stretcher took form. Two islanders from Baum's party jumped in to become its bearers.

Night closed in as they began their trek down to the beach. Jock said, "Sid, I hope you've got this trail marked."

"Way ahead of you, sir," Baum replied as he blinked his flashlight into the darkness ahead. Glowing dimly in its beam was a white strip of cloth tied to a tree. Baum untied it and stuffed it in his pocket. "We've got it marked like this all the way home."

"Good thinking."

"Did you get to see the bombing raid, sir?"

"Yeah."

"How'd they do?"

"Not so great, Sid."

"Speaking of *not so great*, sir…what's gonna happen now with these Japs crawling all over the place?"

"Wish I knew."

"They must be looking for that transmitter of ours…and you're gonna transmit again, ain't you, sir?"

"I'm afraid we have to, Sid."

They were quiet for a few moments. Then Baum said, "Well, at least we're all back together. Safety in numbers, right?"

Chapter Thirteen

The ramshackle building was more an oversized tin awning with open sides. The sign out front glowed in the jeep's headlights: it read OFFICERS' CLUB. Jimmy Ketchum hit the brakes and said, "This must be the place, ma'am."

Jillian pivoted and slid from the passenger seat, stepping to the wooden walkway with high-heeled feet together like a lady gracefully dismounting a horse. She had no intention of giving the crowd of eager officers watching her arrival an upskirt peek. "Pick me up in an hour, Lieutenant," she told Ketchum. "That should give me all the time I need."

He watched the growing crowd of men as they salivated over the prospect of this fine-looking woman joining them for a drink—and a lot more, perhaps, if their overheated imaginations had anything to say about it. "You sure you don't want to carry that buffalo gun of yours, Missus Miles? You might need to fend off some wild beasts in there."

Jillian tossed off the warning with a laugh. "I grew up in the bush, Lieutenant. I've been fending off wild beasts my whole life."

She found Captain Hutchins right where the barman said he'd be, seated in a dark corner with nothing for company but a row of empty Australian beer bottles on the deck beside him. When she stepped up to him and began to introduce herself, the same thought crossed the mind of every other man present: *How come that Section 8 lush gets so lucky?*

Hutchins cut her off halfway through the introduction with an unsteady wave of his hand. "I know who the hell you are," he said, with all the slurred, impotent belligerence a belly-full of beer can provide. "I read the dispatches from HQ, you know."

"Then may I sit down, Captain?"

In one abrupt motion—like a sagging marionette whose strings had suddenly been jerked tight—he shrugged and pointed to the empty chair next to him.

She told him of the discrepancies she'd uncovered in the camp's records.

"You'll have to talk with my sergeant about that."

"I already have, Captain...and he's been most uncooperative. I'm quite sure he, and perhaps *you*, are hiding something."

"I don't know what you're talking about. I may be the C.O. of that place on paper, but I've got nothing to do with it. Knox takes care of business there."

"I heard those exact words earlier today, Captain Hutchins. From Sergeant Knox, of all people. But the question is, what is this *business* he's taking care of?"

At first, Hutchins' face registered confusion, as if running the resettlement camp was the only possible answer to that question. Then the expression on his face changed. She couldn't tell if it now displayed shame, guilt, ignorance...or all of those things put together.

"I couldn't prove anything in a court martial, ma'am, but Knox may have something going on with some guy. Some half-breed civilian scumbag."

"Does this scumbag have a name, Captain?"

"Yeah...Van Flyss. Fritz Van Flyss."

"What can you tell me about him?"

"Not much...but one look at him and you can tell he's a slippery bastard. Probably as dangerous as the damn snakes around here, too. Or at least as dangerous as Knox himself."

Captain Hutchins slumped into his chair. His eyes seemed to shake off the unfocused glaze the beer had put there. What was left was the faraway stare of a shattered man.

He's broken, Jillian thought. *What in bloody hell is he still doing here?*

Her voice softer and sympathetic, she asked, "Captain, I've seen so many like you before...and believe me, I understand. But why hasn't the Army sent you home?"

"Because those assholes say I'm not crazy and I'm sure as hell not wounded. I just need some time and rest, that's all. So they stuck me in this backwater shithole."

"But why? What happened to you?"

"Buna happened, ma'am."

Without a moment's hesitation, Jillian replied, "It happened to all of us, Captain."

Belligerence returned to his voice. "Oh, yeah? What would you know about it, lady?"

"Quite a bit, actually. I was there."

He scowled. "How the hell could—"

"I was master of a coastal freighter, bringing supplies to you Yanks. To make a long story short, I was sunk and taken prisoner by the Japanese."

"But...how...but you're *here* now. How could that be?"

"I got rescued. I was very lucky."

"How long were you...you know...with the Japs?"

"About a year."

His sodden mind wrestled with the simple arithmetic for a moment. "So you've only been back here a few...let's see...a few months?"

"That's correct."

Jillian had a pretty good idea what he was thinking: *The imprisonment...it's made her damaged goods.*

The halting, incomplete question he spoke next proved it.

"Were...were you..."

"Raped? No, Captain. Tortured? Yes."

"Jesus..."

"No, he wasn't there. We were on our own."

Hutchins shifted uneasily in the chair. His eyes were focused on her now and not that illusory refuge of the mind where the war weary sought their escape. For just one moment of clarity, he realized whatever misdeeds Hard Knox had committed running that camp, he could be found equally guilty: *Ignorance won't be an excuse. They'll call it dereliction of duty. A C.O.'s responsible for everything his unit does or fails to do.*

"You'd better be careful, though, ma'am. Like I said, that Knox is a rough customer. Maybe you should just steer clear."

"Captain, I've been a prisoner of the Japanese. I think I can stay one step ahead of some redneck Yank sergeant."

A faint smile crossed his lips. He was beginning to have little doubt she could.

"Could you do me just one favor, ma'am, one Buna survivor to another?"

"And what would that be?"

"If you figure out what kind of racket Knox has going on, give me a heads-up first, so I can maybe try and cover my ass before the shit hits the fan."

She offered her hand and they shook on it. "Agreed. But just one thing, Captain…it's not a question of *if* I figure it out. It's a question of *when*."

Chapter Fourteen

Colonel Dick Molloy wouldn't have been surprised if General Willoughby balled up the message he'd just handed him and threw it back in his face. He braced for the tirade he felt certain was coming.

He wasn't disappointed.

"I've got a squadron full of Fifth Air Force's crack bombardiers telling me they BLEW. THE. SHIT out of those Jap airfields," Willoughby said, his fist pounding the desk once for each syllable in *blew the shit*. "And then, Richard, we got that one little major of yours telling me quite the opposite."

"Sir," Molloy replied, "you wanted *eyes on the ground*, and you got them. If you're not going to believe what Miles is telling us—"

"Oh, shut the hell up, Richard. I don't need lessons in processing intelligence. Not from you."

Willoughby spun his desk chair around and stared out the window. The awkward silence that followed was as intrusive as a stick in the eye. It made Molloy aware of his every breath—every twitch of his muscles—as he stood rigid before the general's desk. He was sure the clock on the wall had stopped. It seemed like a week passed before it clicked off another minute and Willoughby turned his chair to face him once again.

"Even if the information Miles sent is on the money," the general said, "I'm not going to worry my head about it. The Fifth Air Force thinks we wasted a whole lot of their precious gasoline and ordnance with that raid, and they're quite confident that even in the unlikely event those airfields fill up with aircraft overnight, it's nothing they can't handle. As far as they're concerned, the Japs have nothing but inexperienced pilots left, and they'd love to get what's left of the whole damn Jap air fleet in one place so they can knock down those rookies all at once."

To Dick Molloy, that had the stench of wishful thinking and willful ignorance about it. But he said nothing. He knew he'd already lost this battle.

"Besides," the general continued, "the Navy is breaking my balls now that we didn't mention to them about their aircrewmen still being with Miles. They had them listed as *missing in action.* Now they're hot to recover their boys…and they're planning on doing it tomorrow night."

That was the best news Molloy had heard yet.

"But that doesn't give you much time, Richard. We've still got radio contact with Miles?"

"As of thirty minutes ago, we did, sir."

"Good. Let's get with the Navy liaison and coordinate the pickup. They say they've got two subs in the area, and either one can handle it. Now get your ass back to work, and don't let this little *rescue sideshow* get in the way of your real job."

"No problem, sir. Everything is on schedule for the Biak landings."

Willoughby didn't even look up from his desk as he replied, "Very fine, Richard. Dismissed."

Hector Morales was just about to shut down the transmitter when his earphones came alive once more.

Grabbing the code book he'd just put away, he told the islander assisting him, "Get Major Miles. Now!"

The message was still coming in when Jock arrived at the lean-to sheltering the radio. Over Morales' shoulder, he strained to read what was already written down by the dim glow of the receiver's dial. The message was still coming when a breathless Andreas Dyckman joined them.

"It's good news and bad news," Jock told the Dutchman. "The good news is they want to take us off the island tomorrow night."

"I will not go," Dyckman said. "Not now. Not if your Army is coming so soon."

"That's your call," Jock replied. "Whatever you want to do."

"But what is the bad news, Major?"

"They need coordinates for where we want the sub to pick us up."

Dyckman seemed surprised. "A submarine? How will that work?"

"It'll park in deep water a mile or two offshore and send a rubber boat in for us."

Jock knelt and unfolded his map on the ground, lighting it by muffled flashlight. "So where the hell do I tell them? With this piece of crap for a map, their landing party could end up God knows where and we'd never find them in the dark."

"It's a pity," Dyckman said. "We made some excellent maps, but the Japanese have them all now. My daughter Greta and her husband were the cartographers. They'd mapped almost all of the southern island when the Japanese came."

Jock asked, "So they'd be the ones who know this part of the island pretty well, then?"

"Yes, Major…they'd be the *only* ones. But now Greta is dead, as is Lukas."

"I'm real sorry to hear that. But how'd they die? In that evacuation attempt you told me about?"

Dyckman nodded.

"Gee, I'm sorry," Jock said. Turning back to the map, he asked, "So what do you think, Mister Dyckman? Where the hell are we?"

Dyckman leaned over the map and ran his finger along a curved section of coastline, where blue ink met green, both faded by time and the elements and barely distinguishable in the faint light. When his finger came to a stop, he said, "We are here, I believe, on this bay."

The bay he picked—little more than a tiny crescent scooped from the coast—didn't even have a name on the map.

"I won't be able to get a look at this beach until sunrise," Jock said. "Can a boat land here?"

Dyckman replied, "Yes, Major."

Morales looked up from the radio and nodded his agreement. "I saw the beach before the sun set, sir. It'll do."

"Well, it's decided, then," Jock said. He wrote down the coordinates and handed them to his radioman. "Send them quick, Hector, and get that transmitter the hell off the air. Maybe the Japs won't get another chance to track us."

Jock was certain of one thing: even if the Japanese hadn't tracked their signal to this no-name bay, he and his people were in a terrible defensive position, one they'd have to hold for an entire day. They occupied a narrow coastal plain, not quite a mile deep, with a horseshoe of high ground above them and their backs to the sea:

The Japs can lob mortar and artillery fire down from the cliffs to their hearts' content, and there's not a damn thing we can do about it except try to dig into this coral that's like fucking concrete and keep our fingers crossed.

The only thing we've got going for us is there's only one way down here from the high ground—that one steep, skinny foot trail—unless the Japs decide to slide down off that cliff on ropes. But then they'd be the vulnerable ones...and they'd need about fifty miles of rope to get any numbers down here.

So all we've got to do is keep them off that trail... For twenty-four hours.

"Mister Dyckman," he said, "I need four of your armed men who speak good English."

"Why, may I ask, Major?"

"I'm going to take them and one of my Navy guys with the machine gun to the head of the trail. We'll keep the Japs from coming down here so your people can try and get some rest. Until the shooting starts, at least."

"Do you really think they'll come at night?"

"If they know we're here, they just might," Jock replied.

"Take me, sir," Hector Morales said. "I got a good nap before while Sid was out looking for you. He can mind the radio for us."

"You've got a deal, Hector. Grab the thirty cal, then gather up the guys Mister Dyckman picks and meet me at the base of the trail. I'll be along in a minute."

Jock needed that minute to check in on Steve Richards. He was lying beneath a small canvas tarp the islanders had rigged to shelter him from the inevitable rain. His bloody shirt and makeshift field dressing were gone, replaced by a cloth competently wrapped around his abdomen.

"Pretty good-looking bandage, Steve," Jock said. "Who did it?"

Richards' voice was strained, but he was in good spirits. "One of the Dutch guys. Seemed like he'd make a pretty good corpsman. And here I was, expecting some witch doctor remedies with leaves and voodoo chants and stuff."

His voice dropped to a whisper. "I hear we're getting rescued tomorrow night, sir."

"Yeah, you'll be back in your Navy's hands before you know it."

"Maybe I'll even be around to see it."

"You will be, Steve. Just take it nice and easy and we'll get you out of here safe and sound. Like I told you back there, you've got a good wound. You're going to be all right."

Richards couldn't help but smile at the words *good wound*. "I didn't think there could be such a thing, sir. But I guess you've seen a whole lot of them…and you know good from…well…" He let the sentence drop. "But I've got to ask you something. Is ground combat always like that? I mean, so fucking confusing, like you're caught in some machine—you can't even see its parts, but you know damn well they're whirling all around you—and they're trying to rip you to pieces."

"Steve, have you ever heard the saying *anyone who's not confused doesn't understand the situation*? The guy who coined that one had to be talking about ground combat."

Richards nodded. He could find no argument with that piece of wisdom.

"But that Jap, sir…did I kill him?"

"You did, Steve."

He thought that over for a minute. Then he asked, "I really didn't have much of a choice, did I?"

The trail seemed so much steeper in the dark. It was especially tough on Hector Morales as he lugged the heavy .30-caliber machine gun. The only way they knew they had reached the top was when their aching leg muscles told them they weren't climbing anymore.

"Hector," Jock said, "set the thirty cal up right here." He held out a forearm like a signpost. "Now orient it in this direction. Follow my arm. There was a curve in the trail about twenty yards out. You'll be shooting right across it. Nobody should get past."

"What if I can't see 'em, sir?"

"It won't matter, Hector. Just keep your bursts short so you don't blow your ammo all at once. And don't let the barrel climb. Put those rounds out there at knee height, so they can't even crawl under them. I'm going to go set up the others now...spread them out wide on either side of you. Then I'll be right back."

When Jock returned a few minutes later, Morales asked, "Sir, I thought of something when we were getting that last message from HQ. You weren't thinking about going back to the other side of the island again, were you? I mean, you're limping pretty bad and all."

"Why the hell would I do that? We're getting picked up tomorrow."

"I know, but suppose they'd asked you to do another scouting mission. Would you have gone?" He paused, and then added, "I'm betting you would've."

Jock had to stop and think about it. Morales had a point: if he'd been ordered, would he have tried to do it again?

Yeah, I would have tried, at least. But no point pretending to be a hero now by saying it out loud.

"You'd have bet wrong, Hector."

Morales shook his head. "That's not the way I read it, sir. Remember what *Honest Abe* said? You can fool some of the people—"

"Yeah, yeah. I heard that tune a long time ago."

"Just saying, sir. Can I ask you something else?"

"Might as well. Just make it quick."

"How come you call me and Sid by our first names? Naval officers never do that. Ever. It's like they'd die if they ever got informal with subordinates."

"The way I see it, Hector, just consider it my way of showing you guys some respect for the way you've come through out here. Now let's shut the hell up and stay alert."

Chapter Fifteen

Jimmy Ketchum lay on a cot in the Quonset hut's sweltering heat and thought, *If this dump is the guest quarters, I'd hate like hell to see the stockade on this post. I'd rather sleep outside with the snakes and the jungle rats than in this sweatbox...but it's the least I can do for that lady. She's got enough problems right now, with her husband in limbo and all. I swear, she must be tougher than nails.*

The sparse room in a corner of the hut was officially assigned to Jillian Miles; her name had even been neatly printed on the door in chalk by one of Sergeant Knox's minions; her clothes and gear were scattered throughout. But she would never sleep there. She'd burrowed herself a refuge in an adjacent Quonset among the towering stacks of clothing, cots, blankets, and sheets, probably intended for the resettled civilians but yet to be distributed. It was a good hiding place: the building—and its contents—seemed all but forgotten.

To complete their deception, Ketchum would spend the nights in this room meant for her rather than the big, barely occupied tent designated *Visiting Officers' Quarters.* To make sure he'd be awake if the intruders came, he'd rigged noisemakers—tin cans with a few small rocks inside—on the floor near all doors and windows; the same precautions GIs used on jungle perimeters. To keep it dark, he'd pulled the fuses for the ceiling lighting. For emergency communication, he'd hooked up the unused telephone wire strung between the two huts to simple buzzers he'd found lying around. All you had to do was touch a flashlight battery to the wires and the buzzer would wake the dead.

Proud of his handiwork, he reminded himself, *You know what they say about infantrymen—we're skilled generalists. We can do a little bit of everything.*

He wasn't asleep when he heard the first rattle of a noisemaker. Within seconds, he could hear footsteps outside his door...

And then the scrape of the door latch as the knob was turned.

One hand gripping his Thompson's trigger, the other his flashlight, Ketchum slid himself and his weaponry deeper beneath the sheets. He was ready.

The door opened part way, just enough to allow the moonlight seeping through the window to illuminate their faces.

Blacks. Two of them.

One rushed in, batting the mosquito netting around the bed aside...

Ripping away the sheet...

Straddling Ketchum's legs, grabbing his boxer shorts, trying to pull them down...

And then stopping—frozen in place and time—as the muzzle of Ketchum's Thompson was deep in his mouth.

"Maybe you wanna fuck this instead," Ketchum said.

In the flashlight's beam, he caught the other intruder lunging toward the cot. Something in the man's hand glinted like metal...

He's got a shiv.

The angle was almost perfect, one assailant nearly lined up behind the other.

It only took a jerk of the Thompson's muzzle, still in the first man's mouth, to resolve the geometry.

A three-shot burst killed them both—through the mouth, out the neck, into the chest of the man behind.

Scurrying footsteps beyond the door...

Shit, there's another one.

There was no sound of a screen door slamming.

The bastard's still in here, somewhere.

※

Jillian didn't need a buzzer to warn her. The gunshots sufficed.

She grabbed her rifle—the *buffalo gun,* as Jimmy Ketchum referred to it—and slipped her *torch* into the pocket of her shorts. Barefoot and silent, she ventured outside to cover the entrance to Ketchum's hut.

She could hear noises from inside: intermittent sounds of frantic movement—brief but rapid skittering and thumping—like a rat trying to prevent itself from being cornered.

Then, Ketchum's voice: "I'd give it up if I were you, pal. Just come out with your hands up."

The sweep of a flashlight made crazy shadows dance. *Ketchum's scanning the interior,* she thought. *He said "pal"—I reckon that means there's just one.*

The *clomp* of running footsteps on the wooden floor...and then the screen door slammed open as Fritz Van Flyss burst out of the hut, arms and legs flying like a champion sprinter...

And went sprawling over Jillian's outstretched leg.

He struggled to regain his feet and resume his dash, but a foot against his backside pushed him face down into the dirt. He would have tried to get up and run again, but there was something cold and hard pressing behind his ear.

Something larger, not quite as firm—a bare foot, perhaps—was resting against his scrotum, causing him to wince with the anticipation of pain, pending but not yet delivered. He tried to turn his head to see his captor but was blinded by the brilliant beam of a flashlight—her *torch*—aimed right in his face. The Webley revolver in his hand felt wasted, like a trump card played too soon.

"Toss the bloody gun away, wanker," Jillian said, pressing the rifle's muzzle more firmly against the back of his neck.

Van Flyss did as he was told. "You've got this all wrong, miss," he said. "I know why you're here. I know everything. I can help you."

"Bloody rubbish," she replied.

"But I was trying to stop them!"

Standing a few feet away, Jimmy Ketchum stifled a laugh and said, "Get a load of bullshit this guy's peddling. Two of his buddies stone cold dead and he's trying to play hero and cut himself a deal. Some balls, eh?"

Jillian dug her foot into Van Flyss' scrotum, making him whimper.

"Some balls, indeed," she replied. "Why don't you start *helping* by telling us your name, bucko?"

He told her.

"Brilliant!" she said. "Just the scumbag we're looking for. Tie him up, Lieutenant."

"But you need me," Van Flyss protested.

"It looks like I've already *got* you, laddie...and for as long as I bloody want, too."

"You sure had them pegged, ma'am," Ketchum said, "figuring they'd come after you like that."

"They certainly didn't waste any time trying it," she replied. "It just shows how desperate they are."

If only we bloody knew what it is they're so desperate to hide.

"So what are we going to do with him now, ma'am?"

"For starters, we're going to have him locked up for the attempted murder of a Yank officer—*you,* Lieutenant.*"

Ketchum was almost done binding Van Flyss' hands behind his back. But he paused to marvel at what Jillian was doing. She had bound his ankles to allow some movement—a slow, hobbled walk at best. *Baby steps*, she called them. A man could never run away bound like that.

Then she fastened a noose around Van Flyss' neck, like a dog's choke collar and leash. Perfect for leading a prisoner around.

"Where'd you learn to do all that, Missus Miles? The Girl Scouts?"

She laughed and replied, "No, Lieutenant. I learned at the hands of the Japanese." Checking Ketchum's work, she shook her head and added, "You're not doing his hands right at all." She began to retie the rope. "Here...do it this way. He'll chafe the skin off his wrists before he ever gets out of it."

"So I guess they used to tie you POWs up a lot, ma'am?"

"All the bloody time, Lieutenant. The Japs love their ropes."

Chapter Sixteen

They could hear the thunder now as the storm coming off the sea grew closer. Each streak of lightning would illuminate the pitch black rainforest before them like a photographer's flash—an instant of trickster's light, showing them things that existed only in their fears. In those momentary flashes, every dancing shadow could be a soldier of the Emperor advancing toward them. Each of Jock's five men, though only a few yards from the man next to him, felt completely alone.

Jock could sense how anxious they'd become: *If I can't calm them down, it's only a matter of time before someone breaks and gives us away.* He moved quietly along the dispersed line they formed, offering whispered words of reassurance he could only hope they believed.

Even Hans and Josiah seemed much too jumpy. He'd placed them on the flanks because of all Dyckman's people he knew them best and trusted them the most. Now he was beginning to doubt even their composure.

We need this fucking storm rolling in like a hole in the head. If someone starts popping off, we're screwed.

But what can I do? Take their weapons away?

No...but I've got to put the brakes on this train before it derails and we all get killed.

He made the rounds of his men once again, hissing the same command to each in turn, "Do not shoot unless I give the command. Is that clear?"

Each man offered the same, wordless response: a wide-eyed, fearful look of acknowledgement which could mean *Yes, sir*…or it could mean *Are you out of your fucking mind?*

The storm was almost on them; there was only a second or two now between the lightning and thunder. No sooner had a crashing *BOOM* assaulted their ears than the next round of lightning came, with multiple, strobe-like flashes that made the forest come alive with those phantom soldiers.

"Easy, boys," Jock urged, scuttling from man to man once again. "There's nothing out there except—"

But he realized he was wrong. Beyond their left flank—Hans' post—something was definitely out there: the *crunch* of a man's footsteps, stepping gingerly through the brush.

The Dutchman's rifle swung in their direction. Jock grabbed its forestock with one hand. With the other, he waggled a finger in Hans' face: *No!*

Then he held that finger to the man's lips: *Quiet!*

The crunching of footsteps stopped. Whoever it was couldn't be more than fifteen feet away.

Some rustling sounds, and then nothing…

Until they heard the soft groaning of a man, as if he was straining against something. A few muttered words, definitely Japanese.

The poor bastard's trying to take a shit, Jock told himself. *Eating nothing but rice like they do, they probably only crap a little rock-hard pellet about once a week.*

Just like when we eat nothing but K rations, and I'm betting it hurts like hell for them just like it does for us.

But he's too fucking close.

The groaning continued, getting louder.

Sounds like he's giving birth or something.

Still, he's too fucking close.
Is he alone?
Is there a platoon of Japs out there somewhere?
A company?
A battalion?
One step, one stumble, and he walks right into us.
Can't take the chance. But it's got to be done quick....and real quiet.

Jock laid his Thompson next to Hans. Once more, he placed his finger to the man's lips, harder this time: *Quiet. I mean it.*

The Jap's groaning became more insistent.

This guy's about ready to drop his load. It's now or never.

Jock drew his bayonet...

Crept forward...

It was over in a second. He'd never killed a man with a blade before.

But it had gone by the book: stun the victim with a sharp blow to the side of the neck. Pull back his head. Slice his throat.

Done without a sound.

I don't think the son of a bitch even got to finish taking his crap.

In the next flash of lightning, Jock could see just for a moment the man he'd killed, lying on the ground next to the rifle that could no longer save him.

He's so young. Just a kid.
Maybe he was lost.
Bad luck for him.

Then the rain began to fall, a deluge so strong it could wash away everything but the sins of men.

The storm passed and so did the terror of night, finally yielding to the relief and cautious optimism of daybreak. No other Japanese had come their way, as near as Jock and his men could tell. The only weapon used was one bayonet, now wiped clean.

They could take a better look at the dead Japanese soldier. To Jock's surprise, the hapless victim, who looked so young in the brief, harsh flashes of lightning, wore the rank of lieutenant on his collar.

Hector Morales asked, "What are we going to do with this gentleman, sir?"

"When we get relieved in a little bit, we'll take him down with us and bury him, if we can manage to dig a hole in this rock. Can't leave him up here."

"How come?"

"He might have been alone last night, poor bastard, but he belongs to some unit. They just might come looking for him."

Jock rolled the dead man over and checked his pockets. There was nothing out of the ordinary: a small notebook, a pen, a few yen, some pills in a tin—probably quinine. There was also a photograph of a young woman and a few letters, their paper faded, brittle, and tearing at the creases.

His rucksack was a different matter. It had the pungent smell of seafood about it, with good reason: wrapped in crumpled paper was a small fish, probably being hoarded for a private feast.

But it was the wrapping paper that was most surprising. It was a map of Biak; an American map, just like the one Jock carried. There was writing on it, in

English. Where the fish oil hadn't smeared it, the handwriting was fluid, almost decorative.

"That's Mister Simpson's handwriting," Morales said. "I'd know it anywhere. It's all over my radio log." After a long pause, he added, "Maybe he just threw the map away and the Japs found it."

"No," Jock replied, "I'm betting the Japs took it off him, and then *they* threw it away. Our maps are so useless the enemy uses them to wrap fish."

Dyckman shook his head sadly when Jock showed him the fish-stained map. "As I told you, Major, the Japanese have the maps my daughter created. They have no need for these nineteenth century mapmakers' fantasies you Americans carry." He fell silent for a moment before adding, "And I suppose we can deduce the fate of your Mister Simpson, as well. Now that the sun is up, I must take my people away from here, to the mountains in the north. The Japanese are too close—all those radio transmissions you've made. They must know exactly where we are. And as you've said, Major, this place is a trap, hemmed in on all sides."

"Sure," Jock replied, "pull out whenever you're ready. But I need one favor."

"What kind of favor?"

"I need you to leave your crank generator behind, so we can use the transmitter as a homing beacon for the submarine."

Dyckman didn't like that idea one bit. "That is unacceptable, Major Miles. We need the generator if we are to charge the receiver's batteries after you are gone.

It's our only link to the outside world. And why would you not give us the transmitter now, too? You don't have any need for it. The submarine has your coordinates—"

"You mean the coordinates we got from that *mapmakers' fantasy*, as you call it? The ones that might be off by thousands of yards?"

"Really, Major, you must be realistic."

"I *am* being realistic. A miss is as good as a mile in the dark. We need that transmitter—and the generator—to put out a homing signal."

"If you transmit again, the only *homing* that will occur is the Japanese zeroing in on you."

"That's a risk I'll have to take, Mister Dyckman. Now listen...we're not taking that gear with us. We're leaving it behind. You can come back and get it if you need it that badly once we're gone."

"If the Japanese haven't already claimed it, you mean, don't you?"

"I guess that's a risk *you'll* have to take, Mister Dyckman."

The Dutchman scowled, threw up his hands, and began to stomp off. His red hair caught the morning sun and seemed ablaze.

Jock called after him, "So we have an agreement?"

"I wouldn't call it that, Major. You give me no choice."

Chapter Seventeen

Captain Hutchins felt like a man reborn. He was glad he'd stopped drinking the moment Jillian Miles left his table last night. Rather than closing the bar, as was his usual custom, he'd headed straight to his quarters and gotten a good night's sleep, his first in weeks. Waking at 0500, he ate a decent breakfast at the officers' mess and downed several cups of coffee as he read the note once again, the one someone had slipped under his door as he slept.

The note was unsigned but he knew who wrote it. *That lady really kept her word*, he told himself. *This is my "heads up."*

His newfound feeling of well-being was quickly put to the test as he arrived at the provost marshal's office—*his* office. The place was swarming with MPs from 6th Army HQ, led by a lieutenant colonel whose collar brass identified him as *Judge Advocate General's Corps*; in layman's terms, a lawyer. Technical Sergeant Franklin Knox was seated in a corner of the day room, looking unfazed, a burly MP standing on either side of him. He wasn't handcuffed.

Pretty strange to see MPs guarding other MPs, Hutchins told himself.

Several other soldiers from Hutchins' company were seated along the opposite wall, with their own 6th Army MP overseers. The looks on his men's faces varied from bewilderment, to defiance, to terror. They weren't handcuffed, either.

Standing in the middle of the room was Jillian Miles. She didn't bother saying hello. Her first words to

Hutchins were, "That man Van Flyss…the one we put in your nick for attempted murder late last night. He's dead. Hung himself in his cell, they're telling me…if you can believe that."

She looked to the colonel as if saying, *You want to take it from here?*

"Missus Miles' skepticism is well-founded, I'm afraid," the colonel said. "The dead man has considerable blunt force trauma beneath that bushy hair of his, an injury quite inconsistent with hanging. This, Captain Hutchins, appears to be a murder clumsily dressed up to look like a suicide, and it happened in your shop, right under your nose." He relaxed into a chair, folded his arms across his chest, and fixed Hutchins in a damning gaze. "So it's your call what happens next…unless you want it to be my call."

Hutchins had a pretty good idea what the colonel's call would be: *He'll lock every last one of us up—starting with me—and throw away the fucking key.*

He couldn't help but see the look Jillian was giving him. He knew what it meant: *You wanted the chance to cover your ass, one Buna survivor to another. Well, here it is, mate. Better grab it.*

Hutchins seized that chance like a lifeline. "Who was the duty NCO last night, Sergeant Knox?" he asked.

Knox replied as casually as if he was reciting a grocery list: "That would be Sergeant Polito, sir."

Polito, Louis T. Jillian recalled the name and the face. He was the sergeant she saw leading those alleged *Japanese sympathizers* back to the camp. The one who was so arrogant at first, until he realized she worked for the *Supreme Commander.*

The one who looked so terrified now.

"Sergeant Polito," Hutchins continued, "you are under arrest for dereliction of duty." He turned to a 6th Army MP sergeant. "Confine him to the stockade, pending further investigation and possible additional charges."

"But I didn't do anything, sir!"

"That's the trouble, Sergeant," Hutchins replied. "You didn't do anything…and now a prisoner—*your* prisoner—is dead."

As he spoke, he caught the momentary smirk that crossed Knox's face and thought: *That's the look of a man who thinks he's getting away with murder.*

Hutchins continued, "And you, Technical Sergeant Knox, are confined to quarters until further notice."

"Oh, bullshit," Knox said. "You can't do that. You ain't got nothing on me."

"Actually, Sergeant Knox, I can."

"You gotta charge me with something first. Then I demand my right to a fucking court martial."

"Okay, fine. The first charge is insubordination."

Knox scoffed, like this was all a big joke.

"And there'll be many more, Sergeant, I'm quite sure. I've only just begun to peel this little onion of yours."

"You ain't got nothing on me," Knox repeated as the MPs pulled him from his chair. He didn't sound quite so sure this time, though.

But Knox wasn't finished. Before he and his escorts reached the door, he stopped, turned to Jillian, and said, "This is all your fault, lady. That man had a lot of enemies. You had him locked up, disarmed him…a perfect set-up for someone with a gripe to do him in. You got him killed."

"So you knew Mister Van Flyss, then, Sergeant?" she asked.

"Don't make me laugh, lady. Everybody knew him. Even some of your high-falutin' officers. Any one of them could've killed him."

Jillian replied, "Only one problem with that line of reasoning, Sergeant—he was in *your* nick at the time."

"You don't know shit about nothing, lady."

Hutchins said, "That will be quite enough out of you, Sergeant Knox." He motioned to the MPs: *Get him out of here.*

Knox's little empire toppled faster than a house of cards once Sergeant Polito was isolated in a room with the JAG colonel. "I ain't taking the fall for no murder," Polito blurted. "I didn't even desert my post last night…Knox relieved me, all proper, by the book. He told me to go get some coffee over at the mess hall."

The colonel asked, "And when you got back from getting the coffee, you didn't check on the prisoner?"

"Why would I? Knox said everything was under control. Then he took off. When I finally did check, right before sunrise, well…it was me who sounded the alarm and called HQ, wasn't it?"

"So to your knowledge, Sergeant Knox was the only person alone with Van Flyss, aside from you?"

"Yes, sir. This stockade ain't exactly Grand Central Station—ain't much traffic through here even in broad daylight—and he was alive when I went for the coffee. I swear it. And that rope wasn't even in the cell when I locked him up."

The colonel jotted a few notes on his pad. Then he asked, "Do you have any idea why Sergeant Knox might want Mister Van Flyss dead?"

Polito looked as if he was about to be sick. It took him a few moments to hold down the bile and form the words, but finally he replied, "Yeah, I know why. Boy, do I know why..."

He was barely into his rapid-fire description of the black market operation when the colonel stopped him, asking, "You're telling me that, led by their senior NCO, half the men in this company were involved, in one way or another, with the theft and resale of Red Cross relief food and supplies to any and all comers?"

"Not exactly *all comers*, sir. Only to the GIs. Nobody else in this fucking country got any money...not the Aussie *diggers* and surely not the darkies."

There was a look of surprise on the colonel's face. "Is there really much of a market for it?"

"Are you kidding me, sir? We were doing land office business. Maybe you officer-types don't feel much like noticing, but the *doggies* around these parts ain't exactly chowin' down like *the swells*. Some extra rations and stuff come in real handy."

"Why did you go along with it, Sergeant Polito?"

"Knox told us we'd play the game and keep our fucking mouths shut or we'd end up with our asses beatin' the bush for Japs. Or worse."

The colonel asked, "To your knowledge, was Captain Hutchins involved in these events you describe?"

"You kidding, sir? I think this morning was only the third time I even seen him in the months I've been here. He's just a name on an office door."

"So the captain had no idea this was going on?"

"I don't think he knew shit about anything around here, sir."

"Did you receive any money for participating in this...*enterprise*, Sergeant?"

"No, sir, I swear. But *somebody* hadda get the dough. I'm guessing it went to the kingpin of the whole show."

"And that *kingpin* would be Sergeant Knox?"

"Yeah...him and that Van Flyss clown. You know, the dead guy. But there's more, sir...a lot more."

"Go on, Sergeant."

"There's a secret camp, sir," Polito continued. "A *prison* camp...no other word for it. Some of the Dutch at the resettlement camp must've caught wise to what was going on, seeing as how they were barely getting subsistence rations and all. So before they could make a big stink, they got separated from the rest and put in this *special* camp. When we asked why we were doing that—rounding them up and all, like they were criminals instead of people we *liberated*—Knox said he just found out they were Jap sympathizers, and he'd been ordered to keep them on ice."

"*Found out* from who, Sergeant?"

"How the hell would I know, sir?" He tapped the three stripes on his sleeve and added, "Just because I wear these don't mean I get to ask no questions."

"Are men of your company involved in this *prison camp*, Sergeant?"

"Hell, yeah, sir. Where do you think the guards come from?"

"I see," the colonel said. "Let's take a break for a few minutes. I think it's time we brought that lady from

HQ in to hear your deposition. It might provide some answers on the missing refugees she's looking for."

"Is it going to get me in worse trouble if she does hear it?"

"No, Sergeant. I don't believe we could make this mess much worse at the moment."

Polito's chin slumped to his chest. "Just do me one favor, sir. Promise me you'll lock Knox up and throw away the key. Otherwise he's going to kill me for ratting him out. He'll find me somehow and kill me. It won't matter what stockade the Army puts me in." His eyes filled with tears as he added, "Why do you think we all danced to his tune, anyway?"

The colonel shook his head. "Sergeant, if everything you just told me is true, Knox won't be in a position to hunt you or anyone else down. Not from inside a penitentiary."

By midday, a platoon of American MPs from 6th Army descended on the *prison camp* hidden in the forest. Six of Knox's men were on duty there, oblivious to the shitstorm of reckoning going on back at company headquarters. The six were arrested and loaded into a deuce-and-a-half.

An MP lieutenant, bustling about with great purpose, approached Jillian and asked, "What exactly are we supposed to be doing with these civilian prisoners, ma'am?"

"Prisoners?" she replied, trying to keep her temper in check. "*Prisoners*? Clearly, you haven't yet grasped this situation, have you, Lieutenant? These people were being held captive by criminals in your bloody Army. Congratulate yourself—you've just freed them. You're a liberator."

He still didn't get it.

And a stupid wanker, too, she said only to herself.

"I'll make it easy for you, Lieutenant. We're going to feed them and let the medics check them over. After that, we'll transport those that don't need to go straight to hospital back to proper quarters at the resettlement camp. Any questions?"

He still looked confused. "But we're kinda spread thin, ma'am, between cleaning out that secret warehouse and this place. I've only got one empty deuce-and-a-half, ma'am...and there's dozens of these people."

Bloody hell, Jock was right...MPs really are the dimmest of the lot. Even their officers.

"Then we'll have to use that truck as a shuttle, won't we, Lieutenant?"

"Oh...sure...okay, ma'am," he replied. He lingered uncomfortably for a few moments before hurrying off, finally realizing his presence was no longer required.

The prison camp—there was no other term for it—reminded Jillian so much of the Japanese POW camps where she'd lost a year of her life. Tin-roofed huts with screens for walls, hemmed in by a tall, barbed wire fence, could have been created by the same evil architects the Japanese had employed. Fifty-two fair-skinned, painfully thin men and women—European and Eurasian—were confined here:

All less than thirty years of age, Jillian reckoned, *although they look at least a decade older. That's what happens to you when you live without hope.*

They'd been rescued from the Japanese...only to be enslaved and slowly starved by some bad-seed Americans.

She gazed beyond the ramshackle structures to a far corner of this fenced-in hell and saw the small crosses perched atop low mounds of earth. She tried to count them but couldn't; her tremors of outrage became too much to control. It was all too real and personal, a terrifying memory being replayed on a stage where no such horror should ever happen. Sinking to her knees, she began to sob:

And we call the Japanese bloody barbarians...

There was a hand on her shoulder. Jillian looked up to see one of the women standing over her, helping her to her feet. There was something so familiar about her...

That red hair! She was the female prisoner we saw being marched across the road when we first arrived. I'm sure of it.

It was hard to tell who was comforting who as Jillian and the red-haired woman stood in each other's arms.

"I heard you speak," the woman said, her English heavily accented by a lifetime in the Dutch East Indies. "You're Australian. Is it the Aussies who come to save us this time?"

"No...it's still the bloody Yanks, I'm afraid."

The woman's response was in Dutch. The words were lost on Jillian but their invective tone was not.

Jillian's gaze was still on the graveyard. This time she finished counting the crosses—*eleven*—and added the living and the dead in her head.

"So, sixty-three souls in all were brought here?"

"That sounds correct," the red-haired woman replied as she brushed away some windblown hair in her face. As she did, her tattered sleeve slid down, exposing her wrist. Both women had matching scars there, harsh ligature marks imprinted for life by methodical acts of torture.

Mine come only from the Japanese, Jillian told herself. *I hope this woman can say the same.*

Composed enough now to make notes, she asked, "Do you know all their names?"

"Yes. You can begin with mine…I'm Greta Christiansen, nee Dyckman, from the island of Biak."

Chapter Eighteen

Jock, Baum, and Morales took turns carrying Steve Richards down to the beach. The man not holding up one end of the stretcher carried the .30-caliber machine gun. Once they found a seaside patch of trees where they could hide the wounded pilot, Jock said, "Okay, Steve...we're going to leave you here while we go back and get the rest of the stuff. You got everything you need?"

Everything didn't boil down to very much: two canteens of water, a little pouch of food—fresh crab meat and berries, courtesy of Dyckman's people, for which he had no appetite—and his .45 pistol with one bullet in the chamber and nothing left in the magazine. Richards sounded less than convinced when he replied, "Yeah, I'll be fine. You'll be back before sundown, right?"

"It's only about a mile round trip, Steve"—Jock checked his watch—"and it's only 1600 right now. We've still got a couple of hours until sundown."

"But you'll be lugging that transmitter...and that generator, too."

"We'll manage. You just relax. Before you know it, we'll be on that sub."

Jock and the two Navy men made good time on the walk back to the camp. It was deserted, just as they'd suspected it would be. Dyckman and his people had been ready to depart on their trek north the same time they'd set out to bring Richards to the beach. Finding them gone was no surprise.

What was a surprise was finding the transmitter and generator gone, too.

They dropped to the ground as one, sure a million Japanese eyes were close by, watching their every movement. Quickly, though, it dawned on all three of them:

The Japs didn't do this. They're not interested in stealing our transmitter.

They're interested in killing us.

So there's only one explanation where it went.

Hector Morales stood up, scanning the trees for the wire antenna he'd strung there. But it was gone, too. He looked bewildered, like a man who couldn't come to grips with the fact he'd just lost everything he held dear to people he'd come to trust. He just kept shaking his head, unable to say a word.

Sid Baum didn't have any problem finding his words. "Those lousy lying sons of bitches. When it came down to us or them, I always figured they'd fuck us up the ass." He shot Jock an accusing look; its meaning seemed quite clear: *This is all your fault. You trusted that miserable Dutch son of a bitch.*

Then Baum said, "We gotta go after them and take that shit back."

"No," Jock replied. "I'm not getting any of us lost on some wild goose chase."

"But they couldn't have gotten far, dammit…and we know they're going north."

"Am I not speaking fucking English? I said *no*, Baum. Now calm down and forget about it."

"But why, sir?" His tone was less aggressive, as if he suddenly remembered he was talking to a superior.

"*Why*? Because *north* covers a lot of territory—which we don't know from Adam—and with this useless map we've got, we might as well be on the moon. Plus, it's going to get dark on us real quick."

His defiance had collapsed, but Baum's pride was still calling the shots. "We can't let them get away with this shit, sir!"

Sounding more like a priest than a superior officer, Jock replied, "Sid, I know you're a stand-up guy, but this isn't some brawl between street gangs. We're in the jungle. Different rules apply out here, like don't go looking for trouble when you don't know where the hell you are in the first place."

Baum pleaded, "But what are we going to do, sir?"

"Simple. We're going to stick to the plan and be waiting for that sub."

"And if that doesn't pan out?"

"Then we'll have to think of something else, Sid. But at the moment, it's all we've got. So let's get moving. Let's not leave Mister Richards alone any longer than we have to."

Jock and Baum started walking. Morales didn't—he was just standing there, looking toward the bluffs surrounding them.

Baum asked, "You coming, Hec, or what?"

"I hear something," Morales replied. "Listen…"

"I don't hear a fucking thing," Baum said.

"No," Morales replied. "I'm not kidding. Listen."

Then they heard it: the sound of engines…

"Tanks," Jock said.

"SHIT," Baum wailed. "We're boxed in here. What the hell are we going to do against tanks?"

"Don't worry about the damn tanks," Jock replied. "They're pretty far away and they can't come down here. The trail's way too steep and narrow for them. If they try, they'll just slide off and tumble down the cliff. Worry more about any infantry that may be with them."

That came as no comfort to the two Navy men, who seemed frozen in place.

"C'mon, dammit," Jock said, "we need to get the hell away from here...and right fucking now."

They hadn't gotten far when a tank—perched at the edge of the ridge—fired its main gun, targeting the area where the transmitter had been. Baum and Morales flinched, but Jock said, "Hey, that's a good sign. As long as they're shooting this way, there probably isn't any Jap infantry poking around down here. Too much chance of hitting your own guys. The sons of bitches sure got the transmitter's old location dialed in, though, don't they?"

Jock found a spot where he had a good view of the bluff. "Look...there's two tanks sitting up on the ridge," he said. He watched the puffs of smoke from their barrels as the guns fired. A moment later, he heard the reports.

Two more rounds splashed into the ground hundreds of yards away from them.

"Pretty low-caliber stuff," Jock said, "and they're just lobbing it down here blind, like artillery shooting at a spot on the map. Don't worry about them...just keep your eyes peeled for foot patrols. But let's get real wide of where the camp was, just to be safe."

Baum said, "Then it's going to take a lot longer to get back to the beach, sir."

"No shit, Sid."

It was darker than they'd hoped when they got near the beach. The late afternoon sun, which had silhouetted the tanks perched on the ridge so well, had now dropped behind it, shrouding the coastal lowlands in dusky shadow. The spot where they'd left Richards wasn't so easy to find anymore.

We've got to be close, Jock thought. *But if we stumble onto him, he might get panicky and...*

He stopped Baum and Morales, telling them, "Mister Richards is probably going to be really jumpy, lying there listening to those tanks firing. Let's not startle him, okay? Keep calling his name real softly."

They both nodded in agreement. Then Morales said, "Speaking of the tanks, they haven't fired in at least ten minutes."

"Yeah," Baum added, "and if they're not shooting anymore, maybe Jap infantry's on the way?"

"Could be," Jock replied.

"That's just fucking great," Baum said. "Now we've got two different ways to get shot."

Jock smiled and said, "Only two? That's pretty good odds in this game, Sid."

After walking north for ten minutes—and still not coming across Steve Richards—Jock said, "We fucked up. Let's backtrack. We must've been too far north to begin with."

He was right. They backtracked for ten minutes and walked a few minutes more before Richards' frail voice floated out of the darkness: "I'm over here, for cryin' out loud. Geez, you guys are making a hell of a lot of noise. Where the hell've you been? And what's all that shooting back there? Artillery?"

Jock told him about the tanks.

Richards sat up on his stretcher as the three friendly shadows drew closer. But something didn't look right: "Hey...you guys aren't carrying enough stuff. Where's the transmitter?"

The answer stunned Richards into silence for a few moments, until he finally whispered his reply: "Shit. Those bastards..."

"Damn good thing we got to recon this place in the daylight," Jock said. "Otherwise, we'd be just guessing how to defend it." He placed Morales' machine gun so its fire crossed a broad, flat field inland of their position, with few trees to provide cover for attackers. "We'll get the best field of fire for the thirty cal here," he explained. "It should cut down anyone trying to come from the south or west. Sid, you and I will move over a few yards and cover the north."

Their backs were to the east, where there was nothing but the no-name bay and the sea.

"Ain't we all kinda close together, sir?" Baum asked. "You know...like *one hand grenade gets you all?*"

"In the daylight, you'd be right, Sid. But in the dark...we've got to stay close to keep in touch. Otherwise—"

"We could end up shooting at each other, sir?"

"You got it."

Jock checked what was left of the machine gun's only remaining ammo belt. "Should be enough for four or five decent bursts," he told Morales, "but let's do something. I count seven tracers still mixed in...swap them out with ball ammo from the end of the belt. If we get all the way down to those last rounds, we're screwed anyway...it won't matter a damn bit those last shots are tracers."

His gallows humor was infectious. Morales replied, "At least we'll go out in a bright blaze of glory, sir."

"Now you're talking," Jock said. "We've just got to hold on a couple more hours..."

"Yeah, that's all," Baum added, "and pray that fucking sub finds us."

The hours dragged on, marked only by the rhythmic lapping of low waves along the beach, like the languid swish of a clock's pendulum running much too slowly. The moon cast the faintest of glows, yielding a vague, monochrome sketch of shore and water. It wasn't enough light to see the silhouette of a dark vessel, especially a submarine's, with her decks nearly awash and stubby conning tower barely protruding above the sea.

The night brought an end to the sea breeze, and with it, the hope of that breeze helping to carry the faint sound of diesel engines toward shore. "It might not matter," Hector Morales said. "I'll bet when the sub gets close, she'll probably be running on electric, anyway. Much quieter."

Jock shook his head and asked, "You ever been on a sub?"

"No, sir."

"Well, I was, for a couple of days. Believe me, if they're on the surface, they use diesel, period. They can move faster and keep their batteries charged...not to mention the fresh air those engines suck into the sub."

"The fresh air, sir?"

"Yeah. Subs stink to high heaven. You cram about seventy guys who never shower into a stifling little tin can and it gets ripe really fast. Airing the damn boat out whenever you can is a real good thing."

Morales replied, "Right now, I don't care what it smells like, sir, just so it shows up."

Jock looked seaward, cupping his hands against the sides of his head like crude ear trumpets. There was nothing to be heard but the sounds of nature.

"I can feel it in my bones," Baum said. "This ain't gonna work. We're never gonna get picked up." These weren't the words of a frightened man, just one who seemed totally convinced of his fate.

It was the last thing Jock needed to hear: *This is all we fucking need right now...a collapse of morale.*

"Take it easy, Sid," Jock replied. "The night makes everyone a little pessimistic."

"You mean that old shit *it's always darkest before the dawn*, sir? Sorry, but I'm more than pessimistic. I'm fucking certain. It's not gonna happen. Too many ways for it to go sour. Shitty map coordinates, no radio to home on...We're fucked."

Morales threw up his hands. "Ahh, shut up, Sid," he said. "This ain't like you."

"He's right," Jock said. "It's not like you at all, Sid. And it sounds like I've got more faith in your Navy than you do. A hell of a lot more."

Morales mumbled, "That's exactly what I was thinking."

Even though Baum's face was invisible in the darkness, Jock could sense him withdrawing into himself, a man suddenly without hope. *Bad choice of words on my part,* he told himself. *I must've hit a nerve, and Morales piling on was maybe the last straw.*

"I'm not questioning your loyalty to the Navy, Sid, just trying to lighten things up a little."

"I know, sir, and I appreciate that. But it's fate I'm pissed at right now, not the Navy."

Pissed at fate, are you? Well, join the fucking club.

They settled back into their waiting game. Jock turned to listen for the sound of engines on the sea once again, but all he heard was the sloshing of surf.

Chapter Nineteen

Three hours until dawn. There was still no sign of the submarine.

Morales asked Jock, "If it doesn't come, sir, are we going to try and hook up with the Dutchman again?"

"You've been reading my mind, Hector."

"Hey, sir," Baum said, "can I get first punch when we find him again?"

"Negative. I'll be doing the honors personally."

Another hushed voice joined in, a voice they hadn't heard for quite a while. It was Steve Richards saying, "All due respect, sir, but you guys need to shut up for a minute, so you can hear something really interesting—maybe even wonderful—out there."

They all turned to face the sea, listening, hoping…

And there it was: the faint rumble of diesel engines.

"Damn right it's wonderful," Jock said. "That's what our subs sound like."

He picked up the binoculars but found he didn't need them. The sub was coming much closer to shore than he'd imagined, so close he could make out the shadowy outlines of her periscopes and deck guns. She seemed only about half a mile from the beach when she coasted to a stop. A blinker light on the conning tower began flashing its message.

"Sid, you be our signalman," Jock said. "Leave Hector on the machine gun."

"Aye aye, sir," Baum replied.

It took a little over a minute before the sub's message ended. Baum shook his head and said. "You ain't gonna believe this. They want to know who said, *Frankly, my dear, I don't give a damn.*"

"That's an easy one," Jock replied.

"That's swell, but I don't know it."

"Tell them *Rhett Butler.*"

"Who the hell is that, sir?"

"You've never seen *Gone With The Wind*? Clark Gable played him."

"Well that's just fucking wonderful."

Baum blinked the answer with his flashlight. But the sub had another question.

"My aching ass!" Baum said. "Don't these fucking squids like baseball? Now they want to know the name of the president's dog! What the hell is their problem, anyway?"

"Actually, that's pretty simple, too, Sid. The dog's name is Fala."

"Better spell that for me, sir."

Within minutes of the reply from Baum's flashlight, a rubber boat was in the water, making its way to the beach.

Jock told Baum, "Let's you and me get Mister Richards. Once he's in the boat, I'll pull in Morales."

The rubber boat scraped to a stop on the beach. An oarsman drawled, "One of y'all a Major Miles?"

"I'm Miles. Glad to see you guys."

"Still a party of four souls, sir?"

"Affirmative."

"No problem...we got us plenty of room."

As Jock and Baum struggled to get Steve Richards on board, the nerve-wracking jackhammer of Morales' machine gun shattered the stillness of the night.

"Dammit, he's holding the trigger down," Jock said. "I've got to get to him."

First, they had to pass Richards to the two sailors in the boat, who now seemed far more interested in rowing back out to sea.

"Gimme a goddamn minute," Jock told them as Richards was finally nestled in the boat. "Hold the fort here, Sid."

Baum knew why Jock told him to stay: *I'm supposed to keep these squids from taking off without us.*

Jock wasn't even halfway to Morales' position when those last seven rounds in the .30-caliber's belt—the seven tracers—lit up the rainforest like wayward fireworks, bouncing crazily into the air as they careened off trees, the ground, or whatever else was lurking out there. All too soon, the machine gun went silent.

Suddenly there were more tracers flying low over Jock's head, slicing through the trees like brilliant arrows, shearing them like a woodsman's saw run amok. A new sound from offshore now poisoned the night: the deep-throated *poom poom poom* of the sub's 20-millimeter deck gun.

Is this their idea of fire support? Or are they just trying to kill us? And where the fuck is Morales?

There was movement on the ground to his right. He brought his Thompson to bear, tripped over some unseen obstacle...

And went sprawling to the ground.

He landed right next to Hector Morales, who was struggling with something, pulling with all his might.

"Whoa! Hector...what the hell are you doing?"

"The thirty cal, sir...it's stuck. A fucking tree just fell on it."

"FORGET IT. IT'S OUT OF AMMO ANYWAY. C'MON, LET'S GET OUT OF HERE."

He pulled Morales away by his collar and they began the low-crawl back to the beach. The sub's tracers were beacons pointing the way.

Morales said, "Boy, somebody ain't afraid of using tracers, that's for sure."

"What the hell did you see, Hector?"

"I never saw them, sir…but I could *feel* the Japs out there, all around."

"You're sure about that?"

"You don't believe me, sir?"

"I don't know what to believe, Hector. All I know is the only fire I saw was all going one way."

Scurrying along the coral on knees and elbows, Morales was silent for a moment. Then he said, "You think I fucked up, don't you, sir?"

"Not if we get out of here alive in the next couple of seconds."

The 20-millimeter deck gun kept firing at the shore until the submarine was under way. "What are you shooting at?" Jock asked the sub's captain.

"Same thing you were, I suppose," the captain replied.

"Yeah…whatever the hell that was. What took you so long to show up, anyway?"

"Those coordinates we had for you…they weren't worth a shit." He pointed to a spot on the nautical chart about two miles south of the actual pickup location, separated from it by a spit of land. "Your map and my chart certainly don't agree with each other. One of them—maybe both—is way off. We might've never found you if you didn't fire up that radio beacon."

"Wait a minute," Jock said, "*what* radio beacon?"

"The one that steered us right to you." He showed Jock the vectors his crew had plotted from the shore transmitter's signal. "We were expecting that signal a whole lot sooner, but hey…better late than never, right? And the later it got, the higher the tide, so we could risk getting real close to shore."

Jock stared at the chart in stunned silence for a few moments, until a smile began to spread across his face. "I'll be a son of a bitch," he said, "the old Dutchman came through after all. Go figure…"

The captain didn't get it. "What do you mean, Jock?"

"Long story. Let's just say it had a happy ending."

"If you say so. But is your leg okay? You had some trouble getting down the ladder before. You need the doc to look at it?"

"No, I'm okay. It's just my souvenir of Manus Island. The doc's got his hands full with Mister Richards, anyway."

By the time the sun came up, Biak was nothing but a few distant, hazy mountains off the submarine's stern. Jock and the three Navy airmen learned they wouldn't be on board much longer.

"We'll rendezvous with the flying boat here," the sub's captain said as he pointed to a spot on the chart. "You'll be back in Hollandia for lunch."

Chapter Twenty

At the Aitape resettlement camp, the sordid empire of Sergeant Knox and Fritz Van Flyss was still being unraveled. Jillian's first order of business today would be an in-depth interview with Greta Christiansen over breakfast at the camp's mess tent.

"The doctor told me I'll be fine," Greta began. "Quite a bit undernourished at the moment—and malarial, like everyone else—but nothing that can't be dealt with." She took a bite of her scrambled eggs and then, with what seemed to be great reluctance, pushed the rest away. "He did caution me not to eat too much too soon. Our digestive tracts need to get used to—" She stopped herself, as if she suddenly remembered she was talking to another ex-POW, one well familiar with the privations of captivity.

Jillian switched the topic to the question of *Japanese sympathizers.*

"That Van Flyss," Greta said, "he was the real sympathizer. He'd go whichever way the wind blew. When the Japanese were here, he never spent a night within their barbed wire. He was in business with them instead, coming and going as he pleased, housing their *comfort women*, supplying the officers with Australian liquor he'd stolen...practically providing a resort for their high command. If anyone stood in his way, he'd single them out for *special treatment*, and the Japanese were more than glad to oblige."

"Yes, I remember the *special treatments* all too well," Jillian said. She looked at the bruises on Greta's wrists—permanent disfigurements they both shared—

and knew this Dutch woman had endured her share of *special treatments*, too.

"As soon as the Yanks came," Greta continued, "he switched sides in an instant."

"You mean he became an *American sympathizer*?"

"More than that. The trouble is, the Yanks always seem to have lots of money. Nobody else around here does. And money is the root of all evil. They had it, he wanted it. All he had to do was find something very profitable to sell to them."

Jillian asked, "And that *something* was the Red Cross food and supplies meant for you survivors of the Japanese occupation?"

"Yes, and when we found Van Flyss and his natives taking the relief packages away on Yank army trucks, we suspected he was up to no good again, creating a *black market* out of thin air in partnership with the Americans. Before we could even file a complaint with the Red Cross, we were dragged from our quarters like criminals and told we'd been uncovered as Japanese sympathizers. Have you ever heard anything so ridiculous? We knew it was Van Flyss who *identified* us."

"To who did he *identify* you?"

"That beastly Yank sergeant…the one who prowls about like a feral animal."

"Sergeant Knox."

"Yes, that one."

"Just him? No officers?"

"Yes, just the sergeant, as far as I know. In fact, I'd never seen an American officer until yesterday. Nothing but sergeants and common soldiers."

"Interesting," Jillian said. "So what happened next?"

"We were herded onto trucks by American soldiers and driven to that prison camp. We were quite sure we'd been brought there to die, whether by starvation, disease, or God knows what. I even heard Sergeant Knox telling some of his men we were *as good as dead, and we deserved it*." She took a sip of coffee. "So what will happen to Knox, that *hoerenjung*?"

Jillian smiled. She'd been around enough Dutch seamen to know *hoerenjung* meant son of a bitch. "Considering that at the top of his rather lengthy charge sheet is Van Flyss' murder, he could get the firing squad."

Greta relaxed into her chair. "That would be too good for him. Too good for any Yank, as far as I'm concerned. They're all a bunch of ratbags."

"They're not all like that, Greta. Really. Most of them are good blokes."

But the Dutchwoman's skepticism would not be shaken. "I'm not surprised you say that, considering you work for them."

"It's more than that. I'm married to one."

Their conversation ended like a door being slammed, replaced by an awkward silence. Jillian finally broke it by asking, "Can I ask you about your family, Greta?"

"I don't know if I have one anymore."

"Maybe I can help find them," Jillian replied. "Tell me all you can."

Hesitant and guarded at first, Greta settled into the telling of her tale: her life as a wealthy planter's daughter; her and her husband's work mapping the wilderness that was Biak; the last she saw of him as they were separated at a Japanese prison camp; her father, left behind on the island at the mercy of the Japanese.

"You're a mapmaker," Jillian said. "That's very interesting. My husband is an intelligence liaison between the American Army and Air Force, and I believe they've set their sights on Biak…"

Greta sensed Jillian's question before it was asked. Her face screwed up as if she'd just smelled something rotten.

"If you're going to ask me if I'll work for the Americans like you're doing, my answer is this: absolutely not. I won't help those barbarians any more than I'd help the Japanese."

Jillian managed only to say "But Greta, listen to—" before she saw the company clerk barging into the mess tent, making a bee-line for her.

"Missus Miles," he said, "there's an urgent call from HQ on the landline for you."

Jillian cringed at the word *urgent*—there was a good chance it was news of Jock, and it was even odds whether that news was good or bad. Watching the tense uncertainty seize her, the clerk wished he'd phrased his sentence differently. He tried again: "Oh, no, ma'am…they wanted you to know right up front it's urgent in a real good way."

She was breathless from running when she reached the phone. Colonel Molloy's cheerful voice was on the other end, asking her, "How soon can you get yourself to Hollandia, young lady?"

PART II
UNTIL IT ENDS

Chapter Twenty-One

Master Sergeant Melvin Patchett scowled as he watched his commanding officer, Lieutenant Colonel Kit Billingsley, strut like a conquering Caesar on the beach at Biak. With smug satisfaction, the colonel surveyed the mass and might of American men and machines coming ashore to claim the island. *We ain't even set up our damn CP yet*, Patchett told himself, *and already that sorry excuse for a C.O. is playing grand marshal of the victory parade.*

"Sergeant," Billingsley thundered, "this is just another example of the brilliance of Douglas MacArthur."

Patchett replied, "How do you figure that, sir?"

"Just look around you, Sergeant. Do you see any Japanese? Once again, our landing was virtually unopposed."

"Our battalion took three dead and ten wounded, sir. Looks like the other battalions got hit a little worse. Wouldn't exactly call that *unopposed*."

"Small potatoes, Sergeant," Billingsley replied. "Now, as I was saying, MacArthur has the knack for knowing where the Japanese will be weakest. But I think he's outdone himself this time…this island was a *positively inspired* next move for us. We'll be through this place like shit through a goose, and then it's on to Manila…and Tokyo."

"Remains to be seen, don't it, sir? We ain't been here an hour yet, and the Japs never try to fight on the damn beach, anyhow. They let you land…suck you in…and then—"

"That'll be quite enough, Sergeant Patchett. I don't need a lecture on Japanese tactics right now."

Colonel Billingsley's confident façade faded as he spread his map on the hood of the jeep. He stared at it for a moment and then took in a quick panoramic view of the island beyond the beach, trying desperately to reconcile the cartographer's graphics with what the land revealed of itself. Then he returned to the map and the process began all over again. His eyes made that circuit three times before he said, "Our CP...I think it should be right over there." He pointed to a spot on the open beach a few yards away.

"Negative, sir," Patchett replied. "The only ones gonna find us there are the Jap planes come to strafe the beach." He pointed in the opposite direction. "We're supposed to be a couple hundred yards over yonder, just inside the treeline."

Billingsley regained his bluster. "Well then, Sergeant, you'd best get over there and set that CP up on the double."

As Patchett rounded up the battalion headquarters staff, he thought, *And that's the good map, the brand spanking new one! Shit, it's like looking at an aerial photograph that got took five minutes ago...and the damn fool still can't figure out where the fuck he's at. Ink ain't hardly dry on that map it's so new...just like them orders jacking MacArthur's golden boy there up to light colonel.*

I reckon we never knew how good we had it when ol' Jock Miles was running the show here.

"You serious, Top?" Sergeant Bogater Boudreau asked Patchett. "He couldn't even figure where he was on that li'l ol' beach?"

"As I live and breathe, Bogater, that man is a walkin', talkin' *fubar*."

"Nothing we didn't already know, Top." Boudreau leaned over the maps he'd spread on the ground. "But now he doesn't even want me and my boys to recon this road to the airfields *in person* first? Just a fucking *map recon*?"

"That's what the man said. He's in a big rush to get to Tokyo, you see."

"Fuck Tokyo, *mon frère*. Y'all might never even reach Mokmer alive if we don't have ourselves a little look-see first. We only got one good map of this whole fucking island and it stops about a mile north of here. Once we're off it...shit, the fucking road even disappears off the next map sheet...and I ain't believing the terrain's as flat as this antique piece of junk says it is."

"What'd you expect? Damn thing was drawn around the turn of the century. Fucking road probably wasn't even hacked out of this here jungle then."

Bogater fumed for a moment. "Son of a bitch. This is Hollandia all over again, ain't it?"

"You still going on about that, Cajun?"

"Hell yeah I am. We were supposed to be capturing some nice, firm ground for more of MacArthur's precious airfields...looked fucking great on that map from last century, didn't it?...but instead, we're up to our titties in a swamp. *A little too soggy for flight operations*, the brass say, *so let's move ourselves onto this little rock of an island called Wakde instead.* Don't even give us no dry set of clothes or nothing. Fuck me...just once, I'd like to be sure what exactly the damn terrain's gonna be *before* I set foot on one of these shitholes."

"Hey, you knew this landing was gonna be on a dry coral beach, didn't you?"

"I surely did, Top...and I'm *beaucoup* grateful for small favors. But I'm betting them favors just about run out."

※

The downpour had slowed the long column of military traffic to a crawl once again. Jillian fumed, checked her wristwatch, and slid inboard on the jeep's passenger seat as far as she could, trying to keep dry from the rain slashing into the open-sided jeep.

"At least we've got good canvas on top, ma'am," Lieutenant Jimmy Ketchum said as he rode the clutch for traction on the dirt road's slick surface. A little more rain and it would become a quagmire, ending their progress toward Hollandia until the deluge stopped and the ground dried out. It would be the third time their trek from Aitape had been forced to a halt by storms in the past two days.

"Don't worry, ma'am," Ketchum said, "I'll get you there before your husband ships out."

She smiled and patted him gamely on the shoulder. But deep down inside she didn't believe him. It had been five days since Jock had arrived in Hollandia, his odyssey on Biak finally over. It had taken her three days to wrap up her business at the resettlement camp. She'd managed to account for every last refugee of the sixty-three missing from the camp's official roster: fifty-two living, eleven dead. Those still alive, like Greta Christiansen, had been placed in the care of the Red Cross, with the camp now under the direct supervision of 6th Army HQ. The unit originally responsible for the camp—the 106th Military Police Company—was disbanded. Its members were promptly dispersed to other units with two exceptions: the top sergeant, Franklin "Hard" Knox, was in prison at Port Moresby, awaiting court martial for murder and a variety of other serious charges. The company commander, Captain Hutchins, was in the back seat of the jeep.

He'd been quiet the entire trip, despite Jillian's and Ketchum's attempts to engage him in conversation. *I reckon he's in no hurry to get to Hollandia*, Jillian figured. *He knows he's getting sent back to a combat unit. But with all the unspeakable things that went on right under his nose, he's a lucky wanker he's not in a cell right next to Knox.*

Maybe the brass figure this is a better way to punish him.

She checked her watch again: *1025*. When she'd talked to Jock on the landline two days ago—right before she left Aitape—he told her in a conversation that was all too brief he'd be flying back to Wakde Island. He had to be there by sundown on June 21.

Today.

It's over an hour's flight. They'll have to leave by 1600.

And we're still thirty miles from Hollandia.

She returned to the memory of that phone call. They'd only been allowed two minutes on the circuit, but that was all they'd needed to express relief for each other's escapes from mortal danger and plan for their paths to intersect—even just for an hour or two—at Hollandia.

Now that plan was crumbling. The column had stopped moving. The dark shape of the truck off their front bumper was barely visible through the cascades flowing down the windshield. Ketchum shut off the jeep's engine. "Better save the gas, ma'am," he said. "We're going to need it."

The rain was falling in sheets now, washing away the last traces of Jillian's hope she'd get there in time.

Chapter Twenty-Two

The battalion had been on the road to the Mokmer airfields for almost thirty minutes, its three rifle companies in column, just like Colonel Billingsley ordered. Master Sergeant Patchett folded the map sheet for the landing beaches and stuffed it between his helmet liner and steel "pot."

Walking beside him was First Sergeant Tom Hadley of Charlie Company. Hadley asked, "Shouldn't we take out that old Mokmer map sheet now, Top?"

"Why bother, Tom? It ain't worth the damn paper it's printed on. Look at what's happening…the terrain to our right is rising faster than bread in the fucking oven. That map sheet don't show shit about it. We're gonna be fish in a barrel real soon, son."

Hadley laughed. "What the fuck else is new?"

"What we gotta do," Patchett continued, "is get us a company up on that high ground. The boundary with 3rd Battalion is way over thataway. We can't trust those shitheads to cover our flank. I gotta talk to the C.O."

"Get him on the radio," Hadley said.

"Nah…I don't want this broadcast to the whole fucking world for a whole lotta reasons. Better I do it face to face."

Patchett hurried back through the next unit in the column, Able Company. At its tail end he found its commander, Captain Theo Papadakis, with Colonel Billingsley. *The Mad Greek* wasn't happy.

"We need to get us a company up on the high ground, sir," Patchett said to Billingsley.

"That's what I've been trying to tell the colonel, Top," Papadakis added.

"Negative, negative," Billingsley replied. "I'm in contact with 3rd Battalion. They'll move west to cover our flank."

"Begging your pardon, sir," Patchett said, "but that dog won't hunt. Our battalion's gonna be strolling into a shooting gallery in a couple minutes—and we're the fucking targets down in this valley. We gotta cover our own asses *now*, not trust them route-step douchebags to do it for us."

"Just what I was saying," Papadakis mumbled.

Billingsley shook his head. "We can't. It'll just slow us down."

The Mad Greek had seen that look coming over Patchett's face before. He knew what it meant: the colonel was about to be hosed down with some righteous wisdom, hard-won in this war as well as the Great War before it.

"Slow us down, sir?" Patchett began. *"Slow us down?"* We best not get too comfortable over having that li'l Stuart tank out in front, because once we get boxed in here—the sea on one side, this cliff on the other—one pissant anti-tank gun on the road ahead stops him dead in his tracks, and we're stuck in a classic fucking ambush. That'll *slow us down* right quick. If we wanna keep moving, better we control our own fate, sir. And the only way to do that is to get up on that high ground."

He watched for a few moments as Billingsley vacillated silently, and then added, "We didn't come all this way to offer ourselves up like rookies, did we, sir?"

Under his breath, Papadakis offered, "Amen to that."

"Very well," the colonel said. "Papadakis, take your company up on the high ground. Link up with 3rd Battalion and make damn sure you keep them out of your way. We can't slow down, not for a minute."

"Roger, sir," Papadakis replied. He gave Patchett a victorious wink.

"One more thing, sir," Patchett said. "He should take Sergeant Boudreau's recon platoon with him. They can do a hell of a lot more good up there than down here."

Papadakis liked the sound of that so much he had trouble containing his enthusiasm.

Colonel Billingsley hesitated. Patchett and Papadakis knew why: *he's trying to figure out if it's really a good idea...or are we just steamrolling his ass?*

"Time's a-wastin', sir," Patchett reminded the colonel.

"All right, fine. Take Recon with you."

"Roger, sir. I could sure use them."

Patchett said, "Captain Pop, keep your bazooka guys up front. We got that intel about Jap tanks running around, remember?"

"Got it, Top."

As Theo Papadakis hustled off, Billingsley told Patchett, "Let me make it clear, Sergeant—we *will* take those airfields before nightfall."

Patchett smiled and said, "I do admire your confidence, sir."

Kit Billingsley knew that was just another of his sergeant's many cryptic ways of saying, *You're one dumb son of a bitch, ain't you?*

Crouched at the brink, Bogater Boudreau looked down on the road that lay before his battalion's column. Coming into view was the lead Stuart tank, with its small main gun—only 37 millimeter—and several mounted machine guns. It plodded along slowly so the platoon of men on foot behind her could keep up. Farther ahead on the road, he could see something else: two Japanese anti-tank gun emplacements, small caliber also, but with enough punch to knock out the American Stuart.

"I gotta put mortars on those guns," Boudreau told Murphy, his radio operator. "Tell Captain Pop we need a fire mission, shell HE, at these coordinates…"

Then he hesitated, as he tried to reconcile the gun positions with the coordinates on his map. "Dammit…this is gonna be a crap shoot. Don't know where exactly the hell anything is." A few more seconds and he said, "Ah fuck, tell 'em this…"

He read off a set of target coordinates. They were nothing more than his best guess.

Then he said, "Please, dear Lord…don't let me drop them rounds on our own guys down there."

"Or us guys up here, either, Sarge."

The call for fire was made. Twenty seconds later, Murphy reported, "Shot, out…and they say we're coming in weak and barely readable, Sarge."

"Oh, that's fucking great. How's your battery?"

"Brand fucking new, Sarge."

His binoculars trained on the terrain below, Bogater mumbled, "I pray to God them bastards hit close enough so I can see 'em."

One one thousand, two one thousand, three—

Four mortar rounds splashed into the ground, silently at first, a second or two passing until the muffled report of their impact reached the GIs on the high ground.

They landed nowhere near the Japanese guns.

"Son of a fuckin' bitch," Bogater said. "Left four-zero, drop two hundred. Fucking map..."

Murphy relayed the correction. Fifteen seconds later, he said, "Shot, out."

Well, they know we're shooting at them now, sure as shit, Boudreau thought. *At least anti-tank gunners can't up and run near as quick as infantry. But that li'l ol' Stuart keeps on coming right at 'em.*

Four more rounds landed, no more accurate than the first. Different points of impact but still way off.

"KISS MY CAJUN ASS," Bogater said. "Ain't no way that correction got plotted right. Them gunners gotta have our azimuth to target all fucked up. Tell them again, Murph—*Direction TWO NINER ZERO, drop five-zero, goddammit.*"

The RTO crawled to the edge of the precipice with the walkie-talkie still pressed against his ear, waiting for the reply, hoping to see with his own eyes just why on God's green earth this simple exercise in fire direction was so screwed up:

It can't be Sergeant Boudreau's fault....we don't call him "Bullseye Bogater" for nothing.

Twenty seconds passed before he nudged Boudreau and said, "Shot, out."

Maybe the Japanese gunners figured the range was finally right. Or maybe they were afraid they were running out of time, even though the mortar rounds hadn't done so much as flick dirt on them. They fired at the American tank in perfect unison—two barrels bouncing in recoil, spewing smoke as their breeches snapped open—the *whoomp* of their shots finally heard by the distant GIs a second later.

It was the last time the Japanese gunners would fire. A moment later, the next volley of mortar rounds hit, close enough this time to send hot metal fragments slashing through their position like invisible razor blades.

"That's more fucking like it," Bogater said. "Looks like we got about half them yellow fuckers. Tell 'em *Repeat*, Murph. Just *level the bubbles* and don't move a damn knob."

Murphy did what he was told, and then said, "The bastards hit the Stuart, Sarge. It's stopped dead. Didn't you hear it?"

Hatches sprung open on the American tank. An arm flailed from the turret and then fell back inside. Nothing but flames escaped the hull. The squad of GIs walking behind the tank fled to safety. There was nothing they could do to save the tank's crew.

"She's gonna blow sky high," Boudreau said. "Thank God I ain't no tanker. Them contraptions ain't nothing but a pot to get your ass roasted in."

The final four mortar rounds landed. If there were any Japanese gunners still alive, they had already fled.

"We took too fucking long," Boudreau said.

"Maybe the mortar section screwed up," Murphy offered.

"Nah. Our coordinates were for shit. The radios ain't so fucking great, either."

Bogater Boudreau watched as the men of Charlie Company reached the silenced Japanese guns. There were a few, time-delayed *pops* from M1s and Thompsons as the GIs made sure the gunners were really dead. Then they continued the advance at a much slower pace now, waiting for another Stuart from farther back in the column to come forward, push its dead brother off the road, and take its place in the lead.

"Tell Captain Pop we're moving out," Bogater told Murphy. "We gotta stay ahead of the boys down there and be their eyes in the sky."

They hadn't advanced very far when the point man—suddenly agitated—signaled the platoon to *halt and hit the deck*. Boudreau crawled forward to join him.

When he got there, the PFC sputtered, "Tanks, Sarge…four of them! And they ain't ours, that's for damn sure."

"Well I'll be a dumb sumbitch," Bogater said. "Two fucking years in this theater and I ain't never seen me one Jap tank…"

And now there were four, spread wide in a line, not moving but with engines running. They hadn't bothered with camouflage. They stood like steel fortresses among the sparse trees.

"If they got any brains at all," he added, "there's infantry with 'em, too. We just ain't seeing 'em yet. Good thing they ain't seen us, neither. Get Captain Pop up here, on the fucking double."

Chapter Twenty-Three

The downpour stopped. Gears grinding and engines revving, the convoy was moving again. They'd been handed a bonus, too: there was little traffic heading in the opposite direction on the Hollandia-Aitape road. Lieutenant Ketchum was able to race the jeep down the nearly deserted oncoming lane, leapfrogging large portions of the seemingly endless line of vehicles in which they'd been stuck. It was saving time, but the extra speed amplified the bumpiness of the dirt road, often to violent, gut-wrenching levels. Jillian was sure the wheels had left the ground a few times already:

Bloody axles are going to snap right off.

When an oncoming vehicle would appear, Ketchum had to rapidly squeeze the jeep back into the convoy's slower flow, sliding the little vehicle between much larger trucks traveling almost bumper-to-bumper. The hair-raising process was forcing Jillian and Hutchins—who was being thrown around the back seat like a rag doll—to the brink of nausea.

But they were making up time, Jillian was sure. They still had a chance to reach Hollandia before Jock stepped on that plane.

And then all this reckless driving will be worth it, she thought...

Until they came to *the curve.* The thick growth of trees lining the road made the curve blind—you'd never be able to see what might be coming the other way...

Until it was too late.

He downshifted to lose speed and tried to ease right, nestling between a deuce-and-a-half and the three-quarter-ton in front of it...

But there wasn't enough room. The deuce's driver tried to brake hard but his truck began sliding on locked wheels along the slick, muddy surface, barely decelerating as the front bumper hooked the right rear quarter of the jeep. The groan of crunched metal sounded like the devil's hammer pounding the world to shreds.

Trying to get away from the jagged, intruding steel, Hutchins flung himself to the left side of the jeep, hanging over the edge like a sailboat crewman struggling to keep his boat from heeling over.

Ketchum stomped on the brake. The wheels locked, without a hint of deceleration.

He jerked the steering wheel hard left. The jeep's course didn't change a bit.

"I AIN'T GOT HER," he said.

The big truck's momentum was doing the driving now...

Ahead, the nose of another speeding truck popped into view as it rounded the curve, less than a hundred yards away, no more capable of stopping than anyone else...and coming straight at the jeep, now nothing more than the deuce-and-a-half's sidecar.

They'd collide in less time than it would take to draw their final, terrified breaths.

Bogater Boudreau was more worried about Japanese infantry he couldn't see than the tanks he could. Captain

Papadakis had a plan to deal with both. "For openers, we'll call artillery in on them," he told Boudreau and his other platoon leaders. "It probably won't do shit to the tanks, but it should shred any infantry with them. Then, we get our tanks up here. No better weapon against a tank than another tank."

Bogater wanted to believe, but he had a long memory. "You don't think their infantry will be dug in those fucking bunkers like they were at Buna, do you, Captain Pop?"

"I doubt it. The ground's just fucking rock. And this looks like a mobile defense. Those bastards at Buna weren't going anywhere. It was *stay put and die.*"

"Sure hope you're right, sir."

"Anyway," Papadakis continued, "I'm gonna call the colonel and get some tanks up this way. Meanwhile, you get us that artillery."

"They're gonna get plenty of warning we're coming, though, sir," Bogater said. "Our adjustment rounds will probably be way off for openers. I had one hell of a time a while back getting the mortars on targets. Fucking maps…"

"I know, I know…but the guns are only about two miles behind us. Won't be much time of flight. Do all your adjustments with air bursts. Start *waaay* high and walk them down. The artillery's got the same shit map we do—their vertical integral info is gonna be just as fucked up as ours. Ain't no bigger waste than burying a shell in the ground that's supposed to be an air burst."

"Amen to that, sir."

"Just make it happen, Bogater."

The base piece of a 105-millimeter howitzer battery still on the landing beach let the first adjustment round fly. It burst well beyond the Japanese tanks, but the height above ground was much too low—just barely above the treetops. "Drop two hundred, up thirty," he told his radio operator. "Dammit! If that sumbitch was any lower, I woulda lost it in the fucking trees. This turf's a lot higher than this map says it is, that's for damn sure."

Someone crawled up beside him and said, "You wasting rounds again, Bogater?"

He turned angrily toward the voice, and then realized it belonged to Master Sergeant Patchett, who'd come to join him.

Bogater asked, "You been here long, Top?"

"Long enough to watch you fucking up. Where do you reckon that next round's gonna land, son?"

"It'll be a little short, but the burst height oughta be a perfect forty. I'll bracket them in."

"A pack of smokes says you're wrong. You're gonna be long again. Them bastards are closer than you think."

"*Buullllshit*, Top."

"Just you watch, young man."

Patchett was right. The burst height was good—the *perfect forty yards* above the ground—but still well beyond the target.

"Ahh, fuck," Bogater said. "Can I owe you them smokes?"

"Sure can. Now make your last correction, son, and call in holy hell."

Boudreau told his radio man, "Drop five-zero, fire for effect."

"Now you're talking," Patchett said. "Where's Captain Pop?"

"Over yonder," Boudreau replied, pointing to where Papadakis was briefing his platoon leaders. "He's calling for our tank support."

"I'm gonna go listen in," Patchett said, tapping the Cajun on the helmet. "Good luck, son."

Bogater had the howitzer battery deliver the *fire for effect* volley six times—six guns, six shots each: thirty-six high-explosive shells in total. Half were air bursts showering deadly fragments meant for the still-unseen Japanese infantry. The rest rained down to point-detonate on the ground—or with a little luck, hit a tank directly.

But the luck all seemed to be with the Japanese tankers. When the dust settled, none of their armored vehicles appeared to be damaged in any way. Worse, Colonel Billingsley had refused Papadakis' request for tank support. "First, the dumb son of a bitch says the tanks can't climb this gradient," the *Mad Greek* fumed to Patchett. "So I ask him how the hell did these Jap tanks get up here? But it didn't matter a damn bit to him. Says he needs the tanks on the Mokmer road…and them little Stuarts we got ain't designed for fighting other tanks, anyway. So what the fuck good are they? Maybe he just wants to watch them get picked off one by one while they're all hemmed in playing *follow the leader* down there."

Patchett was fuming, too: *I swear on my mama's grave…the longer that golden boy hangs around, the dumber he gets. MacArthur's little parade ground soldier's getting good men killed, that's what it amounts to. I've got a mind to tell—*

But he stopped himself. He hadn't survived a lifetime in *this man's army* by spouting insubordinate remarks and he wasn't going to start now. Instead, he said, "I'll go try and change his mind, Captain Pop. In the meanwhile, you got enough of them bazooka rounds to cover your ass if push comes to shove?"

"Yeah, I think so, Top."

Since he wasn't getting the tanks from Colonel Billingsley, Boudreau did the only thing he could think of: call for more artillery fire. The odds it would do any good were slim, and he knew it. With indirect artillery fire, you'd have to score a direct hit on the tank…and even then, you might not knock it out.

Sure give those sumbitches inside a headache, though.

He couldn't believe the reply that came over the radio from the artillery battery: "Unable. Engaging higher-priority targets. Out."

Now it was Boudreau's turn to fume: *Ain't nothing higher priority in my book than something about to shoot my ass…and just where the fuck are these "higher-priority targets?" Probably those assholes at Third Battalion using them to clear trees outta their way. All we get to stop real live tanks with now is a couple of fucking bazookas…which we ain't never used against a tank, since we ain't never seen one before. Not even sure where to hit the sumbitch so that puny little rocket'll do some damage. The guy tells me he's gonna aim for that split where the turret meets the chassis. Or maybe an engine vent. He better be damn good…I watched enough of them silly things bounce right off log bunkers back on New Guinea.*

The tanks' turrets began to traverse. Their engines revved.

Ah, shit...here we go.

Theo Papadakis figured the terrain gave his company a big advantage: the cliff on the tanks' right flank prevented them from moving in that direction. All he had to do was bottle them up on the other three sides, get his three bazooka teams in close enough to finish off the tanks from the sides or rear, and this obstacle would be breached.

But it was going wrong from the start. There were still Japanese infantry protecting the tanks: *Plenty of 'em, too, dammit...too close to us to call in mortars or artillery.*

We're gonna have to root 'em out like weeds.

The tanks had begun to move, pinwheeling toward the approaching GIs like wagons being circled, adding their machine gun fire to that of their infantry.

If my guys ain't behind a sturdy tree, they probably got hit already...

And sturdy trees seem few and far between around here.

The screaming of the wounded and dying confirmed Papadakis' fear.

But still, dammit...we've got 'em surrounded! A tree or a tank hull only protects you from one direction. Just gotta pop our heads up long enough to get a fix on 'em.

He tried: the bullet that glanced off his steel pot knocked him senseless for a moment.

Bad fucking idea.

One rifle platoon had circled completely behind the tanks. The bazooka team with them would have easy shots at the sides of two tanks—if they could just get a little closer.

They couldn't. The Japanese infantry had set a trap and they'd crawled right into it. Grenades and gunfire took a terrible toll. Among the dead GIs were the two men of a bazooka team. Their weapon was just a mangled, worthless pipe now.

Another bazooka team thought they had a chance: a difficult head-on shot, with a low chance of success...

But they took it.

It glanced off the tank's glacis plate, exploding harmlessly in the air.

And then the tank's machine gun mowed them down.

We're getting creamed, Papadakis told himself.

Bogater Boudreau was thinking the same thing: *Those guys are getting creamed.*

His small recon platoon wasn't supposed to help take on the tanks. Their job was to be the lofty lookouts for the rest of the battalion down on the road. The one bazooka team Captain Papadakis had left with him was strictly for last-ditch defense.

But if them damn tanks keep cutting up Captain Pop's company and break out, they're gonna roll right over our asses. Ain't gonna be much "defense" about it—it'll be a fucking slaughter.

I gotta do something.

From Bogater's position, three of the four Jap tanks were presenting their right side, the fourth its rear. He called the bazooka team over.

"You got a clear shot at every one of those bastards," he told them.

"We're too far away, Sarge," the team's corporal said.

"Then get closer, numbnuts."

Bogater could tell right away neither man was thrilled with that prospect. He jerked the bazooka from the corporal's hands.

"Then I'll do it the fuck myself." He turned to one of his platoon and added, "Simms, take their rockets. You and me gonna go do a little tank hunting."

Simms wasn't reluctant, just skeptical. "You sure you know what you're doing with that thing, Sarge?"

"What's to know? You point it, shoot it, and it's got two wrong ends. That's why you, Corporal Simms, are gonna make damn sure there's no touchholes behind me to get burned up by the rocket blast when I fire."

"I dunno," Simms replied. "I just think this would be a whole lot easier if those cannon-cockers took a little more interest in what the fuck's going on up here."

"Too late for that now, *mon frère*. They'd just kill more of Captain Pop's men, probably."

They started to low-crawl toward the tanks, dragging the bazooka and the satchel of rockets along with them. The hard ground was tough on their knees and elbows. The only cover was the spindly trees that seemed to be getting farther and farther apart.

"I'd feel better about all this crawling," Simms said, "if there was at least some fucking concealment down here. Some high grass…some scrub…anything."

"Stand up if you like," Bogater replied, "and get your ass shot off."

Simms stayed on his belly.

A bullet *zinged* off the ground right next to Boudreau. Then another.

He rolled behind a tree trunk. So did Simms.

Just one problem…

They were behind different tree trunks. Boudreau had only one rocket—the one already loaded into the bazooka. Simms had the rest.

A bullet smacked into the tree protecting Bogater.

He asked Simms, "Can you see who the fuck's shooting at us?"

"Yeah…he's about fifty, sixty yards ahead, shooting prone. Kinda in the open."

"That fucking far? I'll never hit him with this fucking Thompson. Take him with your M1."

Gingerly, Simms leaned around the tree trunk and drew a bead on the Jap sniper. He had a clean shot. No trees in the way.

The *SPLAT* of another bullet against the trunk made him pull back.

Simms said, "How about you spray him so he keeps his fucking head down for a second?"

Bogater stuck the Thompson around the tree and fired a short, wild burst in the sniper's general direction.

That was all it took. The bullets went nowhere near the Jap, but they made him stop firing just for a few moments…

And in those few moments, Simms shot him right through the top of his helmet.

"Those fuckers gotta get stronger helmets, Sarge. Way too flimsy."

"Ours ain't a whole lot better...not for a straight-on shot like that."

A tank rumbled and clattered straight for them. But suddenly, it wheeled left, bullets bouncing harmlessly off its hull and turret. It answered those bullets with machine gun bursts of its own.

"Some GIs are in deep shit over yonder," Bogater said. He was fixated on the tank, watching it turn. "We gotta get closer...and fast."

"We won't get close enough for a shot," Simms replied. "The fucker will be gone."

"Nah...he'll be showing us his ass. Just what we want him to do."

They didn't bother crawling now, just running as low to the ground as they could manage.

One Japanese soldier popped out from behind the tank, more surprised to see them than they were to see him.

Bogater knocked him down with a short burst from the Thompson.

"HERE," Bogater said, dropping to one knee, raising the bazooka to the firing position on his shoulder. "I make it thirty fucking yards...I'm gonna put one right up his ass."

He squeezed the bazooka's trigger.

Nothing happened.

He looked at the back end of the tube, then straight down its bore.

He saw nothing but daylight. The rocket was gone.

"THE FUCKER FELL OUT! GIVE ME ANOTHER ONE!"

Simms didn't want to believe it. "COULDN'T YOU FUCKING TELL?"

"COULDN'T YOU FUCKING SEE THE SUMBITCH FALL OUT?"

Simms ignored him and slipped another rocket into the tube.

"Make damn sure you lock down the lever this time," Bogater said.

"I did the first fucking time," Simms replied, indignant. "You must've snagged it on something. There, it's in...wires are hooked up." He stepped clear of the blast zone. A tap on Boudreau's helmet: "READY."

Bogater pulled the trigger again.

This time, there was a deafening *WHOOSH* as the rocket sped away...

And vanished into an engine vent grill.

A small flash, a dull *pfoomf*... and nothing more. The tank kept rolling away from them, straight toward Captain Pop's men.

Another tank began to pivot, as if looking for a path through the trees to reach the one they just shot.

"Hurry up...another fucking rocket," Bogater said. "Gotta get him while he's still broadside to us."

A *clank* as Simms slid the rocket into the tube. A few moments of fumbling with latching lever and wires...and then another tap on the helmet: "READY."

Bogater squeezed the trigger at the exact instant the first tank exploded in a fog of thick black smoke. It made him flinch and ruined his aim.

The rocket streaked away, glanced off the ground yards short of the second tank, and struck its drive wheel with a surprising loud *POOM*.

The damaged track separated from the wheel and became mangled beneath the tank, now pirouetting on its one good track. After half a revolution it came to a stop, its turret traversing, spitting fire from both its machine guns. It was wounded, immobile, but not dead yet...

At least not until Captain Papadakis' surviving bazooka team put a rocket point blank into its engine compartment. In seconds, it was smoking as furiously as the first tank.

Simms asked, "Those Nips inside even gonna try and get out?"

"Maybe they're already dead," Bogater replied. "Probably choked to death on that burning diesel."

The other two tanks wheeled north and, with engines roaring, raced away. Neither Bogater nor the last of Papadakis' bazooka boys had a clean shot at them. The few rounds fired were Captain Pop's survivors mopping up the last of the Japanese infantry—no more than a squad or two at this point. Abandoned by their tanks, they were surrounded, outgunned, hopeless...

And soon dead.

As the echo of the last shots died out, two GIs approached Boudreau and Simms. One was a captain. He wasn't Theo Papadakis.

"I'm from King Company, Third Battalion," the captain said. "What outfit are you boys with?"

"Recon Platoon, First Battalion," Boudreau replied, "and Able Company's around here somewhere. Or at least what's left of them." Then he saw Papadakis in a clearing still thick with smoke and raced to him. The captain from 3rd Battalion followed.

"Nice dent in that steel pot of yours, sir," Bogater said when he reached Papadakis.

"Yeah...remind me never to stick my head up in that shit again. Man, my neck's killing me from getting jerked back like that."

Bogater asked, "How bad are your guys banged up, sir?"

"Bad. Real bad. Don't know how many for sure yet."

Papadakis gave the other captain a stern once-over and asked, "Let me guess. You're from Third Battalion, right?"

"Yeah. I'm supposed to link up with—"

"Save it, pal. Thanks a shitload for all your fucking help."

"Wait a damn minute," the captain replied. "I couldn't exactly tell where the hell you were supposed to be on this shitty map."

Theo Papadakis walked away, shaking his head, trying to take stock of the dead, the wounded, and those who could carry on...

Because he knew the battle for this island had only just begun.

Chapter Twenty-Four

"Squall's coming, sir," the courier pilot told Jock. "If we wait until 1600 like you want, we might not get out of here today."

Jock checked his watch: *1440.* He thought it over for a moment.

"We'll wait a little longer, Lieutenant."

The pilot didn't want to hear that. He was as keen to get back to his hammock on Wakde Island as Jock was to stay in Hollandia. But he replied, "Yes, sir. Whatever you want. I'll be in Operations if you change your mind."

Jock went back to the feverish work of getting out the new maps—the ones that incorporated every last detail he'd learned during his unintended stay on Biak. He knew the GIs on the ground needed all the info about the Mokmer airfields and the surrounding terrain he could provide:

Published intel updates are all well and good, but a picture is worth a thousand words.

He cursed luck, the Japanese, even himself that those maps weren't in the GIs' hands already.

They would've been...if we hadn't gotten our asses shot down.

He handed over his last page of notes. His part was done now, but the maps still weren't ready for printing. These final bits of information would have to be collated, correlated, and plotted by the team of intelligence officers and NCOs who'd been his constant companions for the past five days, ever since returning from Biak. The information on the maps had to be dead-on or they were no better than the obsolete *fishwrappers* being used right now. *Close enough* wouldn't be good enough. Once printing began—tomorrow, hopefully—it would still be days before they were in the hands of the troops whose lives depended on them.

A voice boomed from the far side of the room. "Miles, what in God's good name are you still doing here?" Every man in the room snapped to attention. Jock spun off his stool, tried snapping to attention, and nearly fell over as his bad leg buckled. Catching himself against the work table, he braced and saw General Willoughby, MacArthur's G2, striding toward him.

A testy wave of the general's hand sufficed for *at ease* and the intel staff went back to their work. His eyes boring into Jock, Willoughby added, "I thought your shop was on Wakde, Major, not here in sunny Hollandia."

"Begging your pardon, sir, but my orders are to return to Wakde not later than tonight."

"Shouldn't you be leaving, then?"

"I just finished my work here, sir. My flight leaves at 1600."

"Cutting it a little close, I'd say, Miles, especially with weather moving in…"

The general paused for a moment, thinking—and then his face lit up with sly revelation. "Oh, I get it. You want to get in that last one with the little Aussie spitfire you've been shacked up with."

"With all due respect, sir, that lady is my wife."

If this was a fucking barroom, I'd put this pompous sack of shit on his ass so fast, stars or no stars.

Willoughby replied, "Well, isn't that hot shit? That'd make you and General MacArthur the only two men in the US Army lucky enough to have their wives in theater with them. I understand the *Supreme Commander's* privilege…but what makes you so fucking special, *Major*?"

"Not special, sir…but like you said, just lucky."

"Hmm…well, give her my love, Miles. By the way, what's the story with your leg?"

"Been sitting too much, sir. It stiffens up."

"It's a good thing you don't need two good legs for a desk job, Major."

Willoughby turned to leave, adding, "Good luck, Miles. Don't miss your flight, now. This war's not going to wait for you."

At the door, he had one more piece of cheerful advice: "Don't knock her up now, son, because if you do, we'll ship her pregnant little ass back to Australia so fast your head will spin."

Jock's leg had loosened up by the time he walked to the airfield's operations shack. He could hide the limp fairly well now, adopting a tender, stiff-legged stride, like a cowboy who'd spent too much time in the saddle.

Maybe I'm even fooling other people besides myself…

But I'll never fool Jill.

Where the hell are you, baby?

He checked his watch, just like he'd done every few minutes for the last hour. Now it read 1545.

The coming storm rolled off the jagged mountains that formed New Guinea's spine as it advanced steadily toward Hollandia. Soon, the airfield would be enveloped in treacherous winds and blinding rain. A takeoff at 1600 was pushing it as far as any sane aviator dared.

A mechanic approached and said, "Better get on board, sir. We're gonna crank 'em up in a second."

"Give me a minute," Jock replied. He'd abandoned any thought of holding her in his arms, kissing her, or sharing a moment of conversation. He'd settle for much less now:

I just need to see her. Just a glimpse to know she's okay. That's all I ask.

The right-hand engine of the little C-45 transport plane sputtered to life, sounding as if it, too, had little interest in setting out on this trip.

He gave one last, longing look toward the airfield's access road, one flicker of hope still burning that a jeep, a truck, a bicycle—anything—would change course and come racing across the ramp toward the plane...

But none did.

Jock flung his bags up into the plane as the left-hand engine now popped and rumbled to life. Hesitantly, he ascended the short ladder to the little tail-dragger's cabin door. At the top step, he turned to take one last look across the ramp...

Through the blur of the whirling propeller, there was a deuce-and-a-half racing toward them head-on. As it drew close, the GI behind the wheel altered course, driving a wide circle around the aircraft. The truck swung around the plane's twin tails and stopped aft of the left wingtip, just a few quick steps from the cabin door. The cab's passenger-side door popped open...

And Jillian jumped down to the ramp.

She looked like she'd been in a brawl. Her skirt and blouse were splotched with mud. There were bruises of vivid purple and yellow on her arms and shins.

Jock's leg didn't betray him as he sprinted to her.

Locked in embrace, she spoke right into his ear to be heard over the din of the plane's engines. "I was afraid this wasn't your aircraft. And that storm on the way..."

"Honey, are you okay? You're all banged up. What the hell happened?"

"We had a bit of a wreck. Only the jeep got hurt, though. No worries."

With time so short, he blurted the unfinished business burdening his mind: "I'm so sorry, honey. I had no business flying those missions and I promise—"

She silenced him with a kiss. Then, stroking his face soothingly, she said, "Baby, baby...we already talked about this on the telephone. You don't need—"

"No...I promise I won't fly any more missions, Jill. I've got no business being in action anymore."

She kissed him once more and said, "Like I told you before, Yank, don't make promises you can't keep."

For just a moment, the contentment of their embrace cancelled every calamity the world had to offer. It even cancelled the racket of the airplane engines idling just feet away.

She asked, "Taking your Atabrine?"

"Every damn day. You?"

"Of course. Malaria is just one of the many little joys we've come to share."

"You know, I'm real proud of what you did at Aitape, Jill..."

"Thanks, baby, but I was just doing my job."

"But—"

The mechanic tapped Jock on the shoulder. "Don't mean to intrude, sir, but we gotta go, right now!"

One long, last kiss.

As he turned toward the plane, Jock said, "But no more of that cloak and dagger stuff for you, okay?"

She smiled and gave him a *thumbs up*.

Then she spoke her reply, softly enough he couldn't possibly hear it over the sawmill buzz of the revving engines: "I won't make promises I can't keep, either."

Halfway up the cabin stairs, he remembered another piece of unfinished business he'd completely forgotten: "THAT MAPMAKER YOU MENTIONED ON THE LANDLINE THE OTHER DAY...DID HE CHANGE HIS MIND ABOUT WORKING FOR US?"

Jillian shook her head and replied, "AFRAID NOT...AND IT WASN'T A HIM. IT WAS A HER."

Watching him climb the boarding steps, she thought, *Bloody hell. His leg...he's trying to hide it but it's acting up again.*

The plane was airborne before Jock made the connection: *Holy shit! That mapmaker...her last name isn't Dyckman by any chance, is it?*

Chapter Twenty-Five

Token resistance were the words Lieutenant Colonel Billingsley used to describe the Japanese infantry's defense of the Mokmer airfields. That might have been technically accurate, but the Japanese guns embedded high in the bluffs to the east were taking a terrific toll on the American tanks. Master Sergeant Patchett looked away in disgust as yet another Stuart rolling across the southern airstrip was knocked out. The enemy round blew the turret cleanly off the chassis, leaving nothing but a flaming hulk, spewing clouds of thick black smoke and a fireworks display of cooked-off rounds.

That makes five we lost in the last hour. Counting the one we lost on the road, half of what we hit the beach with this morning is gone already. And ain't nobody or nothing touching them guns up there. At least my boys got the good sense to stay the hell away from them tanks and not get roasted right along with 'em. Gonna be a long fucking night.

Colonel Billingsley stood beside his jeep, talking on its radio. When his conversation was finished, he told Patchett, "I'm pulling the tanks back for now."

Patchett thought, *First smart thing I heard the man say all day.*

But then Billingsley added, "So my soldiers will just have to finish taking these three airfields without them."

"You mean *after* those guns up there are knocked out, right, sir?"

"Negative, Sergeant. Between the battalion's position here and Able Company's above them on the ridge, we've got those guns isolated. They'll run out of ammo soon enough. We're going to press on and take these airfields before nightfall, per the ops plan."

"Begging your pardon, sir, but that's just faith talking. What the hell good is it to take the airfields if we can't show our faces on 'em without getting our asses blown up? Ain't no airplanes gonna use them, that's for damn sure. We gotta take out them guns before we do anything else."

"The job of taking out those guns is allocated to the Navy, Sergeant. We've got all the fire support we need from them."

Patchett was losing patience. "Sir...the Navy's had just a couple li'l ol' destroyers parked *waaaay* the hell offshore and outta harm's way all day long, trying to duel with them guns long distance. They ain't knocked out shit yet. Ain't even come close."

A picture of unjustified confidence, Billingsley replied, "That's why I've called in supplemental air support. They'll plaster those gun positions with rockets and fifty caliber."

"With all due respect, sir, not a one of them ideas is worth dog squat...and they might even get Able Company boys on top of that ridge killed. How about we get ourselves a couple or three artillery pieces and plaster them guns with direct fire? They won't be missing, neither...not from this close. We can bring 'em in and hide 'em in this treeline right here come nightfall, when them Japs up there can't see shit. At first light, we give 'em hell, quick and simple."

"Negative, Sergeant. My men will be capturing airfields tonight, not waiting for artillerymen to save them."

"Sir, your men gonna be dying in droves if we try to hold this low ground with them guns staring down on us. We're just fish in a fucking barrel. Won't be enough of us left by sundown tomorrow to hold jackshit."

"Oh, come now, Sergeant. That's just a little bit—"

"That's the God's honest truth, sir, that's what it is…and since I reckon their maps are as fucked up as ours, I'd rather have our artillery putting some direct fire rounds *exactly* where I want them than some pilot or swabbie putting them where *he thinks* I want them."

Patchett wasn't sure if the silence that came over Billingsley meant the man was thinking or sulking. He blew a sigh of relief when the colonel finally said, "Fine, we'll bring up the artillery. But make sure our evening situation report to regiment states clearly that our troops are holding the Mokmer airfields."

Patchett smiled; it would be an administrative lie well worth the lives saved. "Affirmative, sir," he replied as he told himself, *Yeah, we're holding it all right, provided we don't dare come out from under cover. And it don't matter what bullshit we write…it ain't gonna fool Colonel Molloy. He's got hisself two good eyes.*

High atop the bluffs overlooking the airfields, Bogater Boudreau had an idea. "Get me that spool of lacing cord Bailey's carrying," he told his radioman, "and get Captain Pop up here. I gotta show him something real quick."

"Sarge, shouldn't we be whispering?" the radioman asked. "There's Japs right down there below us."

"Don't worry about it," Boudreau replied. "They're crammed into a cave, firing a big, loud gun. Their ears are ringing so bad they can't hear shit."

When Theo Papadakis arrived, Boudreau was already well into the test phase of his plan. "That cave right below us," he told the captain, "can't be more than fifty or sixty feet down." Something was dangling down the cliff's face from the spool of cord Bogater held in his hands. Papadakis peered over the edge and saw what it was: a cluster of hand grenades, hanging right above the top edge of the cave opening, perfectly in line with the protruding barrel of its 40-millimeter gun—and invisible to the gunners inside.

"What do you think, sir? A hell of a lot better than waiting for the Navy or some flyboy to put one on the money."

"How many grenades you got tied there, Bogater?"

"Four, sir. Any more than that gets a little unwieldy." He started reeling the grenades back up.

"So you want to lower those grenades down in front of the cave mouth? How you gonna pull the pins?"

"I'm gonna pull them *first*, sir," Boudreau replied. "Then Moose Jorgensen here is gonna heave the whole bunch like he's throwing a runner out at home from center field. As they start to fall, the cord'll go tight...and swing those sumbitches right into the cave. Should be just about the right amount of time for the fuzes to blow, too." He played out more cord, measuring it against his forearm. "I'm adding about five feet to the total length, to make sure them *string bombs* swing *inside* the cave."

Boudreau plunged his bayonet into a crack in the rocky ledge at the spot he'd first dangled the grenades.

"There...that oughta be straight above them bastards." He tied the spool end of the cord to the bayonet grip, then coiled the length that would carry the grenades carefully on the ground.

Jorgensen held the grenades—his arm cocked, ready to throw—as two men stood by to pull their safety pins.

Bogater told Papadakis, "Say the word, sir."

"Wait until they shoot again," Papadakis replied, "so we know they'll be huddled up real close to the gun."

They only had to wait a few moments. The report of the 40 millimeter echoed up the cliff. Papadakis said, "Let her rip, boys."

The pins were pulled, and Jorgensen gave a mighty heave. The cluster of grenades was launched high into the air...

One one thousand...

And then began to arc downward.

Two one thousand...

The coiled cord played out quickly and smoothly.

Three one thousand, four one thousand...

The grenades vanished into the cave mouth.

Five one thousand...

The sound of the explosion was soft and disappointing—just a muted *poom*—but the jet of hot gases that blew from the cave looked more like the blowhole exhalation of a giant whale.

Scraps of wood and gear were blown out and began the long tumble to the plain below.

Two Japanese gunners were blown out, too. The GIs perched on the ledge watched them plummet like sacks all the way to the ground.

Bogater said, "They ain't thrashing around like no man alive would."

The barrel of the 40 millimeter still protruded from the cave mouth but it was unmoving, lifeless.

Captain Papadakis said, "I think we can take out two or three more of those guns the same way."

"Yeah," Bogater replied, reeling up the scorched and severed end of the cord. "A couple more, for sure. The rest are too far down for this little trick to work."

"Hmm...yeah. Makes me wonder, though. You suppose the Japs ever come out of those caves?"

"Not in daylight, that's for damn sure," Bogater said. "Maybe they slide down ropes at night or something. It sure as hell don't look like they climb up here. Wish they would, though. Make killing 'em a whole hell of a lot easier."

The C-45 transport plane shuddered to a stop on the ramp at Wakde Island, seeming just as relieved as its occupants the flight from Hollandia was over. If they'd tried to land a few minutes later, the airfield would have been hidden in darkness. As it was, they came back to an earth shrouded in the deep shadows of dusk.

"I had one hell of a time feeling around for the ground," the pilot said as he and Jock climbed out of the plane. "And this damn thing...if you don't fly it all the way to the chocks, it'll ground loop on you or prang itself in a heartbeat."

"Then I guess you did a hell of a job, Lieutenant," Jock replied. "Thanks for the ride."

Jock's desk at photo recon shop looked like a dump truck had backed up to it and unloaded piles of folders, aerial photographs, and drafts of topographic maps in progress. He took that as a good sign: *If they thought I was dead, the desk would've been cleaned out...or some enterprising soul would have "appropriated" it already.* There was enough work there to keep him busy for weeks.

But there was something he had to do first. He began drafting a message to Jillian back at Hollandia. It took several tries—tearing up page after page of discarded words—until it was as concise as protocol demanded:

Is mapmaker's name Dyckman? If so, tell her father is alive. I know where he is. Maybe that will change her mind? Urgent. We need her.

He felt foolish for how long it had taken him to connect the dots:

That mapmaker's got to be Dyckman's daughter. I mean, how many fucking cartographers could there have been on a little rock like Biak, let alone female ones? Maybe I was starting to believe his whole family was dead, too. Wouldn't that be hot shit, after I was the one telling him not to lose hope.

At the Wakde radio station, the communications officer on duty frowned as he looked at the message Jock had just handed him. "This is civilian affairs stuff, sir," the commo officer said. "That's pretty low priority. It may not even get sent for a couple of days. Maybe you should just put it in an envelope and send it with the dispatches."

He tried to hand Jock a manila envelope, which was promptly batted away. Dispatch pouches were slower than GI mail.

Jock leaned across the desk, close enough this Air Force captain sloughing him off could feel his hot breath on his face. "It's damn *high priority* to the GIs getting their asses shot off on Biak...and it's a hell of a lot more important than those stacks of flyboy requests for pillows and sun tan oil your people are sending right now. Here's the deal, Captain...either this message goes out tonight or you can explain to General Kenney why it didn't."

Dropping Kenney's name was a risky move. The 5th Air Force Commander didn't know Jock from Adam. He probably had only the vaguest notion of what Jock's job at his headquarters was, too; there was a thick layer of staff between them.

And an Air Force commander probably couldn't give a shit less about maps for us dogfaces.

But the bluff worked. The commo officer began to sputter as he shuffled papers on his desk.

"So that's a *yes*, Captain?"

"Ahh...yes, sir. Your message will be copied in Hollandia within the hour."

Chapter Twenty-Six

"Sun's almost up, y'all," Patchett said as his foot nudged the sleeping artilleryman. "Get your boys on them guns and let's do the deed."

The gunners tried to rub the sleep out of their eyes—the little they'd gotten, anyway, after driving up from the beach and digging in their 105-millimeter howitzers in the pitch dark of night. They'd dug the guns' trails in deep: they remembered the last time their battery shot direct fire. One of the pieces had reared up so violently from the recoil, her spades hopped out of the shallow holes her crew had dug, allowing the piece to rocket backwards. As she did, the trails of the *loose cannon* smashed into one of her own crewmen, shattering his leg below the knee.

The artillerymen hustled to their positions. They knew the sooner they got done with this task, the sooner they could rejoin their battery, nestled in a far less hazardous location a mile or so behind the lines. Rounds were assembled and lined up, ready to fire.

"Here's the way it's gonna be, men," Patchett said. "That gentleman standing right there is Captain Grossman. Him and me'll identify them targets for you, since ain't a one of you got a fucking clue where they are in them cliffs. The sun's gonna be up behind 'em in a couple minutes. That'll light us up like Christmas but those caves will still be hiding in shadow. Now like I told y'all before, Able Company is on the high ground above them Jap guns. When Captain Grossman gives 'em the word, they're gonna drop illum with their mortars down the face of the cliffs. That'll blind the Japs a little and light them up for our first-round hits."

The artillerymen seemed surprised at the confident proclamation of *first-round hits*. "It may take a little more than one round a target," a section chief said.

"Bull-fucking-shit," Patchett replied. "Y'all gonna know exactly how far those li'l ol' caves are, 'cause we had all day yesterday to triangulate them. Just put the fucking range mark in that scope of yours on it and pull the damn lanyard."

"It ain't quite that exact, Sarge," the section chief replied.

"It better fucking be *that exact*, numbnuts, because once you pop off a round, them Japs gonna know exactly where you are, too. It's kill or be killed, son. I'd advise you to go with the former."

There were no further comments from the grim-faced artillerymen.

Patchett wasn't finished. "Since the very clever doggies of Recon Platoon done already took out four of them guns, all we gotta do is knock out the other eight. That's four shots per gun, y'all. Now load your first round."

Shells were rammed into both tubes. Breeches slid closed and locked shut with the metallic *click* of their handle locks.

They could feel the warm morning sun on their faces now.

"I'm going to light them up," Captain Grossman said. "Gunners, stand by."

Twenty seconds later, four illumination rounds—spread wide apart—began their synchronized parachute descent down the face of the cliffs. The caves appeared as little more than black pockmarks. Patchett pulled the section chief of one of the howitzers close. Grossman did the same with the other gun chief.

"Okay," Patchett told him as he sighted with an outstretched hand, "first target is down three fingers from the top right cave…got it?"

The section chief held out three fingers, formed the sight picture in his mind, and replied, "Yeah…I got it."

"Then do it, son."

Within seconds, both howitzers roared and bucked like angry dragons as they jerked violently from recoil. A cloud of coral dust was sucked off the ground and mingled with the gun smoke. Time of flight would only be a few seconds.

Eyes pressed against binoculars, Patchett and Grossman could see the impacts a heartbeat before hearing them. Nearly in unison, they yelled, "TARGET!" Both shots had achieved their *first-round hits.*

Just as the light of the first volley of illumination rounds was about to drop out of sight, a second volley began its glide down the cliffs. At the howitzers, new targets were being sighted and rounds loaded.

"So far," Patchett told the gunners, "y'all are on the right side of this *kill or be killed* shit. Let's keep it up."

It took twelve shots of direct fire from the 105-millimeter howitzers to silence the remaining eight guns embedded in the cliffs. The Japs had managed to get off two shots from the last caves to be targeted but they both landed wide, hurting nothing but trees and rock. Patchett suggested, "I'm betting they couldn't traverse far enough to get us, sitting in them caves like they was."

Lee Grossman nodded in agreement. "Probably right, Top."

"I'd better go find where *golden boy* is hiding," Patchett said, "and make damn sure he gets us those tanks back on the double."

"Amen to that, Top."

Patchett had to laugh. "*Amen to that*? Begging your pardon, sir, and no offense meant or nothing, but when the hell did a Jew-fella from New York City start saying things like that?"

"None taken, Top. I guess I've just been around you crackers too long."

They broke into grins as they headed their separate ways.

Colonel Billingsley proved difficult to find. After several radio calls, he finally came on the air. When asked his location, his reply—decoded—said, *I'm with Able Company. Consolidate the battalion's position and await my return.*

Patchett snickered as he read the message: *With Able Company, my ass. I just talked to Captain Pop...they ain't seen hide nor hair of the man since they went up the high ground. Just like him to make hisself scarce when the shit's hitting the fan.*

Another thirty minutes passed before Billingsley finally drove up in his jeep. "I've got good news, Sergeant Patchett," he said in greeting. "I've pulled Able Company off the cliffs. They'll be here in about an hour, and then the entire battalion will be moving out. We're heading west, along the coast."

"Whoa...hold on a minute, sir. Who's covering our right flank, then?"

"That's Third Battalion's responsibility, Sergeant. Captain Papadakis has already coordinated the new boundaries with them."

"Begging your pardon, sir, but I spoke with Captain Pop not too long ago. He says Third Battalion's got one platoon wandering around up there, acting like they couldn't find their asses with both hands. Did Regiment okay this?"

"I don't need Regiment's approval to mass my own troops, Sergeant. I'll fill Colonel Molloy in on the details as soon as we get organized here and—"

"Begging your pardon again, sir, but we *are* organized here. Organized as all hell, as a matter of fact. And I'm just a little bit worried we're giving up the ground over our heads we just spent a day, a night, and the next sunrise getting under our control."

"You're not seeing the big picture, I'm afraid, Sergeant Patchett."

No, sir...I'm seeing it pretty clearly, and it looks like another fucking disaster waiting to happen.

"What about the Stuarts, sir? We getting those tanks back *ASAP*?"

The blank look that came across Billingsley's face could only mean one thing: *He ain't even thought about that.*

"Yes, yes...of course. I'll bring that up with Regiment." Then he stretched like a man who'd just awoken from a long nap. "But first, nature calls, Sergeant."

Billingsley started walking toward the only building on the airfield, a squat wooden structure some thirty yards away that had, no doubt, served as the airfield operations building. "I'm betting there's a proper officers' latrine in that facility," he said, "and I plan to enjoy it."

Patchett wrestled with informing the colonel they'd already been through every inch of that building: *And much of nothing in there, let alone a shitter. I guess Jap officers crap in a hole like everyone else.* But he decided, *Let him find out the hard way.*

Then the world went dark for a moment as if a harsh wind blew out all the light.

When Melvin Patchett came to, he was flat on his face. His helmet lay on the ground beside him like an overturned turtle. He looked behind and saw the building was a pile of smoking rubble.

I never heard me a damn thing. What the hell just happened?

His question was answered immediately: he could see the puff from a tank's main gun barrel, sitting atop the cliffs.

The round slammed into the ground between Patchett and the shattered building, barely missing Billingsley's empty jeep.

Looks like them Jap bastards are playing a card out of our deck now.

He began to curse himself that he'd let the howitzers leave.

But there was a flash from the top of the cliff. The turret of the tank was flipped off its chassis like a cap being popped off its bottle.

Then he heard the dull, time-delayed *poom* of the exploding tank.

Was that Captain Pop's boys did that? Or did Third Battalion finally get their shit together? That tank didn't blow itself up, that's for damn sure.

When Patchett got to the shattered building, Lee Grossman and a few of his men were already there. They were pulling Billingsley's lifeless body from the rubble.

Grossman asked, "What the hell was he in the building for, Top? It's the only good target out here...and he walks right into it?"

Patchett replied with a nonchalant shrug. But a nagging voice in his head kept repeating, *Let him find out the hard way*, like an accusing finger pointing right at him.

Praying to silence that voice, he finally said, "I reckon he did find out the hard way."

Grossman replied, "What the hell are you talking about, Top?"

"Oh, nothing in particular, sir. Maybe he was just looking for some Jap maps. Gotta be better than the crap we got."

"But we already looked. There wasn't shit in there."

"I know, sir. Dammit, I know."

Major Homer Rowe fancied himself a paperwork kind of officer: a behind-the-scenes administrator more comfortable at a desk than bearing the burden of command. One of the original National Guard officers in this division, he was forty-one years old, chubby—although the New Guinea GI diet had shed some twenty pounds from his short, stocky frame. Rowe cursed that weight loss because as the pounds dropped, so did his blood pressure readings. They'd been high, the medics told him—high enough to be sent home if the condition persisted. But twenty pounds lighter, his BP dropped to "borderline," and Homer Rowe would have to continue slogging through the swamps and jungles with the rest of the division, on their way to MacArthur's dreamed-of return to the Philippines. Try as he might, there just wasn't enough food to eat in this tropical sweatbox to maintain weight, let alone gain it back.

He'd done a competent job as battalion XO under the now-deceased Kit Billingsley, just as he had for the previous commander, Jock Miles. Now, as he stood in front of Colonel Molloy, the regimental commander, he sensed his position in *this man's army* was headed for a drastic change.

"Colonel Billingsley's been killed in action," Molloy said. "I need you to step in and take the battalion, Homer."

Rowe swallowed hard and asked, "Will this be a temporary assignment, sir? Until you can get somebody more—"

Molloy cut him off. "Why, Homer? Do you have somewhere else you need to be?"

"No, sir. I just thought—"

"For cryin' out loud, Homer, everything around here is *temporary*. Hell, life is temporary. I realize you've never had a combat command. In fact, you haven't had a command at all since running a National Guard company stateside before the war, have you?"

"That's correct, sir."

"At the moment, though, you're senior. I need you to step up and do the job."

"But what about Lee Grossman, sir? He's eminently promotable to major…and he's got plenty of combat command time."

"Major Rowe, listen to me, and listen good. As far as I'm concerned, First Battalion has some of the finest company commanders and NCOs I've ever had the honor to command. I don't want to alter their chemistry right now. All they need is someone to set priorities for them and show them some leadership. And that's going to be you."

Rowe still seemed as if he was searching for something to say that might change the colonel's mind.

Moving to close the deal, Molloy added, "Besides, you've got the finest battalion top sergeant in the entire theater in Melvin Patchett. You know him well. He'll be of great help to you."

Homer Rowe *did* know Patchett well—and he was scared shitless of him:

That cutthroat could kill me and not give it a second thought if I gave him half a reason.

Chapter Twenty-Seven

Jock had ripped through the dispatches from Hollandia for the past three days, searching for an answer from Jillian. He couldn't be sure if she'd even seen his message, the one asking her—no, *begging*, really—to get that lady mapmaker from Biak on his team.

Maybe she has seen it and already tried to reply...but it's tied up in the same "low-priority" bullshit I had to bluff my way through.

Either way, he still needed the mapmaker's help—there was a big snag in creating the maps the GIs on Biak needed so badly. The photo recon squadron flying out of Wakde Island was doing a great job providing aerial photographs of the island. Those images would be the blueprints for the maps those GIs needed as they advanced through rainforests so dense they might not be able to see twenty yards in front of them. But aerial photographs, shot from an aircraft looking straight down, made the world look flat. Sometimes there were telltale signs that indicated the terrain was rising or falling—the meanderings of steams, rivers, and roads; shadows falling across lower ground—but you were still left with a picture of a world without accurate vertical relief features. Oblique aerial photography—side or angular views of the earth below—could be of some help, but the information they provided could only yield estimates of terrain height, not the exacting figures needed for efficient land navigation, precise artillery fire, and coordinating air support.

To get those exacting figures, you needed surveyed information from the perspective of the ground, and that's what Jock and his team of mapping specialists were not getting. A sergeant who'd been trying all morning to correlate aerial photos with survey data finally threw down his plotter in disgust.

"I don't know what planet this survey team thinks they're mapping, sir," the intel sergeant told Jock, "but they're a day late and a dollar short—again. Somebody needs to straighten their asses out."

"Give me the down and dirty, Sarge."

"It looks to me like they're shooting their plots too close to the instrument, sir…like the guys with the barber poles are afraid to walk out too far away and run into some bad guys. Their data's all over the place. Look here…if you believe the numbers, this tableland's got almost a quarter-mile overhang at its edge. You know that's gotta be bullshit. The best I'm getting is goose eggs on the chart, and I should be getting pinpoints. It's all fucking worthless."

"I've seen this before," Jock said. "The survey teams get real fond of plotting where you've already been and not where you need to go."

"So what're you going to do about it, sir?"

Jock had been considering the answer to that question ever since this problem first reared its ugly head. He kept thinking of the promise he'd made to Jillian at Hollandia as the noise and propwash of the plane taking him back to Wakde swirled impatiently around them. He remembered how she'd responded, too:

Don't make promises you can't keep.

Still, he wished with all his heart he could keep that promise.

But there was another promise he wanted to keep, too: the pledge he'd made to *Duty, Honor, Country* when those gold bars were pinned on his shoulders nine years ago at West Point. Even though the obscenities of war and politics had been doing their best to pervert its meaning, the visceral knot tying him to that pledge hadn't been broken. He felt sure that for a man to do less than he could would only dishonor the dead, the maimed, and those survivors with minds and souls irreparably shattered. Worse, it would give new life to the maniacal dreams of demagogues.

To break that pledge now would be like deciding not to breathe.

The sergeant was still waiting for his answer.

"I guess someone's got to go and give those boys some direction," Jock said.

The sergeant replied, "You, sir? You sure you're up to going back there? I mean, your leg and all..."

Jock smiled and said, "Don't worry about me, Sergeant. How hard can it be to ride around in a survey team's vehicle for a couple of days, anyway?"

Jillian had received Jock's message the night it was sent. But she hadn't replied for one simple reason:

I don't have a bloody answer for him yet.

For those three days since receiving that message, she'd been trying to track down Greta Christiansen. It hadn't been easy: without advising Allied Headquarters, the Red Cross had decided to move the Dutch refugees at Aitape someplace else. Jillian had only sorted out this morning where they were going:

Port Moresby. Nearly six hundred miles as the crow flies across the mountains of New Guinea. The Red Cross was looking to consolidate their efforts to care for their growing collection of refugees in a more *civilized* locale.

Not bloody surprised, Jillian told herself, *after the disgusting spectacle the Yanks put on at Aitape. But they could have at least given me a timely "heads up" about what they were doing.* Mocking herself, she added, *After all, I am the Assistant Australian Adviser for Civilian and Refugee Affairs.*

The refugees wouldn't be flying to Port Moresby, though. They were going by boat, all the way around the eastern tip of New Guinea. It would take almost five days on the slow coastal traders available.

They've already been at sea for three. If I can hop a flight to Port Moresby first thing tomorrow, I can get there ahead of her. I just need to tell that wanker I work for where I'll be.

Standing outside his office door, she thought there was a party going on inside. Her boss, the fat captain—the *wanker* himself—was loudly proclaiming the brilliance of MacArthur to half a dozen of his bootlicking underlings.

With great exuberance, the captain was telling his audience, "He's done it again. The Biak invasion has not only put us within easy reach of the Philippines, but it's stolen the limelight from that little *puddle jump* they call *The Invasion of France*. Not to mention the Navy's tiresome and wasteful island-hopping campaign in the Central Pacific, too. Only a man with the stature of our *Supreme Commander* can achieve something so masterful. Eisenhower and Nimitz are mere schoolboys—babes in the woods, I tell you—compared to the genius that is Douglas MacArthur."

Jillian was surprised the captain's enthralled listeners didn't burst into applause. But it was time to interrupt their naïve, rear-echelon idolatry. She stuck her head in the door and said, "Begging your pardon, Captain, but may I have a word?"

Clearly annoyed by her intrusion, the captain replied, "Go ahead, Missus Miles. What word would you like to have?"

"In private, if you please."

He huffed and fumed for a few moments before sending the others out of the office. "Now what's so all-fired important, Missus Miles?"

She told him.

"Absolutely not," he replied. "I need you here in this office, not traipsing all over New Guinea. Wasn't that little trip to Aitape enough for you?"

She decided not to bother with a rebuttal. *It would be lost on this blockhead, anyway.*

"Actually, Captain, I'm just paying you the courtesy of telling you I'm going."

"I beg to differ, Missus Miles. I'm *ordering* you—"

She cut him off with a laugh. "I don't wear your uniform. You can't order me to do anything."

"Perhaps not, Missus Miles, but I can *fire* you."

"You can try, I suppose...but if I convince this woman to help you Yanks, everyone from your bloody MacArthur on down will be thanking me, not sacking me. And unfortunately, I'm the *only* one who has a chance to convince her. She holds you Americans on a par with the Japanese. And she has good reason."

He simmered for a few moments. When he finally spoke, his tone could only be described as *loathing*:

"You've still got that chip on your shoulder, don't you? You think having been a *prisoner of war* entitles you to do whatever the hell you want."

She put her palms on his desk and leaned across it. He flinched, as if she might spit fire right at him.

"No, you've got that all wrong, Captain. If I've got a chip on my shoulder, as you say, it's because I've been fighting the Japanese one way or the other for more than two years now, while you and all the other tossers in this establishment have done little more than polish your desks. None of you have a bloody clue what war is really like. If you did, you might not be so ready to stick your noses up MacArthur's arse."

The fat captain was sweating profusely now, the khaki of his uniform turning dark around the armpits, the tight collar, and the knot of his necktie. He realized he'd just lost this skirmish...but maybe not the war.

"How will you get there, Missus Miles? You'll be gone for weeks in travel time alone. This command can't tolerate *absentee* civilian workers."

Jillian found that funny. "Weeks? Not bloody likely, I'll be back in two or three days at most."

"How on earth will you accomplish that?"

"Simple. I'll hop on a plane."

"But you're a civilian. Travel on military aircraft is not authorized."

Now she was laughing out loud. "You silly, silly man," she said. "How hard do you suppose it is for a white woman in these parts to bat her eyelashes, show some leg, and hitch a ride on one of your airplanes? Especially one with the credentials I carry from your

Supreme Commander himself? Hell, they'll even be eager to let me fly the bloody thing for a bit."

Jillian didn't have much time if she was going to make that flight to Port Moresby. She'd rushed back to her quarters at Government House to pack. Trying to stuff the last of her things into a rucksack, she was startled by a voice in the doorway.

"What's the big rush, baby?" Jock asked.

Shrieking with delight, she raced toward him. "What in bloody hell are you doing here?"

But once they were locked in that joyful embrace, there was no need for answers.

With a deft backheel, he kicked the door shut.

"Wait, wait," she said as she untangled one of her arms and set the door's lock.

One more kick to clear the bed of the rucksack...

And they collapsed onto the sheets as one, pulling down the mosquito netting with them as they fell.

"I don't...don't...have much time, Jock. I...oh, bloody hell, baby..."

And then they were lost in each other.

When they were finished, they lay side by side, drenched in sweat and contentment. It was Jillian who returned to harsh reality first. She jumped up and stepped out of her rumpled dress. After a quick session at the washstand, she pulled on a fresh shift from the wardrobe.

"I've got to get to Port Moresby, Jock. Greta—your mapmaker—has been sent there. I hadn't been able to find her until this morning."

"So her name's Greta *Dyckman*?"

"That was her maiden name. She's Greta Christiansen now."

"Fantastic. Do whatever it takes to get her on my team, Jill."

"I'll do my best, Yank...but if news of her father won't do it, I won't have anything left to work with." She snatched up the rucksack. "And if I don't hurry, I won't make the courier flight today, either."

"I've got a jeep," he said. "I'll give you a ride to the airfield."

"Brilliant. And while we're driving, you can tell me why it is you're here." A big smile came over her face as she pointed to the disheveled bed. "Or was that the bloody reason?"

As they sped toward the airfield, Jock started to tell her about the surveying problems at Biak and how it was preventing them from creating the maps the GIs needed so desperately. He hadn't gotten to the part about him actually returning there when Jillian said, "Stop the jeep."

There was no need for him to say any more. She'd already figured it out.

When the jeep came to a halt, Jillian climbed out, walked several paces away, and stood there, arms folded across her chest, her back to him.

He killed the engine and said, "Jill, come on. Get back in. It's not what you think."

"It's exactly what I bloody think, Jock."

"But I came all this way just to make sure you heard it from me."

"Thanks for small favors, Yank."

She still wouldn't turn to look at him. So he went to her.

His limp never seemed worse than at that moment. He was grateful she wasn't looking.

What he saw in her eyes surprised him. He'd expected hurt. Instead, there was a clear-eyed gaze far into the distance. Or maybe far into the future.

"How long, Jock?"

"Just a few days, I promise."

"Ahh, there's that word again. No promises, Jock. War doesn't keep them."

She hopped back into the jeep. "Come now, Yank, or I'm going to miss my bloody plane."

Chapter Twenty-Eight

It had been four days since Major Homer Rowe took over 1st Battalion. Melvin Patchett summed up his new commander's performance this way: *The man couldn't organize a pissing contest in a brewery.*

They'd finally managed to mop up the lingering Japanese defenders around the main airfield at Mokmer, as well as the two smaller landing strips at nearby Borokoe and Sorido. But it hadn't been easy, and it had taken much too long—*days* too long, in fact—and Colonel Molloy was fuming over the slow progress. He was beginning to think he'd made a mistake elevating Rowe to battalion commander.

"Major Rowe," Molloy said, "I handed you what is probably the finest fighting battalion in this division, maybe in all of 6th Army...and in no time flat, you turned it into the fuck-up outfit."

Rowe sputtered his answer: "We're...I'm...doing as well as can be expected under the circumstances, Colonel."

"I think those *circumstances* would get a lot better if you got your head out of your ass, Major. For example, I witnessed that little fiasco yesterday, where you sent Charlie Company's assault right through Baker Company's position. If it hadn't been for Captain Grossman's quick thinking, your men would have been killing each other. How'd that happen, Homer? Did you forget where you put Baker Company?"

Rowe's sputtering continued. "No, sir. It's just...well..."

"Never mind, Major. But this is the glorious morning of a brand new day. Do you understand what you've been ordered to do?"

"Yes, sir. We're to move inland, onto the high tableland, and pursue the withdrawing Japanese."

"Not just pursue, Major. Cut them off and finish them. And I want every last one of your companies up on that high ground by noon...without you having them trip all over each other. Is that clear?"

"Yes, sir," Rowe replied, his voice squeaking with stress. "Quite clear."

By noon, the four companies of 1st Battalion had arrived at their objectives on the high tableland. But the area wasn't a wide open plain like their ancient maps indicated. It was a thick rainforest hiding a small village teeming with invisible Japanese. The first American squads blundering their way were quickly cut down.

"We'll envelop the village," Homer Rowe said, his words coming like gasps for breath. "Sergeant Patchett, have Able Company move—"

"Just a damn minute, sir," Patchett replied. "Good plan, except we'd better call in artillery on that village first, before we show our asses again. And we'd better not be too close when it comes down, because with the coordinates we'll be pulling off these fucking maps, only the Good Lord knows where that first round's gonna land. Let's narrow the odds of getting hit by our own guns, okay?"

"I...I suppose, Sergeant," Rowe replied as he began fussing with his map.

It became clear very quickly that the major hadn't a clue where they were.

"I'll take care of calling for fire, sir," Patchett said. "Why don't you make sure our wounded are getting pulled out?"

"Yes, yes...that's a good idea, Sergeant."

As Rowe and his radio operator scurried off, Patchett asked himself, *I wonder if he even knows where the hell he's going?*

As soon as he called the fire mission in on his own radio, Patchett switched frequencies and broadcast a warning on the battalion net: "Every swinging dick better get their asses flat down on the double. Rounds on the way. Your guess is as good as mine where they're gonna hit."

Nobody guessed that first round would land *behind* them—and much too close for comfort.

"Son of a goddamn bitch," Patchett said. "They gotta have the elevation of this place all fucking wrong. Hold on to your hats, boys...next one's gonna come right overhead, close enough to give us all haircuts, probably."

No sooner had Patchett radioed the corrections, a frantic call came in from Major Rowe's radioman: "The C.O.'s down, the C.O.'s down, over."

Patchett replied, "Down? As in *hit*, over?"

"Negative, Sarge, negative. He's just down. Something's wrong with him. Don't know what, over."

Ain't that just ducky? Like we ain't got enough going on right now.

The next adjustment round streaked in, impacting well in front of the huddled GIs this time. It didn't quite reach the village but it was close enough to call, *Add five-zero, fire for effect.*

"Shot, out," Patchett's radioman announced. The rounds were on the way—six each of 105-millimeter high explosive, with point-detonating fuzes.

And they better be right on the fucking money...

A soldier crawled up to Patchett and tugged at his shoulder. "Sarge, there's a couple of trucks coming up the trail behind us."

"Are they GI trucks?"

"Yeah."

"Then they're lost worse than we are, son. Don't worry about 'em. Now watch close..."

The *fire for effect* rounds seemed to do exactly what their name implied. One second, the village was standing, offering a thousand concealed places from which a Japanese soldier could kill Americans.

The next second, it was leveled, looking like a box of giant toothpicks had been spilled and splayed across the ground—a most powerful *effect*. But it was no guarantee of victory. Rubble often yielded fighting positions every bit as good as standing structures. Maybe better.

If the Japanese soldiers in that village weren't dead, maybe they'd been stunned and rendered useless by the blasts just long enough for the GIs to swarm in and finish them.

It only took Patchett a few terse sentences over the radio to get the companies moving into the village:

Able hook in from the left,

Baker from the right;

Charlie—cover Able and Charlie's asses and cut off any Japs running out the back door;

Dog Company—your heavy mortars stay put and provide fire support on call.

That's what we call your classic double envelopment, boys. Y'all make sure you don't shoot each other, now.

"C'mon, son," Patchett told his radioman, "let's go see what's the deal with Major Rowe."

The medic from Dog Company had beaten them there by several minutes. Despite his frantic efforts to revive Rowe, one thing was painfully obvious: *the man's dead.*

"What on God's green Earth happened to him?" Patchett asked.

"Heart attack, I think," the medic replied. "There ain't a mark on him."

"It fucking figures," Patchett said. Then he told his radioman, "Get me Regiment. Maybe we can convince Colonel Molloy to put a *real* combat officer in charge this time. And then call Charlie Company and tell Captain Grossman he's running the battalion in the meantime."

The radioman hadn't yet keyed the microphone when he saw the man coming toward them. He'd know him anywhere—and the limp just made it easier to recognize him at a distance.

"Speaking of *real* combat officers, Sarge, take a look over yonder…"

At first, Melvin Patchett thought he might be dreaming. Or worse, he was seeing a ghost…the ghost of Jock Miles.

But real or imagined, this apparition could speak: "How's the morale around here, Top?"

"Pretty shitty right now…and pardon my French, sir, but just what the fuck are you doing here?"

"Just checking up on your cracker ass. What happened to Major Rowe?"

"Heart attack, Doc says. Four days in command was too much for the man, I reckon."

"He was the C.O.? Did Billingsley finally get kicked upstairs?"

"In a manner of speaking, sir. He bought it those same four days back. Got hisself killed trying to take a shit."

"Well I'll be a son of a bitch. So who's next in line? Lee Grossman?"

"Affirmative. He just got the word about a second ago."

The intermittent crackle of small arms fire from the village swelled to a crescendo. The radioman clamped the handset against his ear, desperate to hear the voices being drowned out by all the noise.

"Charlie Company needs the big mortars, Sarge…and a couple more heavy machine guns. They've got a bunch of Japs on the run."

"Give 'em what they want, son."

He turned to Jock and said, "I gotta get closer, sir. Things are a little hectic right now."

"I'll come with you, Top."

Patchett looked at the walking stick in Jock's left hand: *At least it ain't his shooting hand…and he's still got the good ol' Thompson in the other.*

"Suit yourself, sir. You sure you can keep up?"

"Just watch me, Top."

"Damn glad to have you along then. Be like old times, sir."

Operation Fishwrapper

Captain Lee Grossman was thrilled to see Jock Miles, the man he'd succeeded as Charlie Company commander two years ago in the early days of the Papua campaign. Like every other veteran in the battalion, he desperately wanted to believe Jock had come to take command once again.

"Technically, I'm with Fifth Air Force now, Lee," Jock said. He tapped his walking stick on the ground. "And this bum leg of mine makes my infantry credentials pretty weak."

Patchett added, "Besides, with the job he's in now, he gets to snuggle up with Miss Jillian every chance he gets. Hard for a man to pass up duty like that."

"No, Top, it isn't like that, I'm afraid. Jill and I don't get to see much of each other at all."

With a knowing smile, Patchett replied, "I'm sure you two find a way plenty of times, sir. But now that we done quieted the Japs down for a spell, run it by us again exactly what you're doing here."

"It's simple," Jock said. "Your maps are old and obsolete and I'm going to fix that. I had the same problem when I was stuck on this damn island a couple of weeks ago."

Patchett was surprised. "You been here before, sir?"

"Long story…and it wasn't planned, believe me. But speaking of bad maps, I couldn't help but notice that adjustment round that landed behind you earlier today. It damn near killed me and that survey team of mine. What the hell was that all about?"

"Target elevation error," Patchett replied.

"That stuff's been happening to us all the time, sir," Grossman added. "We just pray we can get eyes on where that first round lands...and that it's not right on top of us."

Jock asked, "Are you setting up registration points for your artillery and mortars?"

Patchett and Grossman exchanged looks like schoolboys caught without their homework. It was Grossman who finally spoke up: "Haven't had much opportunity, sir."

The answer surprised Jock. It wasn't like either of them not to be on top of everything. He asked, "Why the hell not, Lee?"

"Most of our target locations are pretty indistinct, sir. It's hard to find them again when you need them—all the trees look alike. And it's not like we've got maps good enough to record them on."

"I see your point," Jock replied. "But that village you just cleared the Japs out of...you sure as hell better make that a registration point on the double. Your artillery knows exactly where that is now."

"I'll take care of that right quick, sir," Patchett said as he motioned for his radioman to join them.

"Great, Top. Now I need a favor from you guys. That survey team of mine...how about we hook them up with your recon platoon? It just might help the quality of their work a whole lot if they knew someone was watching their backs...someone who wasn't still green behind the ears."

Patchett snickered. "You mean they're a li'l bit skittish about getting their asses out in the boondocks, sir?"

"More than a little bit, Top."

"I reckon you're right, sir. First we've seen of a survey team on this damn island, and we've been the *tip of the spear* ever since we got here. And I'm sure ol' Bogater would be glad to take them under his wing."

Jock smiled at the sound of that name. "That crazy Cajun's got the recon platoon?"

"Affirmative, sir."

"Outstanding. This is getting better by the minute."

Chapter Twenty-Nine

Sergeant Bogater Boudreau thought his leg was being pulled when he was told Major Miles was with the battalion again. He'd replied, "I might've been born at night…but I wasn't born *last* night. So y'all can fuck off."

When he reported to the battalion CP for the survey team briefing, though, he was never so happy to owe someone an apology. "As I live and breathe, sir," Bogater said, "I thought I died and gone to heaven when I saw you standing there. On second thought, forget the dying part. We been through enough of that together, ain't we?"

"Good to see you, too, Bogater. You're a couple of stripes heavier, aren't you?"

"Yessir, seems like the brass think if they give you more stripes, you'll like it here better, the dumb bastards. Present company excepted, of course."

Jock began the briefing by telling the story of the dead Japanese lieutenant's rucksack containing the fish wrapped in an American map. "So as you can see, men, the Japs think as little of our maps as we do."

"Damn, sir," Boudreau said, "maybe we oughta just shitcan this *Operation Alamo* stuff and call this whole fiasco *Operation Fishwrapper*. Fits a whole lot better."

"Not a bad idea, Sergeant Boudreau," Jock replied. "But the reason our maps stink is we still haven't compiled all the data we need to make them worth something. We've got great aerial photos…but they give us a flat world. And as we can see all around us, this place is anything but flat. And there are a lot of terrain

Operation Fishwrapper

features we can't see in an aerial photo, especially with tree cover blocking the view of the ground. We're going to need survey information—*damn good* survey information—to fill in the missing pieces. The survey team and recon platoon are going to work together to get it."

Jock showed them where they'd be working that afternoon: with a grease pencil, he drew a big box on a high-altitude photo that included their current location. "We're going to start here," he said, "and do a continuous survey north, covering a corridor a mile wide all the way across the island. While we're working in First Battalion's area of operations, Sergeant Bogater's recon platoon will provide support for the survey party. How does this play into the big picture? Like this: the division's objective is to hold a line clear across the island. Once we own that line, we'll be able to cut off the Japs trying to withdraw to the west. The Navy will see to it they can't send reinforcements or evacuate anyone by sea, so every Jap we stop here means a man we won't have to fight again someplace else on this rock."

The survey team section chief—a smart-mouthed buck sergeant from Brooklyn named Lynch—was less than thrilled. "In other words, sir, we get to stick our necks out with the toughest job, while the other survey teams get to *fuck the dog* behind the front lines."

Jock smiled when he saw the icy glare Bogater shot the survey sergeant's way. He waited until he was sure Lynch had caught the look, too, and then replied, "Negative, Sergeant Lynch. You've just got the honor of being first. As soon as I'm finished with you guys, I'm going to get the other survey teams in gear, too. They'll be *sticking their necks out* as far as yours, just a little farther down the line from here. Are there any more questions?"

There were none.

"Then good luck to you all. Frequencies and progress reporting times are in the commo section of the ops order. I'll leave you in Sergeant Boudreau's very capable hands."

The survey team seemed in no hurry to get moving. The Cajun draped an arm around Lynch's shoulders and said, "C'mon, *mon frère*, let's get your boys saddled up. You and me gonna be great friends, we are."

Maybe *great friends* was a bit of wishful thinking as Bogater dragged the sullen Lynch and his four terrified PFCs deeper into the rainforest. But at least they were getting the job done properly.

"You don't gotta worry," the Cajun said. "My guys are way, way out all around us. They'll let us know if any Japs are around, believe you me."

He watched Lynch set up a shot on the transit. But something wasn't right; although they were plotting a hill several hundred yards ahead, there was no *stick man* holding the calibrated *barber pole* at its peak for Lynch to target.

"Wait a damn minute," Boudreau said. "How come there ain't nobody up on that hill with one of them sticks?"

"Don't need it," Lynch replied. "It's far enough away to qualify as a distant aiming point."

"Bullshit on that. Even a dumb *coonass* like me knows a distant aiming point gotta be *distant*. I could hit the top of that hill with a rock. And if we get that location wrong, everything you shoot off it's gonna be wrong, too."

Bogater picked up a barber pole off the ground, walked over to one of Lynch's stick men, and shoved the pole into his hands. "Let's go, young man. You and Corporal Simms here are gonna take a little walk up that hill."

"But Sergeant Lynch said I didn't have to."

"I'm changing the sergeant's mind for him, son. Get your ass moving. Simms will hold your hand all the way up there, if you like."

The two men trudged off toward the hill.

"This is all a waste of fucking time," Lynch said. "It ain't gonna matter all that much how I take this shot…pole or not."

Boudreau replied, "It's gonna matter a whole lot to me, Sergeant Lynch, next time I'm calling for fire on that hill and that first round don't get in the ballpark. And it's gonna matter a whole lot to Major Miles, too."

"I don't understand why everybody in your outfit's so willing to eat shit for that gimpy-legged son of a bitch. Does he give out blow jobs on Sunday or—"

The next thing Lynch remembered was being flat on his back, his jaw throbbing like it had been struck by a hammer. Bogater's snarling face hovered over him. The muzzle of the Cajun's Thompson was inches from his face.

"You ever say anything like that in front of any man in this battalion again, he's gonna shoot you dead on the spot. Consider this your warning, *mon frère*. Now get the fuck on your feet and take that plot."

Colonel Molloy studied the piece of paper in silence as the KP poured him and Jock another cup of coffee. The colonel seemed troubled. He was pacing the CP tent with that faraway look on his face all soldiers wore as they struggled to deal with the trials of their profession.

"I don't know what to do about this, Jock," Molloy said, waving the paper in his hand.

"About what, sir?"

"I've never seen anything like this in all my years of soldiering. It's a petition...can you believe that? Signed by every officer and NCO in First Battalion. *Your* old battalion."

Jock cringed. He'd learned a long time ago never to sign your name to anything critical of your command or a higher one. The Army wasn't a democracy; civil institutions didn't cut any ice here. Those who tried to make it work like one endured quick and vicious punishments.

Every officer and NCO. Shit, that sounds like a mutiny. Were my guys—my ex-guys, I suppose—really dumb enough to put their names on something like that en masse?

God, I hope not.

The next sentence Molloy spoke should have brought him great relief.

But it didn't...for a completely different reason.

"Jock, what this paper says is they want you back as their battalion commander."

"But I thought Lee Grossman was supposed to get moved up. He's more than ready."

Molloy laid the petition on the table in front of Jock and pointed to the first signature:

Leon Grossman, Captain, USA.

Right below it was *Melvin Patchett, Master Sergeant, USA.*

Feelings of pride and dread were stirring themselves into a witch's brew in his gut. He wanted the job back. There was no doubt in his mind.

So I limp a little...okay, maybe a lot sometimes. The field grades of this man's army are full of old coots with one physical problem or another.

How can I say no and let my men down?

But how can I say yes and let Jillian down? I'm not a fool...all her talk about "don't make promises" assumed we were talking about staff jobs, not a combat command.

Would she leave me?

What the hell do I do?

"Am I really being offered a choice here, sir?"

"Absolutely, Jock. It's your call. But I think you know what I'd like. There's just one thing—I need an answer by tomorrow morning."

That didn't seem like enough time. *Sleeping on it* wasn't an option, because Jock knew there'd be no sleep tonight with this hanging over his head.

"But sir, how could we make this work? I'm in Fifth Air Force now. That's a whole different chain of command."

"Don't worry about that, Jock. Buck Ziminski and I are classmates from the Point. He didn't just save your ass from getting shipped home when he offered you that job—he was returning a favor."

"A favor...to *you*, sir?"

Molloy nodded. "So he and I are even now. He never figured he'd have you forever. Now I know your leg can be a challenge for you sometimes, Jock..."

"It's not about my leg, sir."

"That's good to hear. And speaking of Buck Ziminski, I heard he was about to promote you to light colonel. I wouldn't mind doing those honors myself, Jock."

That news took Jock by surprise. Promotion had been the last thing on his mind for quite some time.

"But what about the survey teams, sir?"

"Looks like you've already solved that problem, Jock. I'm detaching the survey teams to the individual infantry battalions, continuing what you've started. It was a really good move. It'll keep them on track."

"Sir, if I say yes, can I get back to Hollandia—even just for a day—so I can talk to Jill in person?"

"No can do, Jock. I've been called back there myself. I'm flying out tomorrow morning to brief the *big boss*. I can't have one of my battalion commanders gone at the same time, can I? Especially my best one. I can't have this whole show going to hell in a handbasket overnight. Not again."

The die was cast: Dick Molloy was already talking as if the deal was closed. They both knew it was.

The colonel's body language made it clear the meeting was over. He had one more thing to say: "Tell you what, Jock...write down whatever you want to say to Jillian and I'll deliver it to her personally tomorrow."

He knew it would be the hardest letter he'd ever had to write. All he could do now was hope she'd understand…somehow.

Chapter Thirty

It was just past noon when the ship carrying the Dutch refugees arrived at Port Moresby. Warily, the men and women stepped down the gangplank to be shepherded onto waiting trucks. Jillian stood by, watching the procession, but there was no sign of the woman she'd come to collect.

"Where is Greta Christiansen?" she asked the man from the Red Cross, who was checking off names on a clipboard. Two very disinterested American MPs were by his side.

"Christiansen...Christiansen. Ah, yes. I have her name on the list. It's right here."

"So where in bloody hell is she?"

His tone suddenly pompous, he asked, "And who is asking?"

She showed him her credentials.

His face dropped. Any hint of arrogance was gone. "If she's not on board, Miss Miles—"

"It's *Missus* Miles, thank you."

"Oh, I'm sorry, Missus Miles. But if she's not on board, I have no idea where she is. I can ask these MPs to go and search—"

"No need getting MPs involved," she said. "These people aren't criminals." She called to the ship's first mate standing at the top of the gangplank. "Permission to come aboard?"

With a theatrical flourish, he bowed from the waist while sweeping his arm wide and high in welcome.

Stepping onto the deck, she asked the mate, "Do you know of a Greta Christiansen onboard this vessel?"

He grinned as if she'd just tapped into a juicy subject. "Yes, of course," he replied.

"Well, where the bloody hell is she? I would think she'd be in a hurry to get off this rust bucket."

"Now that we're in port, I'm sure you'll find her in the navigator's quarters, ma'am."

"The navigator's quarters? Why?"

"Turns out they're husband and wife. A real touching story…they both thought the other was dead. Until she turned up on this ship."

The Red Cross man on the wharf was getting anxious. "WELL? IS SHE THERE?" He pointed to his wristwatch.

"NO," Jillian replied with a perfectly straight face. "I'M AFRAID NOT."

He seemed unsure what to do. He paced in a circle at the foot of the gangplank for a few moments, and then stopped to jot something on his clipboard. When he was done, he signaled the trucks and the MPs to be on their way, jumped into a waiting car, and was gone.

"What was all that about?" the first mate asked.

"Much easier than having a little administrative tussle over custody right there on the dock. Let's just say Missus Christiansen has a higher calling at the moment than cooling her heels in another resettlement camp. Show me to the navigator's quarters, please."

It took a lot of knocking—and a few minutes of waiting—before the navigator opened the door to his darkened compartment. Looking past the annoyed and shirtless man in the doorway, Jillian could see Greta inside, hurriedly buttoning her dress. She didn't look thrilled to see who their caller was, either.

"Hello, Greta. I just did you a favor," Jillian said, "and maybe I can do you another."

"If this has anything to do with working for the American barbarians, you already have my answer."

Greta joined her husband in the doorway. Jillian extended her hand to him. "Lukas Christiansen, I presume?"

"You presume correctly, miss," he replied, his tone anything but cordial.

"It's missus, actually. The Dutch government-in-exile will be delighted to know you are alive and well. And a navigator, too! Not a lot of difference between cartography and navigation, is there?"

"What would you know about it?"

Greta provided the answer. "Actually, Lukas, she knows quite a lot. She used to be a ship's master."

"Still am, technically. Just doing some other war work for the Yanks at the moment."

He still wasn't impressed. "It figures. She speaks like a fucking American."

Again his wife filled in the blanks. "That's only because she's married to one, Lukas."

Pleading woman-to-woman now, Greta said, "Jillian, I've only got a few moments left with my husband, the last ones for who knows how long. Please leave us in peace before I must fall back into the chaos of Red Cross hospitality."

"Actually, that was the favor I just did for you, Greta. I told them you weren't on board."

At first, she didn't seem to comprehend. Then, as the short-term implications sunk in—she was free to linger with her husband—she became amused. A few moments later, the long-term implications reared their ugly heads.

"Oh my god, Jillian…you just made me a ghost again! I'm officially *missing*. I don't exist."

"No, no, no, Greta. It won't be like that at all. Have you forgotten what my job is? And who I work for?"

"You can fix it? You can make it right again?"

"Of course. Didn't I *fix it* at Aitape?"

The conversation was making Lukas confused and distrustful. Greta soothed him, holding him close while running her hand through his hair. He started to speak—to hurl more vitriol, no doubt—but Greta *shushed* him with a kiss.

"You said something about *another* favor, Jillian. What would that be?"

"I'm thrilled that you've found your husband again, Greta…but how would you like your father back, too?"

Within a few hours, the two women were on the day's last military flight back to Hollandia. Greta spent their time in the air telling Jillian every detail of Lukas' miraculous story. How, after they were captured by the Japanese and then separated, he'd been placed on a motor barge with other prisoners which headed west toward the Moluccas. The barge swamped in a storm; a few of the male prisoners made it ashore on the Vogelkop Peninsula. The escapees worked their way south, managing to stay just ahead of the advancing wave of Japanese. Hitching a ride at Sorong on a trawler which survived several attacks by Japanese aircraft as it crossed the Banda and Arafura Seas, they finally landed in Darwin. There, Lukas met a Dutch freighter captain desperate for a navigator and willing to overlook the undocumented status of this ragged but talented refugee who knew how to read charts and use a sextant.

Jillian asked, "And he never thought to identify himself to any of the Allied authorities?"

"Let's just say he reveled in his anonymity."

"Like a hermit at sea."

"Exactly. I'm sure it was his way of escaping the war…and the memory of losing me. He was so sure I'd die a prisoner."

Jillian replied, "They love to underestimate us, don't they?"

They landed just before dark and went straight to the Office of Civil Affairs. Her boss was still at his desk. He took one look at Greta and said, "Oh, good grief! Don't tell me this woman is Greta Christiansen."

"Of course she is. She's the reason I went to Port Moresby, remember?"

His voice becoming loud and shrill, the fat captain said, "Good lord, Missus Miles, you've done it all wrong. Don't you realize you've just kidnapped a Dutch citizen?"

"Not true," Jillian replied, not in the least bit concerned by the captain's rage. "She came of her own free will. Isn't that right, Greta?"

Greta had no trouble mimicking Jillian's nonchalance. "Absolutely. I'm here to help."

"THE RED CROSS HAS ALREADY LISTED HER AS *MISSING*. THEY DIDN'T WASTE A SECOND WIRING ME THE REPORT. DO YOU REALIZE THE AMOUNT OF PAPERWORK AND

AGGRAVATION THIS LITTLE STUNT OF YOURS IS GOING TO CAUSE, MISSUS MILES?"

"Actually, Captain, it will cause neither. A simple letter to the Dutch East Indies government-in-exile in Australia will suffice. I can have that prepared and on its way first thing tomorrow morning. By the way, we've turned up her husband alive and well, so we can cross another name off our *missing, presumed dead* list."

He looked about to boil over but Jillian kept on talking. "And as far as the Red Cross goes, they have nothing to be aggravated about. We've just given them one less mouth to feed. As soon as Missus Christiansen signs her statement of employment with Supreme Allied Headquarters, the *baffling mystery* of her whereabouts will be solved to their satisfaction."

The fat captain wasn't going to let it go that easily. "This is all highly irregular, Missus Miles. You've made me and my command look like a bunch of gangsters."

"Oh, that's just bloody bullshit. *War* is highly irregular, Captain. And as far as the *gangster* claim, I think Missus Christiansen would agree—all you Yanks are bloody gangsters. Right, Greta?"

"Correct, Jillian."

"So if you'll excuse us, Captain, we're going to enjoy a drink and a meal at the officers' club. Good night."

They made it as far as the veranda, where Jillian was startled to come face to face with Colonel Molloy.

"What are you doing here, Colonel?" she asked.

"Actually, I was coming to say 'hi' to you. Figured you were still at work." He looked to Greta and asked, "And who do we have here?"

Jillian gave him the lowdown. Molloy was delighted to learn Greta would be offering her mapmaking skills and knowledge of Biak's terrain to the Americans.

"We can certainly use your help," he said. "How soon can you join us on the island?"

Greta replied, "As soon as I can collect some suitable clothes."

"Excellent. I'm sure Jillian can have you decked out in no time. You can fly back with me tomorrow."

Molloy's smile faded; there was something else on his mind. Producing a small envelope from his shirt pocket, he said, "Jillian…this is from Jock. I promised I'd give it to you personally."

"Oh dear lord…is he all right?"

"Yes, yes. He's fine. Perfectly fine." He pressed the envelope into her hand.

Shit. He's being too solicitous. This is bad news. I know it.

"I can't read it out here. It's too dark. Excuse me for a moment."

Back inside the villa, she read Jock's letter with trembling hands. Smiling through her tears, she was touched that his men—some of whom she knew so well—had loved him so much they'd petitioned for his return as their commander. It was easy to understand his bond with them. She felt a bond to those men, too. They'd all been through so much together in the past two years.

I should be jealous.

My husband has two wives…me and his bloody First Battalion.

But how will he manage back in the bush with that leg of his?

Knowing him, I'm afraid he'll find a way.
If those bastards don't take brilliant care of him, though, they'll be answering to me.

She had to stop and pull herself together before she could make it through the last paragraph:

Promises, Jill...I keep remembering what you said about promises. How war doesn't let you keep them. I'd like to believe it, now more than ever. My only fear is that war or not, I've pushed it one broken promise too far this time. I lost you once to the Japs. If I lost you again...this time to my own foolishness...there would be nothing left for me to live for.

She was too overwrought go back outside and face Greta and Colonel Molloy. If she tried to speak, she knew nothing would come out.

Just a few more moments and I'll be right as rain.

That was all it took. When she stepped onto the veranda, Molloy's eyes wouldn't meet hers. Greta, with no such problem, saw the tracks of Jillian's tears glistening even in the dark. She threw her arms around her.

"I'm fine," Jillian said. "I've grown quite accustomed to this insanity."

She asked Molloy, "Really? A bloody petition?"

"Can you believe it?"

"Yes, Colonel, I can. Nothing surprises me about your Army anymore. Tell me...were you there when he made his decision?"

Molloy nodded reluctantly, as if confessing to some transgression against her.

"Was it hard for him?"

He nodded again, this time with a bit more enthusiasm.

"Silly boys," she whispered. "You all can be so *thick*. As if he really had a choice…"

Jillian walked to the veranda's railing. Looking up at the starry sky, she added, "This war is our life…until it ends, one way or another. And there's not a bloody thing we can do about it."

Chapter Thirty-One

By the time Colonel Molloy returned to his regimental HQ on Biak, Bogater Boudreau's new name for the campaign they were waging had stuck fast. It might still officially be *Operation Alamo*, but every man in the regiment was now referring to it as *Operation Fishwrapper*. Jock found himself explaining to the colonel how the new name had come to be.

"So I've got you and your hoodlums to thank for this," Molloy said, trying to sound displeased by the state of affairs.

No one in the regimental CP was fooled. They all knew their colonel wasn't really upset. *Maybe he even likes it*, Jock thought. *He certainly agrees with the sentiment.*

"Think of it as a morale-boosting device, sir," Jock offered. "It puts a smile on the men's faces."

Molloy replied, "Always looking on the bright side, eh, Major Miles?" Then he broke into a devilish smile of his own. "By the way, that'll be the last time anyone calls you *Major* Miles."

He reached into his pocket and produced a silver oak leaf, the insignia of a lieutenant colonel. Unpinning the gold leaf from Jock's collar, he installed the new rank in its place. "I'm sure you'd rather have your wife here doing this," Molloy added, "but at least she can tell you in her own words how she feels."

From another pocket, he produced Jillian's letter.

Jock held it gingerly in his hands, like it might explode if handled too roughly. "I shouldn't read this right here and now, sir."

"Read it whenever you like, *Colonel* Miles. But let me remind you that good things come in threes. You've already seen the first two..."

"So this letter's a good thing, sir?"

Molloy smiled. "I believe you'll find that to be the case, Jock. And now, for that third good thing, just take a look outside the tent."

A GI was helping a red-haired woman unload her gear from Molloy's jeep.

Jock said, "Let me guess...that hair's a dead giveaway. That's got to be Andreas Dyckman's daughter, Greta."

"Yep, that's her. Your wife did one smooth job rounding her up. Come on...you need to meet her. She's quite an interesting lady."

As they shook hands, Greta said, "Very nice to meet you, Colonel Miles...and congratulations on your promotion."

"Thanks. Call me Jock."

"As you wish. Actually, the familiarity shouldn't be a problem. Jillian's told me so much about you I feel I've known you for years. By the way, your wife is an amazingly courageous woman, you know."

"Yeah, tell me about it. She's a hell of a lot tougher than I am."

"And very persuasive, too," Greta added. "I wouldn't be here if it wasn't for her."

They went into the CP tent. A big map of the island hung from a side curtain. Greta took one look at it and whistled in surprise. It sounded like a bomb falling. "Where did you get this sorry relic?" she asked.

"It's the best we've got at the moment," Jock replied. "There are five survey teams at work. We're updating the map at a rate of about twenty square miles a day, when the Japs don't slow us down."

"At that rate, you could be at it for six months or more. My husband and I mapped most of the southern island. It took us over a year."

She went back to studying the map. "Where is my father?" she asked.

"Last I saw of him, he was about here," Jock replied as he pointed to a spot on the east coast. "When I left him and his party two weeks ago, he planned to go north. They had a radio set...a receiver and transmitter. We've tried to raise him a number of times, with no luck. I'm not surprised, though—he never liked to use the transmitter. That may be a good thing, because if you transmit, the Japs can find you real easy."

"Or maybe he thinks you're the Japanese trying to trick him into revealing his position. Did he have any of the maps Lukas and I drew?"

"Nope. He said the Japs ended up getting everything he had."

"Well, there weren't very many. They were all plotted by hand. We didn't have any printing presses for mass production. You haven't captured any maps from the Japanese, have you?"

"No, not yet, I'm afraid."

"Well, the Japanese have had two years to reproduce our maps. Maybe even make their own. There's got to be plenty of decent ones around this island by now. It's a pity you don't have any of them."

Greta stepped back to take in the entire map hanging there in one glance. She frowned while calculating the scope of the task ahead, finally saying, "Oh well, let's get to work. Unfortunately, it's been a few years and I don't have perfect recall, but I'm sure I can fill in a good many blanks for you very quickly. I assume your lack of elevation data is causing you the most problems?"

"You assume correctly," Jock replied.

"Fine. On which area do you need to focus first?"

Jock tore open Jillian's letter the moment he returned to his battalion's CP. Patchett caught a glimpse of him seated in a corner of the tent, reading intently. In all their time together—even those times under fire—he'd never seen Jock looking so apprehensive.

The boss needs a little privacy. I'll come back in a spell.

When Patchett returned, Jock was in exactly the same place, his eyes still glued to the letter. He said nothing, but his demeanor had done an *about face*: he looked relaxed and content.

A man could read a one-page letter about twenty times in the couple of minutes it took to catch me that smoke. Damn if his eyes ain't welled up a bit, though. But look at him grinning like the cat that ate the canary. It's like a ton of weight just got lifted off him.

If she ain't leaving him over this, I reckon she ain't never gonna.

"Good news?" Patchett asked. It was a safe question. He already knew the answer.

"Yeah, Top. Couldn't be any better, all things considered."

By evening, the big map at the regimental CP looked quite different. Working from memory, Greta had provided a vast amount of topographic data for the current area of operations. A team of intel NCOs drew her enhancements by hand onto smaller maps—the *fishwrappers*—for immediate distribution to the infantry and artillery battalions.

"We owe Missus Christiansen here a big note of thanks," Colonel Molloy told his assembled commanders and staff. "In just one day, we've seen a tremendous increase in artillery effectiveness alone...not to mention a marked decrease in the *terrain surprises* which have plagued us from the moment we set foot on this island."

Artillery effectiveness...every man in the room knew how much that meant, especially when firing on mobile targets that don't bother standing still while you're adjusting rounds on them. Before today, it had often taken five or six adjustment rounds before *fire for effect* was called, the forward observers often trying to adjust the unseen impacts by sound alone in the opaque wilderness of the rainforest. A formation of Japanese soldiers could have run hundreds of yards while all that was going on. The *fire for effect* rounds would take only trees as their victims.

But they wouldn't get very far if that first round was close to *on target*—or you were confident enough of the enemy's location to call *fire for effect* right off the bat. Then they wouldn't have a chance to run.

"There's an added bonus," Colonel Molloy said. "Now we have a much better idea where the tanks can actually operate and do us the most good…and the area we're going into tomorrow looks perfect for tanks. Until we hit the coastal cliffs, it's relatively level ground, with room for them to maneuver in the forest. I'll turn it over to the S3 now. He'll give you all the details."

As the briefing wound to a close, Greta went right back to work on the map. Jock walked over and said, "I think I have an idea that might do us both some good."

He had her complete attention. "I'm sure your father's out there, Greta, and I'm betting he's real close—and in a position to provide us some great intel—if we can just get him to talk to us."

She knew immediately what he had in mind. "You want me to send a message in code that he'll know had to come from me, don't you?"

Jock replied, "That's exactly what I was thinking. What kind of code?"

"Something in Dutch. Perhaps the lullaby he used to sing to me as a child."

"It'll have to be short. We don't want him on the air too long."

"No problem, Jock. It's just a little song."

"Great. Let's run it by Colonel Molloy and get his stamp of approval."

Chapter Thirty-Two

Maybe it was the newfound phenomenon of deadly accurate artillery fire sweeping the rainforest ahead of the advancing GIs. Or perhaps it was the clank and squeak of American tank tracks that quickly filled the void, sounding as methodical and inescapable as a meat grinder, whenever the artillery barrage leapt forward. Whatever it was, after that first, decimating contact earlier this morning, what was left of the shattered Japanese formation was fleeing to the north, not bothering to stand and fight. At least not for the time being. The combat veterans in 1st Battalion could not recall a time they'd advanced so quickly. They all were thinking the same thing:

Are they going to run themselves right into the Pacific? Or are we getting suckered as they hot-foot it to a fallback position...where they'll dig in and start kicking our asses?

A rookie PFC in Charlie Company thought jogging a few yards behind the tanks was insanity. "Why the hell don't we just ride on the damn things?" he asked First Sergeant Tom Hadley. "Fuck this *double-time* bullshit."

"*Why*? You're asking *why*, numbnuts? It's because we're in contact, you dumb shit. A tank hull ain't going to give you cover if you're sitting on top of it. And if you get shot off the damn thing, who's going to keep the Nips from hopping on and stuffing a grenade or two into the vents? And one more thing—if you're up on top, when the main gun fires it's like getting kicked in the nuts and punched in the ears at the same time. Trust me...you're better off down here, close to good ol' Mother Earth."

It didn't take more than a few seconds for Tom Hadley's advice to prove true: every man in Charlie Company went sprawling as Japanese machine guns crisscrossed their column. "STAY DOWN BUT KEEP FUCKING MOVING," Hadley called out for the benefit of the rookies, who were curled up as if trying to squeeze their entire bodies into their helmets. The veterans didn't need to be told. They were already yards ahead, low-crawling for dear life. They knew how the Japs worked from hard experience:

Once we're stopped dead, they'll rip us to shreds with mortars. Gotta get out of the kill zone.

They crawled until they could huddle behind the steel mass of the tanks, now slowed as the crewmen scanned for the enemy gunners. The veterans were there a good minute before the rookies finally made it.

"Nice of you to fucking join us," a platoon sergeant told them, his voice nearly drowned out by the staccato *clank clank clank* of bullets ricocheting off the tanks' hulls and the roar of the tanks' guns, returning fire. "You rookies just learned another important lesson in how to stay alive out here."

Another minute and the fight was over as quickly as it had begun. The steel of the tanks prevailed against Japanese armored only in mortal flesh. As their men scoured what was left of the enemy position, Captain Grossman asked First Sergeant Hadley, "What's our casualties, Top?"

"Two wounded, sir, not too badly. They can make it back to the aid station on their own."

Grossman blew a sigh of relief. "There couldn't have been more than a handful of Japs here, Tom. They were dug in deep…that's why the artillery didn't get them. How many bodies did we turn up?"

"Six so far, sir."

"I doubt we'll find more than that. Any blood trails?"

"Not a one, sir."

Giving a Stuart tank a friendly pat on its hull, Grossman said, "I'm starting to like these contraptions more every day. But I'm betting this little skirmish was only a delaying action. We're going to hit a lot more shit as we keep going forward…and I think we just went off the edge of this new map, dammit."

An excited young corporal came running up. "Sir! Top! You've got to see this!" Thrusting the rucksack he was carrying toward them, he added, "Found it under one of them dead Japs."

Grossman and Hadley jumped back in terror. Neither man would take the rucksack. "Did you open that fucking thing already, Corporal?" the first sergeant asked.

"Yeah, sure. It's full of maps and stuff."

"Did it cross your mind it might be booby trapped?"

"I was real careful when I did, First Sergeant."

"Let's hope so," Hadley replied as he took the rucksack.

Just like the corporal said, it contained maps which were far more detailed than the ones the GIs were using. The *stuff* he was referring to turned out to be a sheaf of Japanese Army documents.

Grossman turned to his radio operator and said, "Get Battalion on the line. Tell them we might've just hit the jackpot."

At the regimental communications section, a new radio operator was coming on duty. He took a look at the messages lined up to be sent. On top was that crazy one in Dutch. They'd been sending it since last night, tapping out words they didn't understand in Morse letter for letter. They'd received no reply.

The message contained just two lines:
Slaap kindje slaap,
daar buiten loopt een schaap.

He asked the man he was relieving, "What'd that lady say this meant, anyway?"

"It means something like *Sleep baby sleep, outside there walks a sheep.*"

"Hmm...don't make no fucking sense to me."

"Well, it doesn't have to make sense to you, pal. That's what the colonel wants, so we're gonna keep sending it."

Sliding onto the stool in front of the radio set, he tapped out the Dutch words, just as he had every two hours of his shift last night. When it was done, he shuffled the message back into the queue without giving it another thought. But as he was about to start sending the next message, his headphones came alive with Morse. The characters seemed like gibberish:

Een schaap met witte voetjes,
die drinkt zijn melk zo zoetjes.

It was a moment before he noticed the repetition of those two words: *een schaap.*

"Hey, Sarge," he called out to the section chief, "somebody besides me is talking about sheep in Dutch."

"You mean we finally got an answer?"

"Looks that way."

The sergeant ran to get Greta Christiansen.

By the time Jock arrived at Charlie Company, Lee Grossman had gone over all the maps they'd taken from that Japanese rucksack. They were printed in Japanese, not Dutch, and had detailed topographic information. In addition, symbols that could only be the location of defensive positions had been drawn in by hand. The position the GIs had just overrun—the place they'd found these maps—was clearly listed.

"Look…this place was just an outpost," Grossman told Jock. "According to this map, their main position is about five hundred yards ahead, right in front of Baker Company. If we get Baker to fix the Japs in place with the sea at their backs, I can swing my company around from the left real quick….and Able can swing in from the right. We'll surround them…and finish them. They won't have any chance of getting away."

Jock eyes didn't lift from the map. "Hold on a minute, Lee," he said. "Something's fishy here."

"What do you mean, sir?"

"I don't believe this map, Lee. I've walked across this island before—not quite this far west—but I've still got a pretty good feel for lay of the land. And it's just not as regular as this map wants us to believe. The coast especially...it gets real rough and then cliffs drop off to the coastal lowlands." He scanned the curtain of rainforest all around them. "And you can never really get a good look at what's ahead because the trees hide so much."

"You think it's some kind of set-up, sir? A hoax?"

"Could be. Maybe the Japs at that outpost were supposed to leave those maps behind for us to find, but your guys nailed them before they could pull back. Look at the defensive positions they've drawn in. Do you really think the Japs would occupy low ground rather than high ground?"

"Yeah, I see your point, sir."

Jock rolled up the maps. "How much do you want to bet that if we moved on the position they've got drawn, we'd be the ones trapped on the low ground, while they're above us all around?"

Grossman wasn't in a betting mood. He just nodded.

"They're going to want to make a stand pretty soon," Jock said, "before their backs are flat against the sea. So this is what we're going to do...I'm going to take these maps up to Regiment and see what Missus Christiansen has to say about them. In the meantime, I want the rifle companies to hold their lines right where they are. Each company is to send out a squad-sized recon patrol. Feel around for what's *really* up ahead in this maze of trees."

Chapter Thirty-Three

This damn leg of mine...

When he arrived at the regimental CP, Jock's leg had almost buckled on him as he stepped from the jeep.

"You okay, sir?" his driver asked.

Clinging to the jeep's hood for support, Jock replied, "Yeah...give me a second."

Once inside the tent, he found Greta and her big map weren't there.

"She's at the commo shack, sir," an intel sergeant told him. "Something about *sleeping babies* and *white sheep*."

Jock knew what that meant: the lullaby was now a duet. They'd made contact with her father, Andreas Dyckman.

He struggled back into the jeep. "Drive over to the commo tent," he told his driver.

"But it's right over there, sir...like only twenty yards—"

"Just drive, dammit."

As the jeep rolled to a stop in front of their destination, Jock said, "Hey...I'm sorry I snapped at you back there."

"It's okay, sir. You sure you don't want the doc to have a look at that leg?"

"No time," Jock replied and limped inside.

"My father's right here," Greta told him, pointing to a pin they'd stuck in the map. "We've gotten a fix on him. Apparently, the Japanese haven't...yet."

Jock figured she'd be happy but she wasn't. Her face was stretched tight with worry.

"My father and his people are pushed back against the sea. He says the Japanese are right in front of him, a very large force, very close. He's very talkative all of a sudden. He must be terrified."

Jock unrolled the map in his hand, the one he'd taken from Lee Grossman. Comparing the two maps, two things became quickly apparent. First, the terrain depicted on the map in his hands looked nothing like the features on Greta's map. Second, if the Japs were all around Dyckman—and not where the captured map claimed they were—half of his battalion would have blundered into them as they advanced to attack positions that were nothing more than lines on paper.

Greta took a glance at his map and said, "Where did you get this piece of *stront*?" He wouldn't have been surprised if she spit on it. "It should show sharp, rocky ledges dropping to narrow beaches, Jock, not some gently rolling meadowland."

"It's no good, then?"

"Complete garbage. It's not from anything I drew, I can tell you that. It looks like the Japanese were trying to deceive you."

"Yeah," Jock replied. "That thought crossed my mind."

"We've almost completed the next map sheets—the ones you'll need to go where my father and the Japanese are. We've had to rush since you've covered so much ground today, so they're very rough, I'm afraid. We have no survey data yet to sharpen them up. Everything you see is from my head."

"So we found this Dyckman fellow," Colonel Molloy said, "and he's in deep shit?"

"Yes, sir," Jock replied. "We can't afford to lose him. He's giving us great intel on Jap strength and dispositions."

Molloy studied Greta's map. "Yeah, I see. So we're backing a battalion-sized force of Nips up against the coast and your Dutchman's gotten himself in the way."

"Yes, sir. We've got to get him out of there. We owe it to him...and to Greta."

"Dammit...that's going to slow us way down," Molloy replied, "and my ass is already in a sling because we're eight days into an operation that should have taken three."

"That's not your fault, sir."

Molloy laughed. "Yeah...you and I know that, Jock. But it don't mean jackshit to the boys upstairs." He stared at the map in silence for a few moments more before adding, "All right. I'll take this up with General Freidenburg. But in the meantime, make sure your boys have those Japs bottled up good and tight."

"It would be a very simple rescue, sir," Dick Molloy told General Freidenburg. "Two landing craft—at most—could pluck Dyckman and his people off the beach under cover of night."

"Negative, Richard," the general replied without giving it a moment's thought. "Can't spare the boats.

I'm using them all to send a battalion from Eighty-Second Regiment to hold Owi."

"But there's nobody on that island, sir."

"Maybe not today, Richard, but the Navy's getting real antsy about having to sail so close to it on the way here. If the Japs were to slip in down there with a couple of big guns, maybe some planes and torpedo boats...it could make our resupply efforts on Biak a living hell."

"The Japs are running in the opposite direction, General."

"Are you questioning my tactical judgment, Colonel? You, who've managed to move your regiment a mere ten miles in eight days?"

"No sir, of course not. It's just that..."

"It's just *what*, Richard?"

"It's just...I don't know, sir...It's just a shitty deal to be sacrificing people who've done nothing but help us."

"Spare me the violins, Colonel. This isn't some pity party we're running here. It's a war...and people will die. Or have you forgotten?"

"No sir, I haven't forgotten. But I can't forget about the Dutchman's daughter, either, and how much she's done for us in such a short time. I think we owe it to her, too."

Perhaps the tone of Molloy's remark wasn't what it should have been. A bit more *respect* in his voice might not have changed General Freidenburg's decision, but it might have radically altered the outcome of this meeting.

"Let me tell you something, Colonel Molloy. I don't give a sweet fuck what you think. That split-tail has been here exactly one day and already you make it sound like she's winning the war single-handedly. It's the same kind of bullshit you dispensed to conjure up special privileges for that Major Miles of yours."

"Actually, sir, it's *Colonel* Miles now."

"WHAT? We've *promoted* that man? On what grounds, if I may ask?"

"Well, for openers, sir, he deserved it."

"How so, Colonel? For his sexual prowess? It seems to me you're trying to tailor that man's career so he can share as much sack time as possible with that Australian chippy."

"Sir, the woman you're talking about is his wife, not to mention a valued civilian official of this command. And if what you say is true, Jock Miles wouldn't be on this island leading a battalion again. He'd be back on New Guinea, with the rest of the pencil-pushers...and his wife."

"So not only is my judgment faulty, Colonel, but now I don't know a damn thing about what makes men tick, either. Well, I'll tell you what, Richard Molloy...maybe you shouldn't be *lowering* yourself by working for me, *insightful* as you are. So I'll make it real easy for you—you're relieved of your command. I'll get someone else to give Eighty-First Regiment the kick in the ass it so sorely needs. My adjutant will have orders cut sending you back to Hollandia for reassignment within the hour. Good luck with what's left of your career, *Colonel*."

There was no point trying to fob off the blame on the failures of two dead battalion commanders. There was no point blaming the maps, either. In fact, there was no point blaming anyone but himself. As commander, he was responsible for everything his regiment did or failed to do. Molloy braced, saluted, and walked away, enjoying that brief elation that comes with unexpected liberation. The regrets would come soon enough, he knew, and so would the stinging impact of Freidenburg's last sentence, like the venom of a snakebite slowly taking hold:

Good luck with what's left of your career, Colonel...

For now Dick Molloy knew for certain he would never in his lifetime wear a general's star.

Chapter Thirty-Four

Melvin Patchett was never a man to mince words. He told Jock, "That General Freidenburg don't know whether to scratch his watch or wind his ass. Anyone dumb enough to shitcan a man like Colonel Molloy—probably the best fightin' regimental commander in this whole fucking army—oughta be taken out and shot. It's just criminal what he done, especially now, in the middle of—NO! Cancel that. It's criminal any damn time."

"Gee, Top…for a moment there, I thought you were going to throw in a *with all due respect*."

"Wasn't planning on it this time, sir." Patchett seethed for a few moments longer. "So what are we gonna do about that Dutchman of yours."

"As far as Dyckman goes, I figure we're pretty much on our own at the moment. Command is going to be in a state of *flux* for a day or two, no matter who succeeds Colonel Molloy."

"So we're gonna go ahead and rescue this guy?" Patchett asked.

"Damn right we are, Top. I owe him one hell of a big favor."

"I understand, sir. When?"

"Tonight…before our new boss has a chance to stop us from doing it."

"We better get our asses organized right quick then, sir. Sun's gonna be down before we know it."

At least they now had Greta's latest map, the one that covered the mile from 1st Battalion's present position to the coast. Jock's three rifle company commanders were busy sketching in the details their recon patrols provided.

"We think they're getting ready to hit us, sir," Lee Grossman told Jock. "The way we've got them hemmed in, their only chance is a breakout. Theo's guys may have found out something that makes that scenario real plausible."

Theo Papadakis picked it up from there. "There's a big gap in their line, sir," he said. "My guys went all the way through it and walked far enough to see the beach. Never saw or heard a Jap the whole time."

Grossman added, "It's not like the Nips to leave a hole that big in a defensive perimeter. We didn't fall for their little trick with the maps, so we figure they're scrambling to put together an attack and may have gotten a little disorganized doing it. That's sure happened to us a bunch of times."

Patchett had a different take. "But they ain't done no probing of their own, looking if we got ourselves a weak spot. What if they're planning on pulling all the way back and being evacuated by sea?"

"I don't think so," Jock said. "If they were planning on being evacuated tonight, they'd be down by the beach already. It'd be too chaotic moving a unit that size in the dark, unless they'd already marked exit lanes through the forest and down the cliffs. We asked the Dutchman if they had. He says there's been no sign of it."

"Well, maybe you're right then, sir," Patchett replied. "But since we've got our bearings with this new map and all, why ain't we pasting the shit out of them with artillery right fucking now?"

"That's a great idea, Top...and we're going to do that...just as soon as we've gotten Dyckman and his people out of the way. We don't want them caught in that fire. I owe him that much."

Patchett narrowed his eyes and asked, "Unless, of course, Captain Grossman's correct and the Japs come on us like stink on shit, right?"

"Yeah, of course, Top. You really have to ask that?"

"Just checking, sir. Seems like you got yourself a whole lotta *owing* going on here. I wanna make sure who gets paid off first when push come to shove."

"All right," Jock said. "Let's get down to business. Theo, who led your patrol that found this gap?"

"Sergeant Boudreau, sir."

"Great," Jock replied. "Bogater's going to be my pathfinder on this little romp in the dark."

"Whoa, wait a damn minute," Patchett said. "You ain't really going in there yourself, are you, sir?"

"That's my plan, Top. I'm the only one who knows the Dutchman and his people. It only makes sense I go."

Jock knew what Patchett was thinking: *You really gonna carry yourself around in the dark on that leg?*

"I'm not worried about my leg, Top. You shouldn't be, either."

"As you wish, sir. How big a team you gonna take?"

"Let's keep it small...about ten men. But I'm taking one of the heavy machine guns and a couple of extra walkie-talkies to be on the safe side. Don't want to get out of touch with you guys if the shit hits the fan."

Lieutenant Ben Stone had never seen anything like it: they'd asked for ten volunteers. They got forty-three—and this in an army where *volunteering* didn't really exist. The word was just a euphemism for being *selected* against your will.

Stone was the newest and by far the least experienced rifle company commander in 1st Battalion. He'd only been in New Guinea a month when he was given Baker Company during the mop-up phase of the Hollandia invasion. It had been strictly a matter of attrition: the few lieutenants senior to him had been killed, wounded, or stricken with one tropical disease or another. Compared to Captains Lee Grossman and Theo Papadakis—veteran company commanders who'd outlived the odds of survival many times over—Ben Stone was a neophyte at this savage game and he knew it. He'd never laid eyes on the limping Colonel Jock Miles, the third commander of this battalion he'd served under, until yesterday.

"I don't understand it," Stone said to Theo Papadakis. "Why the hell are all these guys *volunteering*—I mean *actually volunteering*—to get themselves killed trying to save some civilians who got caught in the wrong place at the wrong time?"

"You're pretty new here, Stone," the *Mad Greek* replied, "and there's a shitload of stuff about this outfit you don't understand. But let me tell you this, my friend…those guys are volunteering because Jock Miles *asked* them to, plain and simple."

Darkness is my friend...Darkness is my friend...

Bogater Boudreau figured those words had scrolled through his mind a thousand times, like the news ticker coursing around that building in New York City he'd seen in the picture shows. Maybe if that ticker played long enough, he'd actually start believing its message.

Trouble is, it's too damn dark. I can't see a blasted thing in this forest. But I'm a tracker...a crack scout...and I'm the point man, the GI in front of this column. I'll use what I got: sound, smell, feel—whatever it takes—to give the guys behind me a fighting chance to stay alive.

It was sound that came first, a *clack-clack* he'd heard too many times before:

That's the bolt of an Arisaka rifle...and it's damn close, too, just off to my right.

Bogater stopped and crouched against a tree. Behind him, each GI in the column bumped to a stop against the man in front, like the cars of a long train braking to a halt. They recoiled like a compressed spring, re-established their short intervals, and took up firing positions as Jock crawled forward to join Bogater.

"I'll go around and take him real quiet-like," the Cajun whispered, patting the handle of the bayonet on his web belt. "I won't let him give us away."

"You sure there's only one?" Jock asked. "It's not like Japs to put just one man on an outpost."

"One's all I'm hearing, sir. If there's more, I can come back for help...if I need it."

"No," Jock said. "Too risky going alone. Take a guy with you. Your pick."

"Okay, I pick Simms. He done stuff like this before, too."

It didn't take long. All Jock heard was a muffled cry, a rustling of brush, and a soft *thump*.

Simms emerged from the darkness and told Jock, "You gotta see this, sir."

When they got to Bogater, he was sitting on the ground, hugging his legs against his chest, rocking slowly back and forth. The lifeless body of an islander was lying beside him, the blood from his sliced throat a glistening black pool on the ground.

"Tell me I didn't just fuck up, sir," Bogater said, his voice low and hoarse.

Simms twirled a Japanese Army cap around his forefinger. "What the hell is a native doing with a Nip hat and a Nip rifle, sir? How come nobody told us we'd be fighting the darkies, too?"

Jock rolled the body onto its back. He knew what the man was: *gekken*.

Simms scratched his head. "What the fuck is a *gekken*, sir?"

Jock told them the story as Andreas Dyckman had told it to him. His closing line: "Gekken means *crazy* in Dutch, by the way."

"So who was this crazy guy fighting? Us or the Japs?"

"Both, probably," Jock replied.

"Well, ain't that hot shit," Simms said. "I tell you what, sir...any darkie I see with a rifle, I'm dropping him on the spot."

"Not so fast, Frank," Jock replied. "Like we talked about in the briefing, some of the people we're about to team up with are islanders…and they'll be toting weapons. Their lives depend on it."

"Dammit, sir…this war ain't confusing enough, and now you're telling me there are good darkies and bad darkies on this fucking island and they all look alike?"

"I managed to figure it out, Frank…and you will, too. Just keep your eyes open."

Bogater looked up, his hopeful eyes shimmering in the dim light. "So I didn't fuck up, sir?"

"No, you didn't, Bogater. And you kept it good and quiet. Now let's get this show back on the road. Grab that Arisaka, too."

***

Bogater brought the column to a halt once again. "I reckon this is the rendezvous point, sir...or at least damn close. So where's that Dutchman of yours?"

Before Jock could answer, there was the sound of rifle shots.

"What the hell kind of weapon is that, sir?" Bogater asked. "I ain't never heard me nothing with a *pow* like that."

"It's a Mannlicher, Bogater. German rifle."

"Ain't we in the wrong theater of war to be hearing one of them, sir?"

"No, that's what the Dutchman and his people carry."

Bringing the machine gun to the front, Jock moved his column slowly in the direction from which the shots had come. They didn't have to go far before a voice, in heavily accented English, called out the challenge: "Luxembourg."

Jock replied with the password: "Licorice."

Hans emerged from the darkness. "Good to see you again, Major Miles," he said as they shook hands.

Bogater said, "It's *Colonel* Miles now, *mon frère*."

"Forgive me," Hans replied, "and congratulations, Colonel. But you have Frenchmen in your Army?"

"Sergeant Boudreau is an American," Jock said. "He's *acadie*...a Cajun from Louisiana."

Bogater added, "*Bonsoir*, y'all."

"I'm afraid I don't understand," Hans replied.

"We'll explain later," Jock said. "Where's Mister Dyckman?"

"*Meneer* Dyckman will be here in a moment. He's making sure everyone is accounted for."

"What was that shooting about, Hans?"

"I'm not sure...one of our people trying to kill phantoms, perhaps. If it had been Japanese, they would surely have fired back."

"I was thinking the same thing," Jock replied. "You have much trouble with the *gekken* lately?"

"Perhaps. Two of our islanders went missing last week. It might have been the gekken."

"Well, we just killed one a ways up the trail."

"Only one?" Hans replied, sounding disappointed.

"Yeah, just one."

"Good for you, anyway, Colonel."

Andreas Dyckman stepped from the shadows. "Ah, you are a colonel now, Jock Miles! That is very good."

As they shook hands, Jock said, "Thanks for your help with the submarine. We had to take back all those nasty things we said about you when the transmitter turned up missing."

"You're very welcome, Colonel. As you've come to learn, my way was much better. I still have your transmitter…and now it's allowed you to return the favor."

"Okay," Jock replied, "then we're even. Hans told me you've lost two of your people. That leaves how many—thirty-eight men and women, counting you?"

"Correct, Colonel."

"How many are armed?"

"Twenty-two."

Jock calculated silently for a moment, and then said, "You and I will stay together. Put one of your armed men with us. Split the rest of your people into four equal groups of nine, keeping the number of weapons and women in each group roughly equal. One of my guys will be in charge of each group. Can you be ready to move in five minutes?"

"Yes, Colonel. But I have a question."

"What is it?"

"Your leg…will it carry you? You're limping badly."

"Don't worry about my damn leg, Mister Dyckman."

"Of course. But one more question, if I may?"

"Make it quick, please."

"Can you tell me when I will see my Greta?"

"If all goes well, you'll see her in about an hour."

Those words stunned Dyckman. "You mean…you mean she's actually *here*? On Biak? I didn't realize…"

"She's here, in the flesh, Mister Dyckman."

Chapter Thirty-Five

Lee Grossman was right about the Japanese wanting to break out. They made their move just minutes before 2100, in the pitch dark of the forest floor at night. It began with a diversionary probe at the right side of 1st Battalion's line, quickly and soundly repulsed by a platoon of Theo Papadakis' Able Company.

The main thrust of the breakout, however, was at 1st Battalion's left side, and injected the might of the trapped Japanese battalion between Grossman's Charlie Company and Jock's patrol bringing in Andreas Dyckman and his people.

"We got a fucking herd of elephants headed this way, sir," Bogater Boudreau told Jock as he took up a firing position. "A pretty damn fast herd, too."

In the ghostly glow of Jock's blackout flashlight, Dyckman looked petrified. "We'll be decimated," he said. "I must tell my people to run!"

"The fuck you will," Jock replied. "They'll stay and take cover just like the rest of us. It's the best chance they've got to come out of this alive. Now keep your fucking head down and shut up."

Grossman—call sign *Cleveland Six*—was on the radio calling for artillery fire. "Oh, shit," Bogater said. "Incoming rounds in the fucking dark...and we ain't got time to dig a hole deep enough."

Jock plotted the coordinates of Grossman's fire mission on his map. He breathed a sigh of relief—they were exactly the coordinates he would have called. When Grossman's transmission ended, Jock picked up his walkie-talkie and added, "*Cleveland Six,* this is *Papa*

Six. Make it *Danger Close*, buddy. I'm just west of target. Over."

His body pressed hard against the ground, Bogater's face peeked out from beneath his helmet like a turtle's head from its shell. "These maps from that lady better be as all-fired good as you say they are, sir…or our goose is cooked for sure."

The night sky suddenly lit up with illumination rounds from GI mortars. The rainforest was no longer opaque as a shroud; they could see the shapes of the Japanese darting through the ghostly light and quivering shadows, pushing toward their breakout point…

And headed straight for Jock and his patrol.

The GIs remembered the rule of thumb they'd learned long ago: *if you can count more than five enemy, you're facing a major unit.*

There was no need to count this time…

Fuck. It looks like hundreds of them.

The forest came alive with an uproar of gunfire. The heavy machine gun from Jock's team dealt its mechanized mayhem as it riddled row after row of silhouettes like pop-up targets on a gun range.

The first artillery rounds impacted in a blinding flash…

Right where Grossman had called for them…

And right where Jock hoped they'd be.

"Grossman called it dead on," Jock said. "What do you think of those maps now, Bogater?"

"I'm thinking pretty kindly toward them at the moment, sir," the Cajun replied as more artillery came crashing down like rolling thunder, right on target.

This close-quarters fight became like every other one these combat veterans had been through: a maelstrom of gunfire, explosions, curses, shrieked commands, and the screaming of the wounded. It seemed to take a lifetime but was finished in moments, leaving a caustic stillness in its wake. The lingering, random shots punctuating that stillness sounded like nothing more than a futile venting of frustration. The darkness of night took back the battleground from the garish glow of ordnance, seeking to erase the carnage for at least a little while...until the rising sun would force you to behold it once again.

"Where the hell is your Dutchman, sir?" Bogater asked.

"Damn good question."

Dyckman hadn't gone far. Jock found him twenty yards away, being held down by one of his soldiers.

"He was running around like a crazy man," the GI said. "Figured I'd better hang onto him before he got his ass blown off."

"Good thinking, Marino," Jock said. "Let him up."

Even in the darkness, Dyckman's eyes glowed like a man possessed. Jock gripped his arm so he wouldn't run off again.

I don't think he's afraid, Jock thought. *But he just seems so damn determined....*

Jock suddenly realized what the Dutchman had been trying to do. "You wanted to get to your daughter, didn't you?"

He was calming now, his breath more even, the fierce look in his eyes softening. In a voice little more than a murmur, Dyckman said, "Of course I was. After thinking she was dead the past two years, and then to find she's here...almost close enough to touch...and the war suddenly close enough to lose her again, maybe forever this time. You cannot blame me, can you?"

"I'm not blaming anyone, Mister Dyckman. But running around like a lunatic isn't all that bright in the middle of a battle."

"I realize that, Colonel." His head sunk into his hands. "I need to see her so badly."

"Then follow me," Jock said. "We might almost be there."

Bogater Boudreau could feel the commo wire they'd laid as a trail marker on the outbound leg going slack in his hand. In a few more steps, he reached its frayed end.

"The wire got cut, sir," Bogater told Jock. "Probably by all that artillery, I reckon."

Somewhere out in the dark, laying invisible and useless on the ground, was the rest of the wire that was supposed to guide them back to 1st Battalion's position.

"I could go crawl around and try to find it," Bogater offered. "It couldn't have gone too far."

"Don't bother," Jock replied. "Let's see if we've got a bearing off Grossman's radio." He summoned the GI carrying the walkie-talkie fitted with a direction finding antenna.

"When *Cleveland Six* transmitted a minute ago," the radioman said, "they were at about one-seven-zero degrees, sir. They gotta be close. Signal's so strong it's hard to get an exact fix."

"We haven't moved too far since then," Jock said. "That ought to get us in the ball park. You get that azimuth, Sergeant Boudreau?"

"Yes, sir. One-seven-zero. We can't be more than a couple hundred yards out."

"Affirmative," Jock replied. But he knew *a couple hundred yards* could seem like a thousand miles in the dark.

At least his leg was holding up.

Each step raised their hopes a little further. Walking more quickly now, they cast to the winds the caution they'd employed walking the forest at night. The stumbles and falls that resulted were many, each a noisy circus of clattering weapons, free-rolling helmets, and groans they tried to stifle without much success.

But they were almost home. They were sure of it...

Until the cruel rhythm of a Nambu machine gun shattered that certainty, telling them they weren't home at all. Bullets *zipped* through the column from back to front, each on a mission to ensure Jock and his people would never go home again.

"THEY'RE ON OUR ASS," a voice screamed from Jock's radio. "I GOT GUYS DOWN. WHERE'S THE FUCKING THIRTY CAL?"

"That's Mulcahey," Bogater said, identifying the voice as the sergeant whose group was the *tail end Charlie* of the column. "He should know damn well where the machine gunners are at. They've got their faces planted in the fucking ground just like the rest of us. What the hell we gonna do now, sir?"

Jock was already speaking into his walkie-talkie, telling *Cleveland Six* to relay his fire mission: "From last target, left one hundred, add two hundred, fire for effect, *danger close*, over."

Bogater let out a soft whistle. "Cutting it pretty fine there, ain't we, sir?"

"Better than calling it in on our heads."

"You so sure we ain't, sir?"

They heard the distant *poom* of the guns a second after an artilleryman's voice crackled from the radio: "Shot, over."

"We're about to find out, Bogater," Jock said.

"*Splash*, over," the artilleryman said.

One one thousand...two one thousand...three one thousand...

They heard the rounds crash into the forest, so close they could feel the shock wave of their detonation. The Nambu kept right on firing.

Shit! I either put it too far out...or I just killed a bunch of my own people.

"What do you think, Bogater? Which way do we move it?"

"I'm thinking we're long, sir...but not by much."

"Yeah. Me, too." He keyed the radio: "*Danger close*, direction zero-two-zero, drop five-zero, fire for effect, over."

Ten seconds later, the artilleryman's voice spilled from the radio again: "Shot, over."

If I'm wrong, Jock thought, *I've just killed the rest of us.*

"*Splash,* over."

The rounds hit, the sound of their impact closer this time, the shock wave strong enough to ruffle their tattered, filthy uniforms. The echoes of their explosions quickly subsided, making way for the sweetest silence Jock though he'd ever heard: the Nambu had stopped firing.

There wasn't a second to lose. Jock keyed the walkie-talkie and said, "Get everybody moving." Eager to prevent another stumbling rush, he added, "With all due caution. Let's maintain noise discipline and security this time."

Melvin Patchett's voice came out of the darkness: "You'd better keep them people quiet, sir. We heard y'all a hundred yards out. Japs did, too, I reckon."

Jock replied, "Son of a bitch...the cavalry's here. How close are we to Charlie Company, Top?"

"A couple of yards. Good thing we knew y'all were there, though. Otherwise you'da got caught up in the crossfire. Pretty good call with that artillery, though, sir. Couldn't've done better myself."

"It's a hell of a lot easier when you know exactly where you are. We can thank Missus Christiansen for that. Pretty amazing, considering she drew these last maps from memory."

"They were close enough, that's for damn sure, sir."

Patchett watched as Jock's GIs and Dyckman's people filtered by, most on their own feet. The few wounded—all Americans—were being carried by Dyckman's islanders.

"I plan to thank that lady personal-like, believe you me, sir," Patchett said. "Where's her *pa*, anyway?"

"Oh, shit...don't tell me he's missing again."

"I saw him headed toward the back of the column, sir," Bogater said. "Maybe he was gonna check on his people?"

"Top, get these casualties taken care of. Bogater, you come with me. Let's go escort our Dutch friend out of harm's way once and for all."

"Watch your step, sir," Patchett said. "No guarantee some live Nips still ain't out there."

Jock heard the sound first. He dropped to one knee behind a tree, trying to get a good fix on its direction while he stretched his aching leg.

Bogater crawled to him and asked, "What's going on, sir?"

Jock pointed into the black gloom of the forest. "There's something—or *someone*—out there. Listen. It's pretty close."

The Cajun strained to filter something other than the usual noises of birds and insects. After a few moments he shook his head. "No, sir, ain't hearing a damn—"

Then it happened again: a loud *snap* and *crunch* of underbrush. Footsteps, without a doubt. Probably human, too.

Struggling to his feet, Jock said, "You sure as hell heard that. C'mon...it's this way."

They moved as fast as they dared through the darkness—ten paces, twenty paces, fifty—but found nothing. They heard nothing more, either.

"You notice we've been going up a rise?" Jock asked, repeating out loud what his leg had been silently complaining about for the last few minutes.

"Yes, sir, I surely did."

"Maybe it's more of a hill than we realize. Whoever's out there may already be on the other side and we can't hear him."

"Good bet, sir. So what are we gonna do?"

"We're not stopping now, that's for damn sure."

The incline was steepening. So was the pain in Jock's leg. More than once it threatened to give out. He found himself grabbing the trunks of trees for support.

"You gonna make it, sir? I can go back and get—"

"No, Bogater. We're going to find him, you and me."

They kept climbing until they noticed patches of moonlit sky peeking through the rainforest canopy. "The trees are thinning out a little," Jock said. "We must be almost to the top of this fucking hill."

"I still ain't hearing nothing, sir."

The *clack-clack* of an Arisaka rifle's bolt cycling changed all that. It sounded like it was only a few feet away...

Because it was.

There was a rustle of movement—and Jock found himself at arm's length from another man. Even in darkness, there was no doubt it was a Japanese soldier.

He tried to point the weapon at Jock but there was no room. They were too close.

Jock caught the stock of the rifle with his free hand and held it fast. The long bayonet on its muzzle—only inches from Jock's ear—gave off a dim glint, reflecting what it could of the sparse moonlight.

Jock tried to maneuver his Thompson for a point blank shot but the adversary in his grasp kept twisting, turning, retreating...

It had become an ironic shoving match between heavily armed men.

Jock could see another shape rushing toward them, another glint of moonlight off cold steel, a tousle of light-colored hair on a helmetless head shining pale gray in the moonlight...

Bogater!

The Jap screamed and went limp as the Cajun's bayonet struck deep into him. Jock was finally able to pull the Arisaka free but the motion made him jerk backward. He stumbled, tried to regain his balance...

And then it all went wrong.

It felt like someone had taken a scissor to his thigh muscle. Like a rubber band snapping, his bad leg recoiled and went limp. Jock toppled over, expecting to hit the ground in an instant.

But he kept falling. It was strangely exhilarating—like floating in space without a care—until he bounced off the first tree. He felt no pain from the impact but heard the distinct *pop*, knowing it could only be coming from inside his body.

The plummet continued. By the third collision with a tree, he had lost consciousness.

Chapter Thirty-Six

The new regimental commander hadn't been in the crowded HQ tent more than a moment when, in the thick drawl of the American south, he asked, "Where's that sumbitch Dutchman who caused me all this trouble?"

"He's at the mess tent having breakfast, sir," an intel sergeant replied.

"Well, get his sweet ass over here, on the fucking double. This isn't the *Dick Molloy Benevolent Society* anymore."

As the sergeant scurried from the tent, the new commander told the rest of his staff, "For *all ya'll* who don't know me, my name is Colonel T. Lamar Abernathy. General Freidenburg has sent me to do a little ass-tightening around here, because it seems like this regiment surely needs some. Any of my battalion commanders here yet?"

Across the tent, Lee Grossman raised his hand. "Grossman, sir, acting C.O., First Battalion." He would have given anything not to claim that title.

Abernathy replied with only a frosty, dismissive glare.

Melvin Patchett whispered in Grossman's ear: "I believe there's something about that name of yours the man don't cotton to, sir."

"Probably so, Top. I'll bet he thinks all Jews have horns, too."

Patchett looked at him with mock surprise and replied, "What? Y'all don't?"

The intel sergeant returned with Dyckman and his daughter in tow. Her arm was wrapped protectively around her distraught father. Abernathy wasted no time firing his first salvo at Greta: "You must be that mapmaking woman my predecessor was so all-fired high on." He looked her up and down with a disparaging eye, adding, "Don't be getting too comfortable here, missy. Your services are no longer required."

Lee Grossman started to raise his hand but Patchett grabbed it, whispering, "Let me be the one stirring the shit around here, sir. We don't need to be losing no more good officers."

Patchett put his hand up.

The colonel pointedly ignored him for a few moments. Then a look of unwelcome recognition spread across his face. "Well, as I live and breathe, is that you, Melvin Patchett?"

"Affirmative, sir."

"I thought they would've put an old goat like you out to pasture by now. Imagine my fucking delight when I heard you, of all people, were a battalion *sergeant major* in my regiment," the colonel said, clearly not delighted. "What's on your mind?"

"With all due respect, sir," Patchett said, "this lady's helped us more in a couple days than a whole truckload of staff jockeys done the past year. It just don't make no sense why you'd want to send her packing."

The colonel smirked as he replied, "I can *explain* it to you, Sergeant...but I can't *understand* it for you. So I'm going to say it just once—despite what Dick Molloy might've thought, the US Army can make its own maps just fine and dandy. We don't need no woman around these parts showing us how."

What Patchett wanted to say: *If only that were true, you fucking jackass. I got me a whole bunch of graves full of guys who thought different.*

But a life in *this man's army* had taught him to know better. Grossman wasn't taking any chances on what Patchett might say next, though. He nudged him and whispered, "Keep a lid on it, Top. We don't need to be losing any more good NCOs, either."

Patchett replied, "Relax, sir. I reckon this is about to take care of itself." He motioned toward Greta, who to this point had been calmly taking it all in, and added, "Watch this. She won't be holding her tongue much longer."

In a flash she proved him right. "In other words, Colonel," Greta said, "your General MacArthur has paid me five thousand American dollars for doing next to nothing. I know you Yanks love to throw money away but this is quite extraordinary."

Abernathy flinched. He shot a nasty look at his adjutant, asking the man, "Is this true?"

The adjutant managed to sputter, "Affirmative, sir."

"Why wasn't I informed?"

Any number of explanations crossed the adjutant's mind, none of which would qualify as a satisfactory answer. Instead, he replied, "No excuse, sir."

Abernathy's face turned bright red. "So you're telling me this woman has an *employment contract* with Supreme Allied Headquarters?"

It was a simpler question. All the adjutant had to do this time was nod.

"Very well," Abernathy replied, "we'll deal with this matter later."

Patchett whispered to Grossman, "He won't be dealing with *shit* later. Abernathy always was a little dumber than the average brass hat…but was he really supposing anyone except a GI would work for nothing? Especially in this stink hole?"

Trumped by the daughter, the colonel set his sights on her father. "And you, Mister Dyckman…I need you to explain just what in tarnation you were doing out there that cost one of my battalions its third commander in a week."

In a weary, wavering voice, the Dutchman tried to begin his story by telling how, nearly three weeks before, he'd helped Jock and the crew of the downed PBY Catalina. But Abernathy cut him off. "I'm a busy man, Mister Dyckman. I just want to hear about the events of last night. Bad enough a battalion commander disobeyed orders and went freelance on me but then he goes and gets himself—"

"Begging your pardon, sir," Patchett interrupted, "but the battalion never got no such order."

"Why, that's just a bald-faced lie, Sergeant," Abernathy said. He turned to his S3—the regimental operations officer—and added, "Isn't it, Major?"

The S3 hesitated before replying, "Not exactly, sir. I was there. General Freidenburg told *Colonel Molloy* not to do the rescue mission. And then he fired him on the spot. Nobody thought Colonel Miles would go ahead and—"

"DAMMIT," Abernathy said, "General Freidenburg's dead on the mark when he says this regiment needs some ass-tightening." He fixed Dyckman in his belligerent gaze and asked, "Let's get back to what happened last night. I'm told you took off—just vanished—after Colonel Miles ordered you not to. And I damn sure want to know why."

"It wasn't my intention to disobey Jock's—*Colonel Miles'*—order, sir. But my people were terrified and disorganized. They'd come under fire twice in just a few minutes. I was trying to ease the colonel's load and help lead them to the safety of the American lines."

"And did you manage to do that, Mister Dyckman?"

"No, Colonel, I did not. I'm ashamed to say I got disoriented. After stumbling about in the dark, I walked right up to soldiers I assumed were Americans...but I was wrong. They took me prisoner and began marching me through the forest."

"How many Japs were there?"

"I saw only two."

"So what happened next?"

"The Japanese seemed confused, as if they, too, were lost. I tried to escape while they were engaged in some hushed discussion—it sounded like an argument—but failed. They bound me to a tree, argued some more...and then one of them leveled his bayonet at my chest. Another man suddenly appeared out of nowhere—I only found out later it was Colonel Miles—and he grappled with the soldier about to stab me. While they fought, Sergeant Boudreau arrived and bayoneted the Japanese soldier...and then Colonel Miles was gone, fallen off the ridge."

"If you couldn't tell it was Miles, how the hell did you know it was this *Boudreau* fellow?"

"Sergeant Boudreau didn't fall off the ridge, Colonel. He stayed right there with me."

"What about the other Jap? What happened to him?"

"I have no idea, Colonel. Perhaps he fled."

"And perhaps you were in cahoots with those Japs all along, Mister Dyckman, leading them to my position?"

"I do not know the meaning of *cahoots*, Colonel."

Keeping her anger in check, Greta provided the translation. "It means *collaborator*, Papa. I've heard such nonsense from the Americans before."

The Dutchman's face flared red as his hair with rage. "I can assure you, Colonel, that allegation is absurd beyond belief."

Abernathy fumed for a few moments. Then he asked Lee Grossman, "Captain, does this man's story agree with what your people told you?"

"Yes, sir. To the letter."

"Well, ain't that just the cat's ass," Abernathy said. "But at least I've got me a forest full of dead Japs I won't need to be chasing anymore. We should have this little ol' island sewed up in a week or two."

"Lord help us," Patchett whispered. "The man ain't found the latrine yet and he's predicting a lickety-split victory."

As they walked back to their battalion CP, Patchett told Grossman, "I blame myself. I shoulda never let him go out there with that leg of his."

"No, Top...none of us could've stopped him. It's all our faults. We never should've asked him to come back in the first place. That damn letter..."

Lost in their thoughts and regrets, they walked on. Grossman finally broke the silence: "But he's come back from the dead before, you know."

Patchett shook his head. "A game-legged man's one thing, Lee. A one-legged man's something different altogether."

Chapter Thirty-Seven

Six months later—December 24, 1944

1900 hours

Jock took a long swallow from the bottle of Australian beer. "I don't think I'll ever get used to the concept of Christmas in the middle of summer."

Jillian replied, "No more than I could get used to it in the middle of winter, buried in snow." She slid a little closer to him on the veranda's wicker settee, careful not to disturb his leg, which was set in a fresh cast after its latest surgery.

"But you've never even seen snow, Jill."

"And from what I've heard, I'd like to keep it that way, Yank. Your Massachusetts sounds frightfully cold and dreary to me."

The sun had dropped behind the mountains west of Brisbane. The city they looked out on was in deep shadow, but the horizon across the Pacific could still be seen clearly. "Nautical twilight," Jillian said, a wistfulness in her voice.

Jock asked, "You miss being on the sea, don't you, babe?"

"Bloody hell, Jock, I'm six months up the duff. Going to sea will have to wait a while. A very long while." She leaned against the seat back, shifting in search of physical comfort that being with child was making more elusive by the day. Still, she found a reason to smile as she patted her swelling belly. "See what can happen? That one fleeting moment in Hollandia…there was so little time…and we were so wrapped up in it we didn't bother to use a bloody johnny."

"Any regrets, Jill?"

"Just one. That I didn't leave a steaming pile of horse shit on MacArthur's desk when I got kicked out of New Guinea."

The Christmas revelers inside the house were growing boisterous. "Aunt Margaret certainly knows how to throw a party," Jillian said. "Sounds like she's breaking out the good stuff right about now. She'll want us to make an appearance soon, you know."

Jock glanced at the empty wheelchair beside them and said, "Not quite yet, if that's all right."

She knew why he was in no great hurry to join the party. He'd fielded quite enough well-meaning questions about his injuries. Nothing was more tiresome—and more depressing—for a *true warrior* than having to play the *wounded warrior*. This holiday furlough from the orthopedic ward had been a godsend for his morale—but it was only temporary.

"Do you really have to be back in hospital the day after Christmas?" she asked. "It seems like such a pitifully short time."

"You know the answer to that, Jill."

"You could go AWOL, you know."

He wasn't sure if she was joking or not.

"You're kidding, right?"

She'd been half-serious, even though she was fully aware he had to return. There was still one more operation scheduled on his leg—the one that would determine if he could ever use it to walk again. Even if that operation was a smashing success, though, he could never go back to field duty; his ravaged quadriceps would never allow it. But with the help of a cane, he'd at least be able to stand on his own two legs once more.

"Of course I'm kidding, Jock. But before we get *shanghaied* into the party, I need to give you your Christmas present."

"Wait," he replied as he gently placed a hand on her midsection. "You're already giving me the greatest present a man could ask for. I don't need anything more."

She kissed him on the cheek. "Well, laddie, you're going to get it anyway."

"Let me go first," he said. Reaching under the wheelchair's cushion, he produced a small box. "Here, Jill...our very first Christmas actually spent together...and already there are three of us!"

Removing the wrapping paper, her eyes opened wide with surprise when the name of Brisbane's most expensive jewelry store was revealed. She gasped when she saw the gold necklace inside. He helped clasp it around her neck. Running her fingers through the glittering strands, she said, "It's so beautiful! But how in bloody hell can you afford this, Jock? Your bloody Army hasn't even paid you in months."

"That payroll *snafu* finally got straightened out, Jill. Remind me never to get transferred from the Army to the Air Force and back again. The bean counters just can't keep up."

"So you spent all your back pay on this necklace, silly boy?"

"Yeah...pretty much. I've never been able to buy you anything before."

She kissed him again, this time full on the mouth. They let it linger.

"Thank you, sweetie," she whispered in his ear. "I love it. And now, for your present."

She retrieved an envelope from the pocket of her maternity top. Handing it to him, she added, "*Ta da*! Welcome to the Forbes family, Jock Miles."

The paperwork within seemed all in order, signed and stamped by various officials of the Queensland and Canberra governments. Its language was tortuously legal. As best as Jock could tell from a quick scan, the papers made him part owner of Forbes-Weipa Company.

"I gave you some of my shares," Jillian explained. "I wanted to split it fifty-fifty but since you're a Yank— *a bloody foreigner*—you can't own more than fifteen percent of an Aussie business. So that's what you've gotten."

He looked bewildered as he stammered, "But...but all I got you...was the necklace."

She burst out laughing. "Oh, Jock...that's so sweet. But Aunt Margaret insists: if you're going to be knocking up her favorite niece, you're going to have to be a man of *considerable* means. And now you are."

"But wait a minute," Jock said. "Your company—"

She corrected him: "*Our* company."

"All right, *our* company does lots of business with the US Government up on Cape York, leasing them all that land, the harbor facilities, and lord knows what else. I'm an official of that government, so doesn't that put me in a conflict of interest?"

She took the paperwork from his hand, turned a page and pointed to a clause. "It says right here you—and I, your wife—will be recusing ourselves from all dealings with the US Government as long as you're serving in its armed forces."

"But what business *is* there right now besides dealings with the US Government?"

With a mischievous smile, Jillian replied, "Oh, baby...you have no idea how much more there is."

She gave him a few minutes of silence to process his startling change of fortune. When that silence finally begged to be broken, she asked, "Sweetie, how did you manage to actually buy this necklace while you were cooped up in hospital?"

"Oh, that was easy. Colonel Molloy did the buying for me. Since General Freidenburg canned him back on Biak, his staff job here in Brisbane doesn't take up a whole lot of his time. He's been trying like hell to get a slot in the Philippines, but that campaign's practically won already."

"Jock, this whole war is practically won. The Nips are finished. Just a few more months..."

"You're sure of that, eh?"

"Bloody right I am."

"I don't know, Jill...maybe we can push them all the way back to their home islands. But to invade those islands...well, that's going to be a whole different story."

"I think you're giving the Japanese far too much credit. They may be vicious little bastards when they have the upper hand, but they're beaten now and they know it. The past two years have been just one long retreat for them. This *kamikaze* rubbish they've started is just the final, desperate act. Once that's played out, they'll have nothing left."

"The closer to Japan, the harder it's going to get, Jill. You know what the GIs are saying right now about when the war will end and they can all go home? *The Golden Gate in '48*."

"Don't be ridiculous. Our son will be three years old by then."

"Whoa...wait a minute, Jill. Our *son*? How do you know it'll be a boy?"

"I can tell, Jock. I just know...just like I know this war will be over before you'll ever be fit for any kind of duty again. Even to ride a desk." She paused, and then, with a contented smile, added, "And that makes me feel very good inside. We've finally stepped off MacArthur's merry-go-round. Paid a steep price, too, but it's done at last."

She saw the wistful look come over his face as he gazed at his uniform blouse draped over the wheelchair's arm. In the rapidly fading light, the golden crossed rifles of an infantryman and the silver oak leaf of a lieutenant colonel struggled to outshine each other. Within a few moments, however, the contest ended. Both insignia dissolved into the colorless veil of dusk.

Just a featureless silhouette in profile now, Jock said, "I'll have to get used to not being a soldier anymore, I guess."

Jillian took him in her arms. "Jock, you'll *always* be a soldier...and a bloody brilliant one, too. You have nothing left to prove. It's just time for someone else to do the actual fighting."

She glanced down at her belly. Speaking to the tiny person growing within, she said, "But mark my words, little man, it won't be you."

***

More Novels by William Peter Grasso

After surviving a deadly plane crash, Jock Miles is handed a new mission: neutralize a mountaintop observation post on Japanese-held Manus Island so MacArthur's invasion fleet en route to Hollandia, New Guinea, can arrive undetected. Jock's team seizes and holds the observation post with the help of a clever deception. But when they learn of a POW camp deep in the island's treacherous jungle, it opens old wounds for Jock and his men: the disappearance—and presumed death—of Jillian Forbes at Buna a year before. There's only one risky way to find out if she's a prisoner there…and doing so puts their entire mission in serious jeopardy.

Port Moresby was bad. Buna was worse.

The WW2 alternative history adventure of Jock Miles continues as MacArthur orders American and Australian forces to seize Buna in Papua New Guinea. Once again, the Allied high command underestimates the Japanese defenders, plunging Jock and his men into a battle they're not equipped to win. Worse, jungle diseases, treacherous terrain, and the tactical fantasies of deluded generals become adversaries every bit as deadly as the Japanese. Sick, exhausted, and outgunned, Jock's battalion is ordered to spearhead an amphibious assault against the well-entrenched enemy. It's a suicide mission—but with ingenious help from an unexpected source, there might be a way to avoid the certain slaughter and take Buna. For Jock, though, victory comes at a dreadful price.

Alternative history takes center stage as *Operation Long Jump,* the second book in the Jock Miles World War 2 adventure series, plunges us into the horrors of combat in the rainforests of Papua New Guinea. As a prelude to the Allied invasion, Jock Miles and his men seize the Japanese observation post on the mountain overlooking Port Moresby. The main invasion that follows quickly degenerates to a bloody stalemate, as the inexperienced, demoralized, and poorly led GIs struggle against the stubborn enemy. Seeking a way to crack the impenetrable Japanese defenses, infantry officer Jock finds himself in a new role—aerial observer. He's teamed with rookie pilot John Worth, in a prequel to his role as hero of Grasso's *East Wind Returns.* Together, they struggle to expose the Japanese defenses—while highly exposed themselves—in their slow and vulnerable spotter plane. The enemy is not the only thing troubling Jock: his Australian lover, Jillian Forbes, has found a new and dangerous way to contribute to the war effort.

LONG WALK TO THE SUN

A NOVEL BY
WILLIAM PETER GRASSO

In this alternate history adventure set in WW2's early days, a crippled US military struggles to defend vulnerable Australia against the unstoppable Japanese forces. When a Japanese regiment lands on Australia's desolate and undefended Cape York Peninsula, Jock Miles, a US Army captain disgraced despite heroic actions at Pearl Harbor, is ordered to locate the enemy's elusive command post.

Conceived in politics rather than sound tactics, the futile mission is a "show of faith" by the American war leaders meant to do little more than bolster their flagging Australian ally. For Jock Miles and the men of his patrol, it's a death sentence: their enemy is superior in men, material, firepower, and combat experience. Even if the Japanese don't kill them, the vast distances they must cover on foot in the treacherous natural realm of Cape York just might. When Jock joins forces with Jillian Forbes, an indomitable woman with her own checkered past who refused to evacuate in the face of the Japanese threat, the dim prospects of the Allied war effort begin to brighten in surprising ways.

Congressman. Presidential candidate. Murderer. Leonard Pilcher is all of these things.

As an American pilot interned in Sweden during WWII, he kills one of his own crewmen and gets away with it. Two people have witnessed the murder—American airman Joe Gelardi and his secret Swedish lover, Pola Nilsson-MacLeish—but they cannot speak out without paying a devastating price. Tormented by their guilt and separated by a vast ocean after the war, Joe and Pola maintain the silence that haunts them both...until 1960, when Congressman Pilcher's campaign for his party's nomination for president gains momentum. As he dons the guise of war hero, one female reporter, anxious to break into the "boy's club" of TV news, fights to uncover the truth against the far-reaching power of the Pilcher family's wealth, power that can do any wrong it chooses—even kill—and remain unpunished. Just as the nomination seems within Pilcher's grasp, Pola reappears to enlist Joe's help in finally exposing Pilcher for the criminal he really is. As the passion of their wartime romance rekindles, they must struggle to bring Pilcher down before becoming his next victims.

EAST WIND RETURNS

William Peter Grasso

A young but veteran photo recon pilot in WWII finds the fate of the greatest invasion in history--and the life of the nurse he loves--resting perilously on his shoulders.

"East Wind Returns" is a story of World War II set in July-November 1945 which explores a very different road to that conflict's historic conclusion. The American war leaders grapple with a crippling setback: Their secret atomic bomb does not work. The invasion of Japan seems the only option to bring the war to a close. When those leaders suppress intelligence of a Japanese atomic weapon poised against the invasion forces, it falls to photo reconnaissance pilot John Worth to find the Japanese device. Political intrigue is mixed with passionate romance and exciting aerial action--the terror of enemy fighters, anti-aircraft fire, mechanical malfunctions, deadly weather, and the Kamikaze. When shot down by friendly fire over southern Japan during the American invasion, Worth leads the desperate mission that seeks to deactivate the device.

Printed in Great Britain
by Amazon